A FROZEN GRAVE

DETECTIVE REBECCA ELLIS BOOK 2

ROBIN MAHLE

INKUBATOR
BOOKS

Published by Inkubator Books
www.inkubatorbooks.com

ISBN (eBook): 978-1-83756-146-9
ISBN (Paperback): 978-1-83756-147-6
ISBN (Hardback): 978-1-83756-148-3

1

A burst of wind gathered the falling snow, swirling it around the pick-up on the side of the road. A layer of white had formed on the truck's hood and roof as it remained parked on the earthy shoulder. One front and one rear tire rutted the soft ground, while the others rested firmly on the pavement. A light dusting of snow had already layered the empty lane.

Inside the truck, keys dangled from the ignition. The gale howled through the window, left cracked. Static from the radio cut into the emergency broadcast, breaking up the transmission as the truck's battery drained.

"Snowfall is expected to continue through the night in the first major storm of the season. Authorities are asking citizens to stay off the roads while crews prepare to clear the streets. Six feet of snow is projected to fall in the Bangor area."

A dense forest lay next to the road, where trees swayed and branches snapped under the growing weight of the flurry. A place where hikers explored and hunters hunted. Deep inside that forest, the turgid, hazy brown eyes of a dead man stared up at the night sky, white flakes descending like stars traveling at cosmic speeds.

Hours passed and snow collected atop him until he coalesced with his surroundings.

As light came again, the storm was over. The forest, quiet. All that remained were beautiful white mounds covering every surface—except one. A tiny scrap of an orange vest peeked out like a beacon calling for help. But out here, well beyond the trails, no one would see it. No one would know how a man had come to be here, and worst of all, no one would care.

ERICKA CHISOLM ZIPPED her weatherproof jacket as the northern wind kicked up. Friend and hiking companion Gina Holder hadn't been as prepared, donning only a thick fleece. With a judging eye, Ericka examined her. "Are you sure you aren't cold? The deeper we get along the trail, the more shade we'll have. We can go back to the car and grab my wool hat."

Gina, a young woman of barely twenty-three, brushed off the idea. "I'm fine. We'll warm up when we start walking anyway."

"All right." Ericka took a drink from her sports bottle and secured the lid. "First hike of the spring. Let's do it."

They traversed over patches of melting snow that glistened on the forest floor. Tree branches sprouted new leaves that would soon form a thick canopy over the trail. And with a blue sky above, it was the perfect spring day in Bangor, Maine.

The trails in City Forest, a 680-acre preserve that lay on the north-east edge of the city, were utilized year-round for hiking, biking, and cross-country skiing.

"Thanks for coming with me today. I needed this." Ericka closed her eyes and inhaled the crisp, fresh air.

"Break-ups are never easy, I get that. So I'm here for you." Gina patted Ericka's back. "I was actually thinking maybe I could set you up with a friend of—"

"Uh, thanks, but no thanks," Ericka cut in. "I appreciate the sentiment, but I think I just want to take some time for myself, you know?"

"Call it a back-up plan, then." Gina looked out over the trail. "It's quiet out here."

"We got an early start. It's nice though, right?" Ericka asked.

"It is."

The young women carried on, taking measured steps to avoid the slick moss that still covered parts of the trail. Twigs and large branches lay near, having fallen under the weight of the heavy winter snow.

"You know, I was thinking," Gina began. "Why don't you move in with me? It'd be cheap, and it would help me out too. It'd be a blast, right?"

Ericka smiled, but soon lowered her gaze. "It would be a blast."

Gina appeared to take notice. "You think he might come back, don't you?"

"Am I that transparent? I know it's crazy to hold out hope like that, but—"

"Oh my God." Gina stopped cold and thrust out her arm. "Wait."

Ericka stumbled over herself as they came to an abrupt halt. "What's wrong?" She watched as Gina canvassed the area. "Hey, what's going—"

"Where are we?"

"We're on the trail," Ericka replied. "What do you mean?"

"No, where are we exactly?" Gina pressed. "How far have we walked?"

Ericka checked the map on her phone to pinpoint their location. "Looks like we're near the preserve. See." She aimed the screen at her friend.

Gina looked closely at the little blue dot that indicated their position. "This isn't hunting season, right?"

"No. That's, like, late fall and early winter, I think. I'm pretty sure it ends in December. Gina, what's going on? You're starting to scare me."

She aimed her index finger to the right of the trail. "Look out that way. Do you see it? Way out there. At least a hundred feet or so."

With some confusion, Ericka glanced back at her friend. "Do you have bionic eyes or something? How can you see through all the trees?" She squinted ahead.

Gina touched Ericka's cheek and gently aimed her head. "Okay, now do you see it? The orange thing out there, behind the logs."

Ericka craned her neck with a narrow gaze. "Yeah, I see it now. What is it?"

Gina walked on. "I think I know, but I need to be sure. Come with me." She veered off the trail and into the woods. "When was the last big snow?"

"A couple weeks ago."

"Yeah, that sounds about right." Gina hurried through the rugged terrain, stepping over downed trees and boulders, climbing over low shrubs until she reached the spot. She looked back. "Ericka, hurry."

"I'm coming. Jeez, it's not easy to walk through here—you know, off the trail."

"Yeah, I get it. We're not supposed to be in here. Just come on." Gina waited for her friend to reach her. "Okay, it's over there, beyond that log."

Ericka looked once again. "What do you think it is?"

Gina approached the bright orange vest that lay beneath the forest debris. She thrust her hand over her mouth a moment.

"What?" Ericka finally reached her. "What are we looking at?" But before Gina could answer, Ericka saw what she had seen. The vest was mostly obscured by decaying leaves and twigs from the forest floor. The ice was still melting, turning the ground to mud and slowly revealing what had been concealed. "Oh my God. Call the police."

DETECTIVE REBECCA ELLIS jotted in her notebook while the sarge briefed the team from behind the podium. She'd been with the Bangor Police Department for more than a decade, following in the footsteps of her now retired father, Hank Ellis. The thirty-four-year-old had worked hard to build her own reputation and come out from his shadow.

Next to her sat Detective Euan McCallister, with whom Ellis had partnered on the troubling Claire Allen murder. Tall and lean with deep-set brown eyes, he wore his brown hair a little long with waves on top. Older than her by a few years, the somewhat mysterious Boston transplant held back his reasons for making the unusual move to the smaller police department.

Behind Ellis were Detectives Connor Bevins and Lori Fletcher, or "Fletch" as she was called. They traded barbs with some excitement, seemingly drawing the ire of the sarge.

"You two got something you want to add?" Sergeant James Abbott set down his marker as he finished listing the active investigations on the whiteboard behind him. The commander of the Criminal Investigation Division removed his reading glasses and smoothed his button-down shirt over his hefty paunch. "No? Then that's it for now. I suggest you go on about your day and stay safe out there."

Ellis stood from the long rectangular table and dropped her notebook into her laptop bag. Wearing a dark gray jacket and dress pants, she stood at about five-foot-eight and wore her blond hair just above her shoulders. While most considered her to be pretty, with large hazel eyes and an oval face, Ellis never put much stock in those things. She took care of herself and kept moderately fit, but it was a necessary component of her job. She glanced over at McCallister. "I'll see you back upstairs." As she entered the lobby and headed for the stairs, footsteps trotted up behind her.

McCallister reached her just as she grabbed the railing. "Hey, so, that fraud investigation you and Gabby worked on, sounds like it's all wrapped up?"

"It is. Gabby had been tracking the suspect's movements through his banking transactions and it led her to the guy's mom."

"Sounds like our resident cyber-expert came through again," he replied.

"There was never any doubt," she replied. "Later in the day, she told us where he was, and he was arrested last night." Ellis climbed the stairs.

McCallister trailed by a step. "Congratulations. Bryce and I are headed out to—"

"Becca, Euan?"

They stopped and turned back when Abbott called out to them.

Ellis raised her chin. "What's up, Sarge?"

He aimed a meaty finger at them. "Come on back down, would you?" Abbott waited a moment for their return. "Listen, a call came into Dispatch while we were in the briefing. A body was found in City Forest. Been there a while, by the sounds of it. I need you two to go and check it out. Euan, I know you and Bryce have something in the fire, so I want you to hand it off to either Gabby or Fletch."

"Yes, sir," he replied. "Are we doing this now?"

Abbott scratched the side of his bulbous nose. "The body won't be getting any deader. Regardless, you'd better take a look. Check with Dispatch for the GPS coordinates. Bangor Land Trust officials are already onsite and waiting for you."

"We're on our way." Ellis headed toward Dispatch but stopped and turned back to McCallister. "I'll get the details and meet you outside. I'm driving."

"Yes, ma'am." McCallister climbed the stairs toward the bullpen.

Dispatch Officer Liz Varney was sitting at her desk when Ellis entered. "Hey, Liz. Sarge mentioned the call about the body in City Forest. You have a location for me?"

"That, I do." Varney typed in the command and the printer kicked on. As it spat out the report, she reached for it, then turned to Ellis. "Here you go."

She scanned the document. "This is near Kittredge Road."

"Yep," Varney replied, smoothing down a rogue strand of brunette hair that sprang from her tight bun.

Ellis raised her gaze to the ceiling as she recalled the location. "Isn't that the preserve?"

"Somewhere in the vicinity, I believe."

Ellis clicked her tongue. "Thanks."

She returned to the lobby, and it appeared McCallister had beaten her outside. She noticed him standing at her white Chevy Tahoe. She pushed through the exit and walked toward him.

His arms crossed, he tapped at his wrist with a smile. "What took you so long?"

"Some of us have to do the heavy lifting. I got the location. Get in." Ellis climbed behind the wheel and pressed the ignition, waiting for McCallister to close his door. "How much do you know about the BLT?"

He buckled his seat belt. "Besides the fact it's a delicious sandwich?"

She gave him the side-eye. "Funny. The BLT is the Bangor Land Trust. They operate the Bangor City Forest and other public open spaces. The forest is about 680 acres. Lots of trails that are used pretty much year-round." She handed him the call sheet and reversed out of the parking lot. "That's the GPS location."

"All right."

"Since you're unfamiliar," Ellis continued, "based on that location, it looks like the body was discovered very near, if not inside, the Northeast Penjajawoc Preserve."

"Is there something special about that place?" McCallister asked.

"October through about mid-December, it's used for hunting deer." Ellis drove on to northbound I-95. "Are you an outdoorsman?"

He scoffed. "Me? No. I'm a straight up Townie."

"You don't live in Boston anymore," Ellis replied.

"I do not, but the outdoors for me extends to a walk along the Penobscot near my apartment downtown. What about you? You grew up mostly in Bangor. Do much camping with your pops?"

She let loose an audible grunt. "No, he was always too busy working. But I did spend one summer in middle school at an archery camp."

McCallister turned down his lips and nodded. "Archery? Huh, I never would've guessed."

"Oh yeah." A corner of her mouth ticked up. "I have a wide range of knowledge on a lot of weaponry."

"Good to know. I'll be sure not to piss you off."

Ellis exited the highway and continued north toward

Kittredge Road. "This is one of the main entrances. We should see BLT cars up ahead soon."

McCallister tilted his head in her direction. "What else do we know about this situation?"

"BLT officials were notified by two hikers. A couple of women in their twenties. They came across the body and scurried back to the security building. Told them what they saw, and BLT drove out there. Dispatch got the call shortly after they confirmed." Ellis pointed ahead. "I think that's them." She slowed her approach and pulled over to the shoulder behind several government vehicles. "Let's talk to these guys and see where we're at."

The detectives stepped out of the four-wheel drive SUV. The sun shone bright this morning, but the air still had that nip of early spring to it.

Ellis led the way toward the BLT officials, who huddled in conversation. She reached for her badge. "Morning. Detective Ellis. This is my partner, Detective McCallister."

An older gentleman, slim with a deeply lined face, wore a black trapper hat and forestry uniform. He outstretched his hand. "Thank you both for coming out. I'm Jeff Brogan, BLT. The two hikers who made this unfortunate discovery are in the main building near the entrance. I'm sure you'll want to speak with them."

"Of course." Ellis turned around in the direction of the woods. "Can you show us what they found?"

"Yes, ma'am. Why don't you both follow me?" Brogan set off into the trees.

"Where's the nearest trail from here?" Ellis kept a close eye over the grounds as she followed.

Brogan pointed north. "Up there a ways. One of the hikers spotted the body from a fair distance. They came over to investigate."

"Can you tell me if this is part of the preserve?" she continued.

"It is, actually." Brogan reached the location, where two other staffers awaited. "We've been keeping watch in the event other hikers get interested in what's going on over here. But it's been fairly quiet today. Not surprising, as the spring season is only just getting started." He turned to his colleagues. "Bangor PD is here. Give them some room, yeah?" When they took several steps back, Brogan turned to Ellis. "Okay, here you are."

Ellis nodded at McCallister, as they moved in to where the body of a man lay on the ground beneath mud, debris, and ice. "Did the hikers touch anything?"

Brogan stepped in. "No, ma'am. That's what they told me."

She squatted low and raised her eyes to McCallister. "Come take a look." When he joined her, she continued, "This body's been here a while, just looking at the state of decomp, even if he was frozen, and he's wearing an orange vest."

"He was a hunter," McCallister said. "But looking at his clothes, he isn't dressed like one. Certainly not one prepared for the weather."

"Hunters are required to wear safety vests to stay visible, but you're right. The state of the clothing...It appears torn or maybe—burned. And I don't see any gunshot wounds." It was then she noticed the dead man's face. "And what's going on with his skin?"

McCallister focused his attention. "Jesus. What happened to his face? That's not decomp. Frostbite, maybe?"

Ellis leaned in for a closer look. "It looks like his lips are peeling. His cheeks and down his chin and neck." She turned back to him. "Are these burns?"

His eyes raked over the dead man. "Not like any burns I've

seen. And no obvious bullet entry wounds, like you said, but I can't see his backside. I'm hesitant to move him until we get a truck here ready to take him to the medical examiner."

"I agree. There is evidence scavengers got to him, but not as much as I would've expected, all things considered." Ellis got to her feet and turned back to Brogan. "When is hunting season exactly?"

"October fifteenth to December tenth," he replied.

McCallister grumbled. "The beginning of winter."

"Let's get a truck out here. We need an autopsy ASAP. In the meantime, did you check for ID?" she asked.

"Yes, ma'am. I did it myself and used caution. I found no identification on the body."

She looked at McCallister. "What kind of hunter comes out here with no ID?"

2

E llis drove behind the coroner's van which carried the body to Augusta, where the chief medical examiner's office was located. She tapped her fingers on the steering wheel, considering how best to proceed. "If we can get an approximation of when the man died, we'll run a search for missing persons around that time frame. And when we get a cause of death, that'll tell us what we're dealing with."

McCallister rubbed his smooth chin as he peered through the windshield. "I'm not sure I buy the idea this man died of natural causes or from exposure."

Ellis raised her brow. "Not if those burns on his face were recent."

"That would mean someone timed it right and knew his body wouldn't be found until spring, and this possibly bought him some time to cover it up," McCallister replied.

"If this was set up, it seems strange they'd leave a bright orange vest on the body if they hadn't wanted him to be found." Ellis made the turn to exit the highway.

He turned down his lips. "Fair point, but he would've had ID on him had that not been the case."

She trailed the van into the parking lot of the ME's office. "And this is why we're here; to determine whether this is a murder investigation or whether we get to knock on some family's door telling them we found their long lost dad dead in the woods because he hadn't been prepared for the elements." Ellis opened her door to step out and took notice of McCallister's far-off stare. "What's wrong?"

He returned a curious gaze. "I was just thinking, if it is some poor hunter who died from a heart attack or something, wouldn't our department have been brought in when the family called looking for him? A search would've been conducted."

Ellis tilted her head. "You are absolutely right. We can check the files when we get back to the station, but I don't recall getting a call like that this past winter. So, if there's no report, no family coming forward. Huh...you know, if we were keeping score, I'd say the point goes to foul play."

McCallister stepped out of the Tahoe and joined Ellis as they entered the building. She reached the administration desk and retrieved her badge. "Detective Ellis. The body that just came in? We'd like to see the ME right away, please."

"Yes, ma'am. I'll let him know you're here." He picked up the phone and soon returned his attention to her. "He's coming up now."

"Thank you." She aimed her sights to the double doors ahead and, when they opened, a man in a white coat emerged. "Dr. Rivera, hello."

"Detective Ellis." He offered his hand. "I'd say it's good to see you, but it rarely is in these instances."

"Yeah, sorry about that." She returned the greeting. "You remember Detective McCallister?"

"I do, indeed."

They exchanged a brief greeting when McCallister seemed ready to cut to the chase. "The man who was just brought in from City Forest—"

"Yes, uh, come on back." He waved them on. "As you know, given his fresh arrival, I haven't had the opportunity to so much as set eyes on him, but I'll do my best to answer your questions." Dr. Rivera entered the intake room and snatched a pair of latex gloves from a box mounted on the wall. After the detectives walked in, he closed the door. "So, what is it I can do for you in the short term?"

"He's a John Doe," Ellis replied. "His identity is our first priority, then cause of death."

The doctor approached the refrigerator and opened the steel door. "I did say *short term*, but let me take a look." He pulled out a metal slab, where a body lay under a white sheet.

Rivera pulled down the sheet and proceeded to take several moments to study it. "No obvious injuries." He appeared to zero in on the John Doe's face. "Except for these lesions on his mouth and neck. Hmm. I'll need to figure that out. One thing is certain, he's been dead a long time. I'd venture to say weeks, maybe months." The doctor slid his hands around the skull and turned it left. "Large contusion at the back of the head."

Ellis stepped in. "Does it appear to be from an object?"

"If you're asking whether I think it came from a weapon of some sort, I can't say right now. Could be from a fall, and it happened peri-mortem." He turned the head right, peering inside the ears and eyes, carefully parting the lips to see inside the mouth. "These skin abrasions are troubling."

"How so?" McCallister asked.

"Well, at first glance, they appear to be burns. An odd find in a victim who, circumstantially, would have no cause for them."

"His clothes looked like they had holes burned in them too," Ellis added.

Rivera continued to examine the torso, arms, legs. "Some postmortem wounds that looked to have been caused by animals. No ligature marks. No other bruising." He raised the man's right hand and looked closely at the fingertips. "A fair amount of material under the nails. We'll check that out, of course."

Ellis set her eyes on Rivera. "What will be your next steps?"

"We'll pull fingerprints first, then we'll try to find a match to dental records. That'll be my first step in determining this man's identity. The fact he's wearing an orange vest suggests he was hunting. Could also be a hiker during hunting season. I wouldn't dismiss the possibility of cardiac arrest either." Rivera set his sights on Ellis. "It's just too soon to say, Detective. I need time to perform the autopsy."

"One thing we noticed, Doc, was that he didn't appear to be dressed for cold weather," Ellis replied.

"And if he was hunting," McCallister cut in, "makes sense he'd be wearing a camo jacket—or any jacket, really. And then he'd put on the safety vest over that."

Ellis crossed her arms. "How soon can you get to work?"

"My stock answer is that it'll take a few days, at least. Longer for labs to come back," Dr. Rivera replied. "But I will do what I can for you."

"Thank you for your time, Doctor," Ellis replied. "Let us know what you find as soon as you can."

"You know I will, Detective."

"We'll show ourselves out," she added. "Thanks again." Ellis was quiet as they left the coroner's office and made their way back to her SUV. She unlocked the door and stepped inside, keeping her eyes fixed ahead. When McCallister climbed in, she fired up the engine. "This guy's been dead, we assume, for months."

"That's how it currently appears," he replied.

Ellis grabbed the column shifter and pulled the gear into reverse. "No self-respecting hunter would go out in the middle of winter that unprepared for the elements."

"And unless he was hunting with his bare hands, he would've had gear with him, too. Probably a hunting license as well." McCallister buckled his seat belt.

"Exactly." Ellis drove onto the road ahead. "It doesn't sound like he was hunting for anything to me, especially if the doctor finds those apparent burns are recent. It sounds like he was the hunted."

THE SECOND FLOOR of the Bangor police station was home to the Criminal Investigation Division (CID). The six detectives employed handled every criminal case from robbery to grand theft, and from drugs to murder. In a city of roughly 30,000, their resources could easily be stretched thin.

It also meant that each of the detectives worked a range of investigations. While they had their specialties—for instance, Detective Gabby Lewis was a computer forensics expert—they had to be ready to handle any case that Abbott tossed their way.

So when Ellis and McCallister returned to the station house to brief Sergeant Abbott on the body found in City Forest, it seemed he considered this an opportunity for Detective Bevins to get his feet wet in homicide.

Abbott focused on Ellis with a probing stare as he sat behind his desk. "Your gut is telling you this is foul play, is that right?"

"At first blush, yes." She glanced at McCallister for agreement, who nodded his response.

Abbott drew in a deep breath and clasped his hands. "All right, here's the deal, stay on top of the ME. See what he finds. And if he finds evidence of murder, I want you both to bring in Bevins."

Ellis furrowed her brow. "You want three of us to work on a single investigation?"

"Look, I get three's a crowd, but the kid needs the experience. He's a good detective. And with only six of you on the team, each has to know what the hell they're doing on any given investigation. Besides..." Abbott gestured to them. "Who better to learn from than you two? Combined, you're the most experienced homicide detectives this department has. You don't know what this case is yet, but if your hunch is right, then bring in the kid. Trust me, it'll humble him. Homicides tend to do that."

Ellis pushed off the chair. "Yes, sir. We'll hold the ME's feet to the fire and see where this thing goes. In the meantime, our plan is to determine whether anyone is out there looking for our John Doe."

McCallister got to his feet and eyed Abbott. "Thank you, sir."

The detectives walked side-by-side down the corridor and back into the bullpen, when Ellis stopped cold. "You know I do my best to look out for Connor, and I might be the only one. But I need to know you're not going to push back on this."

"Why would I?" McCallister asked. "He rubs most of us the wrong way, but hell, I probably wasn't that much different at his age. I wasn't even a detective at his age, but I get it. It's fine. You won't have to worry about me." He shot her a glance. "So who's going to tell him?"

Ellis caught sight of Bevins at his desk and nudged McCallister. "We both do it now."

Twenty-five-year-old Connor Bevins was the youngest detective on the force. With a face that belonged on the cover of a magazine, the kid was cocky, and his know-it-all attitude was off-putting to the rest of the team. When they stopped at his desk, he returned a crooked stare. "What's up? Why are you both staring at me like that?"

"We might be looking at a homicide and Abbott thinks it's a good idea for you to assist." Ellis raised her shoulder. "You in?"

And as if Bevins was a child who had just been told he was going to Disneyland, his face lit up. "Seriously?"

"Yep," she replied. "Like I said, we *might* have a murder. We're waiting on the ME to perform the autopsy. In the meantime, we need to lay the groundwork, so how about you run a missing persons report for the last six months and see what turns up?"

"All right then. I'm on it," Bevins replied, turning serious again.

Ellis dipped her head. "Get back to us as soon as you can."

"You can count on it."

She started back to her desk and sat down, raising the lid of her laptop. "Where does that leave us?"

McCallister arrived at his desk next to hers and grabbed his phone from his jacket. "I'll ask the coroner to send over the fingerprints ASAP. We might stand a better chance at getting results quicker if we run them through the database ourselves. Then he can keep his focus on the rest of it." With his phone to his ear, he eyed her. "It won't take long for Bevins to pull the missing persons' report. I'll let you two run on that."

"Oh, I get it." Ellis nodded. "You want me to be the babysitter."

He returned a grin. "You said it. Not me."

"Uh-huh." Her phone buzzed, and she noted the caller ID before answering, "Hey Dad, what's up?"

"They're moving your brother to a rehab facility next week," Hank replied.

"Why? He still has at least ninety days left on his sentence." She felt McCallister's eyes land on her.

"They're transferring him because he's proven himself in there. Proven that he can be a productive member of society again. So, they're giving him a chance to do that, but he has to successfully complete rehab first."

Ellis rubbed the back of her neck. "Who did you have to collect the favor from this time, Dad?"

"No, you don't get to call me out like that. Carter did this. I didn't pull strings."

She scoffed. "Okay. So where are they sending him? What facility?"

"Cochran House. He'll reside there and still be required to check in with a parole officer daily," Hank replied.

"And how is Carter planning on paying for this, or are you planning to dip into your retirement to bail him out once again?"

"Becca, I'm not gonna argue with you about this over the phone. He's getting out and getting the help he needs. If that means I need to help financially, then that's what I'm going to do."

She glanced at McCallister, who quickly diverted his attention. "Okay, Dad. We'll talk about this tonight. I have to go." Ellis ended the call. "How much of that did you pick up?"

McCallister turned sheepish. "Enough. I'm sorry, Becca. I know your relationship with your brother is strained."

"Strained is a polite way of putting it." She noticed Bevins approach. "Hey, you got something for us?"

"I do." He dropped the report onto her desk. "I ran it for

the past six months. Narrowed it down to males aged twenty-five to fifty, and that's what turned up."

She reached for the report. "This is for the entire state?"

"Yes." Bevins shoved his hands into his pockets. "Figured it was best to cast a wide net."

"Good work," McCallister said.

"It's just a report. I've run these before." Bevins pulled out a chair to sit.

There was that arrogance taking center stage again. Ellis let the comment slide and continued to read the report. "Nothing? How is that possible?"

"Nothing?" McCallister set down his phone and peered over her shoulder.

"Younger men," Ellis added. "A couple of younger guys in their twenties; both from Portland. Our guy was at least in his thirties, maybe early forties."

McCallister sighed. "And based on this report, Portland PD believe those men had headed west to leave the state."

"So that leaves our John Doe out in the cold, literally." She looked at Bevins. "We'll keep looking."

Bevins spun around but stopped and turned back. "Hey, thanks for this, guys."

"For what?" Ellis asked.

He shrugged. "You know how much I've wanted to work on a homicide and you're giving me a chance. So, for what it's worth, thanks."

ELLIS KNOCKED on her father's front door before opening it. "Dad? It's me." She walked inside and secured it behind her. Just ahead was the living room, and she spotted him in his recliner, watching television. "Dad, you awake?"

"It's nine o'clock, kid. Of course I'm awake." He pulled up in the chair. "Did you bring me anything?"

She shed her light jacket and continued inside. "Like what? I figured you'd eaten dinner already."

"Some ice cream would've been nice."

Ellis sat down on the sofa. "Sorry, it's barely 40 degrees outside. Ice cream wasn't exactly at the top of my mind."

Hank chuckled and turned down the volume on the television. "I suppose not. How was work?"

"Might have a homicide on my hands."

"Might?" He shifted his focus to her. "Is the victim still alive or something?"

Ellis cracked a smile. "No, Dad. We found a body and we don't know if he was murdered, or died of exposure or natural causes. In fact, we don't know much of anything at the moment. I'm sure we'll get something back from the medical examiner as soon as possible."

"You want me to put in a call for you? I know those fellas down there pretty well," Hank replied.

"I got it handled, Dad, but thanks for the offer." She folded her hands in her lap. "Tell me about what's going on with Carter."

"Like I said earlier today, he's getting transferred to a rehab facility." Hank captured her eyes. "Becca, this is good news. That boy doesn't need to be sitting in a jail cell, all right? I think you know that. He's done everything right in there. So, his lawyer requested the transfer, and it was approved."

"Did you call the lawyer?" she asked. "I'm sure it wasn't cheap to get him to file the request."

"This isn't about money. It's about getting Carter the help he needs." Hank coughed into his elbow.

"You want some water?" Without waiting for an answer, Ellis retreated to the kitchen. On her return, she handed him a bottle. "That cough's been hanging on a while. Don't you think you should maybe go see your doctor about it? You smoked for twenty-five years."

He accepted the glass and took a long sip. "And it's been almost fifteen since I quit, so what's your point?"

Ellis returned to the sofa. "My point is, you should be worrying about taking care of yourself and let Carter do the same. Being in jail is probably the best place for him. You have any idea how easy it is for addicts to get hold of drugs while they're in rehab? I'm not saying prison is much better, but it is a little."

"He's going and that's that," Hank replied. "Besides, it's no skin off your teeth, you understand? You aren't footing the bill for it."

"No, but you are. And that's where I have a problem. It isn't like your retirement from the force is all that great. You know that."

"I know a lot of things, Becca. But the most important is that my son and my daughter are safe and healthy." Hank set down the bottle. "Why don't you tell me about this body you found?"

3

On a clear morning a lot like the day before, Ellis entered the lobby of the station. Freshly brewed coffee imbued her senses as she noticed officers carrying steaming paper cups in one hand and toasted bagels in another. It reminded her she hadn't eaten yet, so when her phone buzzed in her pocket, it offered a distraction from the hunger pangs. "Dr. Rivera, good morning. I was just getting ready to call you."

"Detective Ellis, I was hoping you and Detective McCallister might come down here this morning. I have some information for you on your John Doe."

She climbed the stairs and stopped at the top landing as McCallister appeared before her. "We can do that. Give me a few minutes and we'll head out."

"See you soon."

Ellis ended the call and eyed McCallister. "Rivera wants to see us about John Doe."

He dipped his head. "He found something he didn't like, if he wants to do this in person."

"Maybe so," she replied. "Let's grab Bevins and we'll

ride out together." Ellis continued into the bullpen and stopped at Bevins' desk. "Get your things. We're taking a trip."

"Where to?" he asked.

"Augusta. The ME has news for us." She returned to the staircase with McCallister beside her, not given the chance to sit at her desk for even a moment or to grab one of those bagels from the break room.

Bevins hurried to catch up to them, while he pulled on his black suit jacket. "Why do you think he wants to meet in person?"

"That usually only happens when they find something out of the ordinary and want to be certain nothing was overlooked," Ellis began. "So, if we're all together, he can go through it with us and he'll be able to say that he consulted with the department before publishing his findings."

"This is a cover-your-ass trip?" Bevins asked.

"Probably," McCallister cut in. "Happened in Boston pretty often. These coroners are on the hook for a lot of things. They like to be certain before writing their reports."

Ellis carried on until she reached the bottom step on the first floor. "We live in a litigious society, Connor. You want to work a homicide? Be ready for a lot of CYA." She walked outside and noticed how quickly the sky had gone from blue to gray, as low clouds settled in.

Once inside her SUV, her attention was drawn to the other side, where McCallister and Bevins looked to be in some kind of a dispute. She rolled down the passenger window. "Guys, get in." When Bevins climbed onto the front passenger seat, her lips twisted into a grin. "You must've called shotgun first, huh?" Ellis glanced into the rearview mirror and noticed a sour-faced McCallister in the back seat. "If this is what I have to look forward to with you two..." She trailed off and pressed the starter.

ON THEIR ARRIVAL at the Augusta ME's office, light rain hung in the air. Ellis slipped on her weatherproof jacket and stepped outside, raising the hood over her short blond hair. "Let's get inside before it starts pouring on us." She hurried to the entrance, leaving the men behind. When they caught up to her, she zeroed in on Bevins. "Connor, is this your first time seeing a dead body?"

He raised his chin, appearing mildly affronted, but soon softened his air. "Yeah, it is. I'll be fine. I can handle it. If my West Point training taught me—"

"Oh boy." McCallister rolled his eyes. "We get it, okay? You're a smart guy. What Ellis was probably about to say was, be prepared. Your gut will do a few flip flops, but hold your shit together, you got it? You're representing Bangor PD. Don't embarrass us."

Ellis jerked a thumb toward McCallister. "What he said. Now, let's get inside." She walked into the lobby, and it seemed the man behind the counter immediately recalled her.

"You're back," he said.

"And I brought another friend." She continued ahead toward the desk. "Dr. Rivera's expecting us."

"I'll call him up now." The man made the call and then turned back to Ellis. "I'll push the button to unlock the doors. You three can go back."

"Thanks." Ellis walked on toward the double doors and heard the click. She stepped into the stark hallway, with Bevins and McCallister behind her. The door to the autopsy room lay ahead and Ellis stepped inside. "Dr. Rivera, good morning."

The doctor turned away from the body and pulled off his latex gloves, offering a hand to Ellis. "Detective Ellis, good to see you again." He turned to McCallister. "And you, Detective McCallister."

"Morning, Doc." McCallister gestured to Bevins. "This is Detective Bevins. He'll be working with us on this investigation."

"Detective." Rivera nodded before turning back to the body. "I performed the autopsy yesterday after moving it to the top of the list. What little authority I have around here works in my favor on occasion."

"We appreciate it, Doctor," Ellis replied. "What did you learn?"

"This is all still preliminary until the tox screen and DNA come back, which could change things." He retrieved another pair of gloves and slipped them on before pulling down the sheet to expose their John Doe.

Bevins approached the body with measured steps and Ellis watched his lips curl for a moment before he appeared to swallow hard.

Dr. Rivera focused on the body, but not before a sideways glance at the apparent greenhorn in the room. "The autopsy revealed tissue damage along the esophagus and the stomach lining. This coincides with the burns we saw around his mouth and neck, and on the clothing. A sizable contusion and laceration on the back of his head, which I've concluded happened before he died. It does not appear to have been from a blunt instrument."

"So it could have been from a fall?" McCallister asked.

"I'm not ruling it out." Rivera shined a light inside the nostrils. "The interior of the nose appears to have burns as well."

"What could do that—the burns, I mean?" Bevins asked.

"I won't have the toxicology report for a few days, so I'm still making some assumptions here. But I did find a small amount of blood in the thoracic cavity, which suggests the damaged organs bled postmortem. Had the damage been done while the man was alive, the bleeding would've been far more significant. He would've suffered convulsions, vomiting. Frankly, it would've been a very painful death. What I believe happened is that a chemical of some sort was forced into his mouth after he died."

"After." She nodded. "And have you identified him?"

"We found dental records that match our analysis of the skull, cavities, and other dental work. It was just confirmed this morning, actually, after our call. And I will also say this —I'm all but certain this man has been dead for months. Best guess for now, given the state of decomp, is two, maybe three months. I'll be able to narrow that down with a few more tests. It does not appear he had been moved during that time. I found evidence of insects in his ear canals, nose and mouth. Bite marks from small animals that had been there for some time." He returned to a desk near the back and grabbed a sheet of paper. On his return, he handed it to Ellis.

"That would put his death in this past December or January." She walked toward her partners and began to read. "Terry Satchel. Forty-one years old. Bangor resident." She eyed McCallister. "Why didn't he come up on the missing persons?"

"Is he single? Maybe he doesn't have family, or doesn't have family here and doesn't stay in touch with family elsewhere," McCallister replied.

"The guy has to have friends, doesn't he?" Bevins asked. "How does someone just die and no one notices?"

"You'd be surprised." Ellis turned back to the doctor. "Are you concluding this as a suspicious death?"

He crossed his arms. "Given the nature of how this man was found—the injury to the skull happening before he ingested the chemicals that damaged his organs—I won't officially make that conclusion, but unofficially . . ."

"Got it." Ellis peered again at the report. "All right. Mr. Terry Satchel, homicide victim." She looked at her partners. "We should get started."

THE MANNER in which Satchel was apparently murdered left Ellis to consider the killing had been an act of retaliation, but for what? The only way to figure that out was to understand the kind of man he was.

That information would only come about when they learned where he lived, worked, and whether he had any family. And as the detectives had made progress on that front at the station, it hadn't taken long to retrieve the details.

It was Bevins who caught the first break. Ellis noticed his hurried approach to her desk and called out to McCallister. "Heads up."

With a triumphant stride, Bevins held up the file. "Terry Satchel's address. Not just that. I have his cell phone number, social security, and employer. The guy worked at Connex Solutions."

"Who's next of kin?" McCallister asked.

Bevins opened the file to read on. "Parents are deceased. No siblings. An aunt who lives in Connecticut." He peered up at McCallister. "She's in a retirement home and suffers from dementia."

"She won't be much help," Ellis cut in. "So we go to his employer and find out when they last saw him. Rivera estimates Satchel died in December or January and that his body had not been moved from where he was found. We'll see if that tracks with the last time his employer saw him. We should go now."

Bevins spun on his heel. "I'll grab my things."

Ellis pulled on her light jacket and tossed her bag over

her shoulder. McCallister grabbed his jacket from the back of his chair, and she glanced at him. "How about you drive, and I'll take shotgun? I don't want a repeat of this morning."

He snatched his keys from his desk drawer and cracked a smile. "Big day for me."

Ellis set her hand on his shoulder. "I gotta let you lead once in a while, so I don't shake that fragile male ego."

He pointed a finger gun at her and clicked his tongue. "There's that wit I've come to know."

The rainstorm had passed by the time they walked to the parking lot. The spring sun took the chill out of the air and Ellis slipped on her sunglasses before stepping into the passenger seat of McCallister's black Ford Interceptor.

Bevins slipped onto the back seat and closed his door. "What happens now? Are we allowed to tell the employer this guy's dead when we haven't talked to his only family?"

"Yes, we can tell them." Ellis glanced over her shoulder at him. "What I'm interested in learning is whether Satchel quit, got fired, or just didn't show up one day. And if he didn't show up, did anyone question it?"

"Yeah, cool. Okay." Bevins buckled his seat belt. "Still seems kind of strange that this guy had no friends out looking for him."

McCallister drove on, making his way to the highway on-ramp. "All depends on whether they believed something happened to him. We don't know much about Satchel yet, but talking to the employer is a solid first step."

"And just like any other investigation," Ellis cut in, "we'll check out his home, work on finding whatever friends he did have and talk to them, too. In regard to procedure, there isn't much difference between a homicide and other cases you've worked. You find the clues and see where they take you."

"Yeah, sure," Bevins said. "The only difference is that a man is dead."

Ellis nodded. "Well, there's that."

McCallister pointed ahead. "That's the place. Right there."

Ellis took notice of the large facility. "Connex Solutions. Do we know what they do?"

"Manufacturing," Bevins replied. "I didn't dig too deep into it, though."

"Got it." She waited until McCallister stopped the car. "This looks to be a pretty large company with a lot of staff— just look at the parking lot." She stepped out and examined the plant.

McCallister headed toward her. "I suppose we'll want to speak to the company officers before talking to Satchel's boss."

She waited for Bevins to catch up and continued. "Let's get it out in the open right away that we're working a homicide, even if Rivera hasn't officially declared it. Homicides scare people and they're more likely to speak the truth." Ellis carried on toward the entrance and opened the large glass doors. As the detectives entered, she noticed the interior's industrial design. Tall ceilings. Concrete floor. Metal columns and staircases. "Afternoon." She led them to the security desk, with her badge in hand. "Detective Ellis, Bangor PD. These are my partners, Detectives McCallister and Bevins. We'd like to speak with an officer of the company."

The young woman, with a pleasant smile and soft brown hair, tilted her head. "Do you have an appointment, ma'am?"

"No, we don't," Ellis replied. "But this is official police business, so if you would be so kind as to get someone who has authority to come down and talk to us."

"Yes, Detective. Of course." The girl fumbled with the phone and made the call. "Mr. Goyer, um, there's some detectives here to see you." She paused a moment. "Uh, not you specifically, sir, but someone with authority." She nodded.

"Okay, thank you. I'll let them know." She ended the call. "Mr. Goyer is the Vice President of Operations. He's the senior-most officer here at the moment."

"That'll do. Thank you." Ellis leaned into Bevins and softened her tone. "If Hank taught me anything, it was to always throw out the whole 'it's a police matter' argument. Gets them every time."

"She's right," McCallister added. "No one likes to talk to us, so they're usually more than willing to pawn us off on whoever's at the top of the food chain."

Bevins shoved his hands in his pockets. "Duly noted."

Within moments, a towering, middle-aged man in a dark suit approached them. His serious mien put Ellis on notice, as she considered whether he had suspected the reason for their arrival. She offered her hand. "Mr. Goyer?"

"Yes, ma'am." He accepted the greeting. "And you are?"

"Detective Ellis. This is Detective McCallister and Detective Bevins. We'd like to talk with you in private."

"Of course. We have a conference room just down this hall. Follow me." Goyer set his sights on the girl at the front desk. "Hold my calls, Josie."

"Yes, sir."

Ellis's sharp-eyed nature kicked in as they trailed the lanky gentleman. The highly polished executive seemed in stark contrast to the nature of the business, as other employees passed by. Most appeared to be line workers dressed in coveralls with safety goggles on their heads.

"Right through here, please." Goyer gestured for them to enter. "I take it you're not here to collect for the Police Benevolent Foundation or some such charitable resource."

"Not exactly, Mr. Goyer." Ellis entered the room and stepped aside to make way for the others.

McCallister was close behind. "But we're happy to accept any donation."

"I'll be sure to check with Bookkeeping to see where we stand." Goyer closed the door and motioned to the table. "Please, have a seat. Can I get you anything? Something to drink?"

McCallister waved his hand. "No, thank—"

"I'll take some water, if you don't mind," Bevins cut in.

"Of course." Goyer eyed Ellis. "Anything for you, Detective Ellis?"

"I'm fine, thank you." She delivered a disapproving side-eye to Bevins.

Goyer walked to the credenza on the back wall and retrieved a bottle from the small refrigerator tucked inside. On his return, he handed the bottle to Bevins. "Here you are, sir."

"Thanks." Bevins twisted off the lid and gulped down half the bottle.

Ellis turned her attention to Goyer. "Sir, we're here about an employee of yours: Mr. Terry Satchel."

He took his seat at the head of the table and glanced up, as if thinking about the name. "Satchel. Oh, that's right." Goyer returned his attention to Ellis. "He hasn't worked here in some time. Why? What's this about?"

"He's dead, Mr. Goyer," McCallister jumped in.

The man caught his breath for a moment. "Oh, I see. That is terrible news. I'm afraid I hadn't heard about that. When did this happen?"

"His body was found in City Forest yesterday, sir," Ellis continued. "The coroner's office was able to ID him just this morning, so we ran a background check and discovered this was where he worked up until December, maybe January."

"That sounds right. It has been months, to my knowledge. But did you say you found his body?"

Ellis hardened her gaze. "Foul play is suspected, Mr.

Goyer, so we'd appreciate learning more about him. Any friends he had here. Had he been fired? Did he quit?"

An awkward grin twisted his lips as though he was grappling with the notion. "Well, Detective, given this news, I think it best if I bring our in-house counsel into this conversation."

This was where her hackles raised, and she wasn't alone. McCallister let slip a grunt of displeasure while Bevins raised his brow. "If you feel that's necessary," she added.

Goyer cocked his head. "It's always necessary, Detective."

4

The door to the conference room opened and Ellis stepped into the hall. "Thank you for your time, Mr. Goyer, Ms. Lunt."

"Of course," Goyer replied. "And Ms. Lunt will gladly accompany you to the shop floor to talk with a few of Mr. Satchel's co-workers."

"Thank you." Ellis raised her index finger. "Give me a moment with my partners?" She walked to the other end of hall, where McCallister and Bevins caught up to her. "We didn't get much out of that, except these guys wanted to make sure they won't be getting sued anytime soon."

"Agreed," McCallister replied. "But they won't release his employment records without a subpoena, claiming privacy rights."

"The guy's dead," Bevins cut in. "What rights govern his privacy now?"

"It speaks to their lack of cooperation, which gives me pause," Ellis added. "At least they're willing to let us talk to his co-workers."

"I wonder what they'll have to say, knowing Satchel said he was going on vacation and never returned," Bevins said.

"We're about to find out." Ellis returned to the lawyer. "Ms. Lunt, if you wouldn't mind showing us to the floor, so we can speak to a few people."

"Of course." Lunt carried on downstairs to the floor where line workers stood at machines and conveyor belts. The full-waisted woman in a blue silk blouse and black pencil skirt reached the bottom. "Here we are, Detectives."

Ellis took in the vast facility. "This place is huge."

"Yes, ma'am. We're one of the largest employers in the city," Lunt replied.

"And what is it you said you make around here?" McCallister asked.

"We fabricate rubber components for machinery. O-rings, and things of that nature." She walked toward a nearby office. "I'll introduce you to the foreman. He can find the people you'll want to speak with."

"Thank you." Ellis eyed the shop floor again. It appeared that a hundred or more people worked down here. Equipment as far as the eye could see.

"Right through here." Lunt stepped inside the office. "Harry, I have detectives with the Bangor police department who would like to speak with you. Mr. Goyer's already okayed it."

The unassuming man appeared to be in his early sixties and removed his glasses. He stood from behind his desk and donned a pleasant expression. With thinning light blond hair and a high forehead, he looked the part. The blue button-down with rolled-up sleeves, beige dress pants, and sensible black work shoes completed the look. "Of course. What can I do for you folks?"

Ellis took a step inside. "An employee of yours, Terry Satchel. Do you know him?"

"Sure. He worked here a while back. Up and quit on us, though."

"I'm afraid he's dead, sir," she said. "And it does appear he died under suspicious circumstances."

"Oh my God." The man slowly returned to his chair. "When?"

"We aren't exactly sure yet," McCallister cut in. "His body was found in City Forest early yesterday by a couple of hikers. Sir, we're here to speak to some of Mr. Satchel's co-workers, friends. Anyone who can give us some idea of when they last saw him."

"Uh, yeah, okay." He peered at Lunt. "And all this has been authorized?"

"Yes, it has," she replied.

"All right then." He got to his feet again, though appeared unsteady. "I suppose the best person to talk to will be Scooter. He and Terry were close."

"Scooter?" Ellis asked.

"Scott Littleton. Everyone calls him Scooter." He headed to the door. "I'll go get him."

After he disappeared on the shop floor, Ellis looked through the office window. It was only moments later when she spotted Harry with another at his side. A younger man, possibly only in his late twenties.

The door opened and Harry walked inside. "Detectives, this is Scooter, uh, Scott Littleton. I mentioned you had news about Terry."

"Where is he?" Littleton hooked his thumbs through the belt loops on his coveralls. "I haven't heard from him in months. Dude just ghosted me, and I don't even know why."

Ellis's eyes raked over the younger man. Short brown hair, a goatee to match. Somewhat scrawny. "I'm sorry, Mr. Littleton, but Mr. Satchel is dead. We believe foul play was involved."

"The hell?" Littleton stumbled back. "Are you saying Terry was killed?"

"Yes, sir, we are," McCallister said. "And it's important that you answer a few questions for us. I'm sure this is a terrible shock, but do you think you can speak to us about him?"

"Son of a bitch." He scratched his furry chin. "Yeah, of course. Terry was my friend. I just can't believe this. Are you sure?"

"We're sure," Ellis replied.

"Well, all right." Littleton dropped onto a side chair. "I'll answer what I can."

———

JANICE BUXTON PULLED the lever to seal the outer ring as it lay on the conveyor belt. The forty-five-year-old with bleached hair and smoker's lips glanced into Harry's office, while Scooter talked to folks who looked a lot like cops. Her first thought was that they'd found him. Cops only showed up when someone was dead, so it wasn't looking like Terry was going to walk onto the shop floor at any moment. After months of radio silence, Janice wondered what had happened to him.

But if they had found him, what had happened? Plenty of people had stood to lose a lot if he had opened his mouth, as he'd threatened to do several times before. And she'd warned him. But Terry was stubborn as hell, and he was going to do what he wanted, no matter the cost. "But for it to cost this much?"

Her co-worker pulled out an earplug. "You say something, Janice?" he asked.

She waved him off and returned to the tedious task, but not before a sideways glance at Harry's office again. Janice couldn't help but think that if Terry was dead, then he'd gone and pushed them too far. And if she pushed too, chances were good she'd end up just like him.

———

THE WRECKED SCHOONER was a dive bar a few blocks away from Connex Solutions, where Scott "Scooter" Littleton had worked for the past three years. He perched on a stool, and the barman placed a pint glass in front of him.

"You want to start a tab, Scooter?" he asked.

"Why not?" He reached for his wallet and set down a credit card. "Got some bad news today."

The bartender grabbed the credit card. "Oh yeah? What's that?"

"A friend of mine was killed. Like, murdered."

"Are you shitting me?" he asked.

"Nah, man. I wish I was. Dude was my friend." He eyed the bartender. "You remember Terry, don't you? Big guy. Weighed about a buck ninety-five. Kind of loud."

"Terry? Hell yeah, I remember him. Dude's dead? Ah, man. I'm sorry to hear that. Listen, that one's on me, all right?"

"Thanks." Scooter set his sights on the television screens above the bar. He sipped on his draft beer and caught movement from the corner of his eye.

"Scooter?"

He turned his gaze. "Wayne? Hey, man. I take it you heard?"

Wayne Byrd was a lissome man with a pallid face. Light-brown hair and deep crow's feet around his blue eyes. Always insisted that too much sun would give him cancer, so he went the other direction and avoided it altogether. "They called me in, too. It's a shame, isn't it?"

"Yeah, it is. Terry was a good friend to me, you know?"

Scooter pulled off his baseball cap and set it on the bar top. "So the cops talked to you too, huh?"

"They did." He shrugged. "Not that I had a whole hell of a lot to tell them. I just thought Terry got fed up with the place and quit. Took off."

"Me, too." Scooter slumped forward. "I should've checked on him, man. What the hell kind of friend was I to him that I couldn't bother going to his house?"

"Look, you can't blame yourself. It was probably some random thing, you know?" Wayne raised is finger to garner the barman's attention. "Can't stop that kind of shit from happening, no matter what you do."

"Guess not." Scooter sipped on his beer. "What'd they ask you?"

"I don't know. The usual, I guess. How long I knew him. Were we close friends and shit. I don't know. The man had no wife and kids. Kinda feel bad no one knew where he was all this time. We came here, of course. Shared a few brewskies. That's about it."

"Yeah, well, I guess we were closer," he replied. "Goddam. I just can't believe someone killed him. I mean, that shit only happens on TV, right?"

"Not anymore."

Scooter tossed back the last of the pint. "I do remember something that happened not long before he left."

"What was that?" Wayne asked.

"I didn't say anything to the cops, mainly because I don't remember much about it except that you were there."

Byrd aimed his thumb at his chest. "I was?"

"Yeah, I'm sure it was you. It was on the shop floor after lunch or something. I don't exactly remember. But it was you."

"Okay, so what happened, if it was me, 'cause I don't remember anything happening with Terry."

"Like I said, it wasn't like I was standing right there, but seemed to me you two were in a heated discussion," Littleton replied.

Byrd waved his hand. "Well, hell, that could've been on any given day. You know what Terry was like. He hated the job. Missed a lot of work. So, if I chewed his ass at some point, does that come as a surprise?"

"Maybe not." He shrugged. "I remember you being plenty pissed off. Like your face was all red. I think one of the other guys, maybe it was Harry himself, got between you two to break it up."

Byrd set his sights on the television. "Like I said, Terry wasn't the most reliable guy and if I got hot over him, like you say, then I guess I did."

Littleton returned an uncertain gaze. "Yeah, I guess you did."

POLICE TAPE SURROUNDED the trees where the body of Terry Satchel was found. Yellow tags lay on the ground where the police had marked the precise location of the victim. No sign of police or Land Trust officers this late at night. But in the darkness, finding the one piece of information that would reveal just exactly what happened to Satchel would be nearly impossible. Nevertheless, the clock was ticking. Bangor PD had put three detectives on this case and now that they'd talked to the co-workers, it was only a matter of time before they found what he now sought.

The two-door black Mercedes' engine idled as it sat roadside near where the body had been found. Exhaust drifted into the air and was visible in the night sky. Sitting inside was a dark-haired man with a thick brow and a square jaw. He picked up his phone and made the call. "It's me. I don't know what you expect me to find out here..."

"You need to find that phone," the man on the other end replied.

"Even if I did, do you really think it would still work?" He shook his head and peered out over the woods. "It's a lost cause, man. Whatever's done is done and we'll have to clean up the mess. That's what I'm here for."

"And the cop?" he continued.

"If we need to send a message, a reminder, then I can make that happen. You just tell me when." The engine in the Mercedes AMG roared, as he pressed on the gas. "I need to get the hell out of here before someone sees me."

THE MANAGER of the apartment complex where Terry Satchel lived stood behind the counter in the lobby. "Like I told you, Detective, Terry's been gone a long time. I had his things cleared out when no rent came."

"What did you do with his stuff?" Ellis asked.

"Put it in a storage unit. I'm required to keep the belongings there for six months. After that, I have the right to sell it off." He looked away. "Guess I'll have to do that now."

"We'd like to take a look inside the unit," McCallister said. "Does anyone live in his apartment now?"

"Of course. I can't leave a place empty like that. But I can let you into the storage unit. It's just across the street, as a matter of fact. Helps keep moving costs down."

"Can you show us now?" Ellis continued.

"Yes, ma'am." The manager grabbed a set of keys from the back wall and walked out from behind the counter. He turned to one of his staff. "Mind the fort, would you?"

"Sure."

The manager pushed through the exit and walked into the parking lot. He pointed his index finger ahead. "It's just over here."

Ellis walked alongside McCallister. "You think Connor's pissed he's not here with us?"

"I know he's supposed to assist but to shadow our every move is just a waste of resources. He'll be fine doing some of the grunt work." McCallister looked at her. "He might not be happy about it, but we all have to do things we don't want to do."

She chuckled. "That's true. I don't know if Connor realizes what he signed up for."

"The kid will figure it out," McCallister replied. "What do you think we'll find inside the unit?"

Ellis shrugged. "I don't know, maybe the chemicals he drank? That would be a good start."

The manager reached the gate and entered the code. "It's just inside. Not far."

The detectives followed him and soon arrived at the unit.

He keyed the padlock and rolled up the door. "There you are, Detectives. Have at it. But if you have to take anything out, just..."

"It'll be included in the chain of evidence," Ellis replied. "We appreciate the help."

"Sure thing." The manager handed her the lock. "Just bring back the key when you're done."

After he walked away, Ellis stepped inside the cold brick-and-concrete unit and scanned what few boxes and furniture were stacked inside. "He didn't have much, did he?"

McCallister shook his head. "Doesn't look like it. But if we don't dig deep into this guy's life, we aren't going to get very far."

"The manager just threw everything in garbage bags. This

guy's entire life is in a bunch of black garbage bags." She squatted low to open one of them. "Clothes."

"I got clothes over here too. A few dishes," McCallister said. "His co-workers said he didn't do much outside of work. Looks like he didn't do much at home either."

"What about a car?" She returned upright. "Let's get Bevins on that too. See if he can find a car registered to Satchel."

"You got it." He returned to the bags and continued to open each one. "He wasn't a hunter, not by the look of the things he owns here."

"Doesn't seem that way. So how did he find himself in the woods wearing a safety vest?"

"With chemical burns in his organs," McCallister added.

Ellis's phone rang and she glanced at the caller ID. "Who the hell is this?" It was then that she pressed the call button to answer. "Detective Ellis."

"Uh, yeah, is this the detective that I talked to at Connex yesterday morning?"

"Yes, sir. Who is this?" She returned a concerned look at McCallister.

"This is Scott Littleton."

"Yes, of course. Mr. Littleton. I remember you," she replied. "How can I help you?"

"Well, I think maybe I can help *you*, Detective."

"Is that so? I'm all ears, Mr. Littleton," Ellis said.

At this, McCallister moved in.

"So a while back, I mean, like I don't know the exact date, but it wasn't that long before Terry disappeared."

"Okay." Ellis placed the call on speaker. "Go on."

"Terry was a good guy, but everyone knows he didn't like his job. And so I think some people got rubbed the wrong way by his attitude, you know?"

"Sure," Ellis replied.

"Anyway, I remember seeing this dust-up between Terry and Wayne Byrd. I think you talked with him yesterday too."

"The name rings a bell," she began. "What happened with this dust-up, Mr. Littleton?" She turned up the volume on her phone.

"I wasn't up close and personal when it happened, but I do remember Wayne getting plenty mad at Terry. Like I said, I don't know what it was about, but I want to say it was only days later that Terry disappeared. So it got me thinking, you know, maybe something happened between those two."

"Do you think the argument didn't end there?" Ellis asked. "Is it possible it carried over to after-hours?"

"I can't say for sure, but you know, Terry didn't have enemies, ma'am. He probably should've quit the job a long time ago, 'cause he just wasn't interested in it, but I can't think of anyone else who had a beef with him, except maybe Wayne."

"We did speak to Mr. Byrd, but he didn't mention any of this," Ellis continued. "And frankly, neither did you."

"Well, I should have. Seems kind of important to me, now that I think about it," Littleton said.

"Is there anything else you can think of?" she pressed on.

"Nah, that was it."

Ellis noticed a mild slur in his tone. "Mr. Littleton, please don't take this the wrong way, but have you been drinking?"

"My friend was killed, Detective. I took the day off work and I'm sitting in my apartment by myself. So yeah, I've had a couple beers. But this doesn't have anything to do with what I'm telling you. Now, Wayne's been a good guy to me, but I'm telling you, he has a temper sometimes. You can ask other people at work about it too."

"Okay, well, thank you, Mr. Littleton. We will follow up on what you've said. And I am sorry for your loss." She ended the call and set her eyes on McCallister. "Byrd said absolutely nothing about this yesterday."

He rubbed his lightly stubbled cheek. "Which means he thought it was something."

BEVINS CARRIED himself with overconfidence on most days, but today, his haughtiness was especially abundant. And was the first thing Detective Bryce Pelletier noticed on his approach. While Pelletier was a man probably too kind for his own good, Bevins cranked the arrogance dial to ten. He threw his arm around Pelletier as they met at the bullpen. "Hey, man. How's it going?"

"Good," Pelletier replied. "I hear you're working with Becca and Euan on that murder investigation." Bryce Pelletier had been with BPD for a couple of years after he transferred out of the Portland police department. The slightly pudgy thirty-three-year-old with light hair, worn short, and stark blue eyes chalked up Bevins' attitude to youth. Though he was certain there was more to it than that. People who put on airs, as Bevins had, generally had a confidence issue they kept well hidden. "How's the case going?" he continued. "You need any help with anything?"

Bevins waved his hand. "Nah, I got this. In fact, I just got a text from Becca asking me to run BMV records to get details on the victim's car. I was just walking back to my desk to do that."

"Cool. All right, man. Well, I'll let you get back to it."

Bevins raised his chin. "Cool. Catch up with you later."

Pelletier carried on into the hall toward the kitchen and spotted Detective Lewis inside. "Hey, Gabby. How's it going?"

"Fine. You?" She grabbed a bottle of water from the refrigerator.

"Good. Yeah. Did you hear Abbott pulled three of us to work that murder case?"

"I did hear that. Connor has to learn somehow, I guess. He thinks it's some kind of badge of honor or something," she replied. "I think he's in for a rude awakening."

"Serves him right. He thinks he knows everything. I worked in Homicide in Portland long enough to know those cases will eat you alive." Pelletier dropped a few quarters into the vending machine and pressed a button. A bag of M&M's crashed to the bottom. "Guess we'll find out if all his bluster gets him anywhere."

Lewis approached him and placed a hand on his shoulder. Out of all the detectives, she was the only one with kids and often doled out motherly advice. The cyber-expert with long dark braids twisted at the back drew her full lips into a smile. "It'll humble him for sure. And then he'll learn. They always do."

"Yeah. See ya, Gabby." Pelletier ripped open the packet of candy and started back into the bullpen. He noticed Ellis and McCallister approaching in the distance and locked eyes with Ellis. He missed working with her. Now, whenever a homicide popped up on the radar, the case went to Ellis and the brooding loner Euan McCallister. Pelletier scoffed. The man looked like he'd walked straight out of some noir novel, even now as they drew near.

Ellis donned a smile. "Hey, Bryce. Got some of them for me?"

He furrowed his brow. "Huh?"

"The candy." She pointed to the bag of M&M's. "You have a couple to spare?"

"Oh, yeah, sure." He freed an awkward laugh. "Here you go."

"Thanks." She plunked one into her mouth. "We just got

back from searching the victim's storage unit and need to do a write-up. I'll catch up with you later?"

"Sure." He nodded graciously as she made a one-eighty and continued into the bullpen.

McCallister offered a casual bow and followed her.

Pelletier wondered if he'd ever have the nerve to disclose his feelings for her. Thing was, he was fairly certain the man who'd just left had feelings for her too, so what chance did he stand?

ELLIS SAT DOWN and swiveled her chair toward McCallister's desk. "It is strange we didn't find a laptop or a computer. No cell phone either."

He set down his bag and dropped into his chair. "I can understand the phone, assuming it was on him at the time of death. But he had a decent-paying job. He must've owned a laptop or tablet."

"Makes me think either the building manager has sticky fingers, or someone else got to his things before we did," Ellis added. "I'm going to see if Connor had any luck with the vehicle registration." She walked over to his desk. "Hi. Sorry about earlier—"

Bevins set down the pen in his hand and raised his brow. "You mean you guys leaving me out in the cold?"

"We hardly left you in the cold. The legwork still has to be done by someone." She shifted her stance. "So, have you had any luck?"

Bevins caught sight of McCallister and waited for him to join them. "Satchel is the registered owner of a 2015 GMC pickup. Tags are still current."

"And yet, this truck is nowhere to be found," Ellis replied. "Whoever wanted him gone went through a lot of trouble to make that happen. No computer in his belongings, and now, no truck."

McCallister folded his arms. "Why make it so easy to find his body, and then attempt to make it look like some kind of a hunting accident? Would've been more believable had his truck been found nearby."

"And the truck wasn't reported stolen?" Ellis continued.

"Nope." Bevins flipped through his notes. "In fact, the tags had been renewed last November. That tracks if we're thinking he was killed in December or January. If we can get access to his bank account, I can find out who his phone carrier was, assuming he paid by check or EFT. Otherwise, we'd have to check every phone carrier and ask them to search whether Satchel had an account with them. That's the only way we'll obtain phone records, which I assume is what you'll be asking me for next."

"As a matter of fact, it is. But there are a couple of ways we can get banking and phone details." Ellis began to count on her fingers. "His former employer, because he probably had direct deposit. The manager at his apartment complex would have a record of payments and contact information. And, of course, utility payments. Let's pursue those avenues so we can get access to bank records. Look for recent activity, first and foremost. That'll give us a trail to follow." She looked at McCallister. "In the meantime, we'll speak with Wayne Byrd again and see what he has to say for himself."

5

After asking around, word had it that Wayne Byrd could often be found at the Wrecked Schooner. As the workday drew to an end, that was where Ellis and McCallister landed.

Ellis parked near the back and kept her sights aimed on the door to the dive bar. "Hopefully, he's had a few. It's more likely we'll get the truth from him."

McCallister opened his door. "I wouldn't count on a confession, if that's what you're thinking."

"If only it was that easy." She stepped out into the cool evening air. A nice change of pace from what had been a brutal winter, in more ways than one.

McCallister took the lead and opened the door for her.

"Thanks." Ellis walked inside the aptly named bar, whose nautical theme may have been a tad overdone. She spied five patrons, who sat at the bar, and around a dozen or more at the tables or playing pool. "Do you see him?"

He tossed an onward glance. "Isn't that him at the end of the bar?"

"Good eye." She started toward the willowy man with deep wrinkles and light blue eyes. "Excuse me, Mr. Byrd?"

He returned a sideways glance. "You're those cops from work. What the hell do you want?"

A welcoming tone, if there ever was one. "Yes, sir. We spoke at Connex yesterday morning. Detective Ellis." She gestured to McCallister. "This is my partner, Detective McCallister. Would you mind if we sat down at one of the tables and talked for a few minutes?"

He regarded her with a close eye. "How did you know I was here? You following me or something?"

"No, sir. Lucky guess. This place is pretty close to the plant," she replied.

Byrd grunted and got up from the stool, grabbing his bottle of beer. "Fine." He started toward a table near the back and sat down. When they joined him, he continued, "I'm guessing this is about Terry."

"Yes, sir." Ellis pulled out a chair to sit. "When we first spoke to you yesterday, you mentioned that Terry wasn't a close friend but that you occasionally hung out."

"Yeah, that's right. Usually here. Why?" Byrd threw back a swig of beer.

McCallister leaned over his elbows that rested on the table. "We're looking for more details about his life, sir. It seems he just up and vanished. Do you know if Mr. Satchel was a hunter?"

Byrd scoffed. "I have no idea. Like I said, we weren't that close."

"When was the last time you saw him?" McCallister asked.

"Like I said at the shop, I saw him at work on December third, and then I didn't see him anymore," Byrd replied.

"Did you two have an argument that day or in the previous few days?" Ellis continued.

Byrd returned a curious gaze and chuckled. "Who told you that? Scooter?"

"Does it matter?" she asked.

"It does if you think I had something to do with what happened to Terry. Is that what you think?" He glanced between them. "You two think I killed him?"

McCallister raised a preemptive hand. "No one's being accused of anything, Mr. Byrd."

The man appeared flustered for a moment before taking another drink of his beer.

Ellis cleared her throat to garner his attention. "It stands to reason you'd think that, Mr. Byrd. After all, why else would cops come talk to you again? Thing is, we don't know what exactly happened to Mr. Satchel and that's why we're here." She watched as Byrd seemed to soften his stance. "So I'd like to ask you again, Mr. Byrd, did you and Mr. Satchel have an argument when you last saw him?"

He eyed the detectives and rubbed his prominent forehead. "Yeah—sort of. I mean, Terry was Terry. He was a good guy, but he hated his job. Everyone knew that. And if there was ever any opportunity to cause trouble, then he would be the guy to take it." Byrd paused a moment. "So on that day, he started talking to me. It was calm at first. Then he started talking about how management was screwing him over. How they were lying to people. I mean, it was just usual Terry stuff." He shrugged. "I guess I wasn't in the mood for it that day and I called him out. Said if he hated it so much, then he should quit. Although I might've used less polite words."

"And what happened then?" Ellis asked. "Did he leave, or did he keep pushing you?"

"I don't remember exactly. I think he trashed the company a little more and then I told him to go f— off so I could get back to work. That was pretty much it."

McCallister set a curious eye on him. "When we called

you in to speak with you yesterday, you didn't mention any of this. Frankly, you didn't seem all that surprised we were there, asking about Mr. Satchel to begin with. Is there a reason for that?"

Ellis noticed Byrd's gaze roam, as though he was looking for someone. "If there's something else you can tell us, Mr. Byrd, we'd appreciate it."

He raised a shoulder. "Nah, I mean, I didn't think I came off that way, but maybe I did. Maybe Terry was just the kind of guy that trouble followed, you know?"

THE THREE-BEDROOM bungalow that had been home to Ellis and her ex-husband appeared just ahead. The porch light burned as she pulled onto the driveway. Her SUV was too big to fit in the puny single-car garage, one of the reasons she considered moving. The other was the fact that Andrew had lived there, too. While he was long out of her life, pieces of him remained. She never cared much for reminders of the past.

Ellis stepped out of her SUV and headed toward the front door, with her keys in hand. After stepping inside, she walked to her bedroom and changed into sweatpants and a T-shirt, securing her weapon in the lockbox in her bedside table.

She returned to the living room and switched on the television. Staring blankly at the screen, Ellis considered what Wayne Byrd had said about Terry Satchel when they had spoken to him earlier at the bar. If he was as hot-headed as Byrd proclaimed, maybe he'd pissed off the wrong person. But it was the look the man gave that perhaps concerned her more. Byrd looked like a man under surveillance, or at least one who believed he might've been under surveillance.

It occurred to her that Satchel could've been indebted to

someone. Maybe he was a gambler. Owed the wrong people. And if Byrd knew those same people, it would stand to reason why he was fearful. There had to be a way to learn more about Satchel. He must've had a digital footprint—but without a device or account information, how could she find out? This was a man who seemingly had few friends and no close family. His belongings revealed nothing.

"It's too clean." Ellis picked up her phone. "Gabby, hey, it's Becca. Is this a bad time?"

"No, not at all. I'm just curled up on my couch with a book. The boys are playing video games in their rooms. What's going on? Are you all right?"

"Yeah, no, I'm fine," she replied. "I was just thinking about this case—Terry Satchel."

"Right, yeah. Abbott had you bring in Connor with you and Euan."

"That's the one. And that's all fine, no problems—yet. But I called because this guy, this Satchel, we haven't found a computer or laptop. No phone or tablet. Connor ran a background on him, so we have his employment history. No arrest record. I need to know more about him."

"Well, I'll tell you the best way—search his name online," Lewis replied. "People have no idea the amount of information about them that exists online. Now, you say you don't have the guy's phone or computer, and that's a hindrance for sure, but you have other resources. The online search is the quickest and easiest way to start, but you also have a background for social media accounts. Run that and see what turns up. If the guy was online, you'll see it."

"Thanks, I'll do that, Gabby. I appreciate your help and I'll see you in the morning."

"You got it. See you then."

When Ellis ended the call, the answer was obvious. No

one was a ghost in this day and age. Dead or alive, everyone had a digital footprint.

As she began her search, her phone rang and she quickly answered. "Piper, hey, what's going on?"

"Becca, are you at home?"

She picked up on the tension in her best friend's voice. "Yes, why?"

"You mind if I stop by? I'm only a few minutes away."

"Everything okay?" Ellis pressed on.

"Just—can I just come by?"

Yeah, there was a problem here. "Of course. I'll see you in a few minutes."

"Thanks." Piper hung up.

The call ended and Ellis felt her heart racing. Something had happened and now she would have to wait to find out what it was. She and Piper had been friends since high school and were as close as sisters to this day. Piper lived in a luxury condo downtown and was a successful realtor. She liked to party and was still single. Ellis might've been that way, too, had she not been a cop. But the call was unusual. Piper Dixon rarely needed anyone, but it seemed as though she needed her friend right now.

Ellis spotted Piper's black BMW through the window as she parked out front. Her friend stepped out of her car and walked up the path toward the front door. Ellis shot up to open it. And when she did, Piper appeared shaken, darting her gaze as though fear gripped her. "Piper? Are you okay?"

"I'm fine. I'm fine." She thrust up her hands. "Can we just go inside, please?"

"Come in." Ellis stepped aside. "Sit down on the couch. I'll get you some water."

"Thanks." Piper made her way to the sofa and sat down. "I'm sorry to bother you. I know it's getting late—for you."

"Don't think twice about it." Ellis returned with a bottle of water and sat down next to her. "Okay, you don't look good, Piper. Tell me what's going on."

"I was being stupid, Becca." She took a drink.

"What do you mean?"

"I mean"—she set down the bottle and held Ellis's gaze— "I met this guy earlier at happy hour. Good looking. Tall. Nice body. Wore a hell of an expensive suit. We hung out. Had a few drinks. He seemed nice."

Ellis felt the shoe was about to drop. "Then what happened?"

"He asked me to go home with him. I said I had to get up early tomorrow and that we could go out another time..."

Ellis felt her heart pound in her chest. "Go on."

Piper picked at her fingernails. "He walked me to my car. No one was around. Not that I saw, anyway. So, I grabbed my keys to unlock the door and he grabbed my arm—hard. I told him to let me go. He said I was going to drive us to my place, and that was all there was to it."

"Jesus, Piper." Ellis turned away, her face heated with anger.

"I managed to get away, Becca. I ran and hid for, like, an hour. I wanted to be sure he was gone."

"Did you call the cops?" she asked.

Piper shook her head. "No. I mean, nothing happened."

"The hell it didn't. He nearly attacked you, Piper, and you were lucky enough to get away before anything happened." She got to her feet. "You need to file a report. You know the guy's name, right?"

"Yeah. But, Becca, I don't want to file a report. I just wanted to come here and see you. I need a friend right now."

"I'm trying to be your friend," Ellis replied.

"No, you're being a cop." Piper raised her eyes to meet hers. "Look, I was buzzed, okay? If I file a report, that'll be the first thing I have to admit to. I mean, I didn't drive, but I was going to. Don't you see that? I screwed up, Becca. I'm just grateful I got away."

Ellis considered Piper's words and pressed her hand on her forehead. "Okay. No police report. Can you at least do one thing for me?"

"What?" she asked.

Ellis firmed her stance. "Give me his name."

PIPER HAD FALLEN ASLEEP, and Ellis made sure of that. It was late, but the bar would still be open. What happened to her friend couldn't stand, so she was going to that bar downtown to find out more about this man, Tom Sutton, who'd tried to attack Piper.

While chances were good he wouldn't be there, Ellis planned to start asking questions. Piper hadn't wanted to go to the police; fine. But fortunately, her best friend was a cop and Ellis wasn't about to let this man get away with what he'd done—or tried to do—because she'd come across men like that before. The idea this was the first time the man had done this didn't hold water.

Ellis walked inside the two-story bar that overlooked the river. The upscale spot was busy as she navigated through the crowd. The bouncer almost hadn't let her in, given her attire, which was a T-shirt with a jacket, and a pair of faded jeans. But when she showed him her badge, he quickly stepped aside. She elbowed her way to clear a spot along the bar and caught the attention of the barman.

"What can I get you?" he shouted.

"I'm looking for Tom Sutton. You know him?"

The young man with broad shoulders narrowed his gaze. "You a cop? You look like a cop."

She nodded. "Do you know Sutton?"

He turned down his lips. "Name doesn't ring a bell. What's he look like?"

"Tall, athletic build. Wears a nice suit."

The bartender gestured to the crowd. "Lady, you just described half the dudes in here."

She smiled. "Thanks anyway."

"Sorry."

Ellis turned around and peered out over the crowd. He was right. Most of the men in here matched her description. But she had a name. And that was a good start.

FROM BEHIND THE wheel of his Mercedes AMG, the man with the thick brow and dark hair peered through the windshield. An image on his phone appeared as he swiped open the screen. A quick glance between the photo and the woman, who now walked out of the bar, confirmed his suspicions. "Hello, Detective Ellis." He waited for the pretty blond cop to reach the parking lot and watched her climb into a big white Chevy SUV. "Where are we off to, huh? Back home? Back to your friend, Piper?"

He waited while she pulled away and started toward the bridge before he caught sight of her rear license plate. He grabbed his phone and snapped a few pictures.

After a few moments, he pressed the ignition and checked his sideview mirror. The SUV's tail-lights dimmed as it gained distance. He turned around and headed in the same direction, following carefully to avoid detection. After all, this detective's father was the legendary Hank Ellis. If she was half as good at her job as he had been, extreme caution was in order.

On exiting the thoroughfare, he continued to trail her as she made a turn onto a neighborhood street. It was time to fall back. If he were to continue along the road, she would see him. He opened his phone and dropped a pin on his location. "Until next time, Rebecca."

CONNOR BEVINS never had trouble with women. If anything, he had a hard time fending them off. Case in point, the beautiful woman who lay next to him now. He'd met her at a bar, pretty typical scenario. And when she asked if he would go home with her, well, what was he going to say? No?

And this was where he always ended up. The thorny post-sex, laying in someone else's bed, in someone else's home, situation when all he wanted to do was pull on his clothes and leave. It was usually the same excuse...

"*I better get going. I have to be in early tomorrow. Working on a big case.*" Only this time, he was working on a big case, and bragging about it seemed juvenile. A man was dead and, for the first time, he understood the seriousness of it.

All this young woman knew was that he was a detective. It often impressed girls his age. Most of them were barely out of college and usually still had a roommate, and had only begun to work their way up the ladder.

"You sure you can't stay?" she asked, eyeing him with the same look he'd seen on her face at the bar.

He pulled on his pants and T-shirt. "Sorry, no. But I had a great time." Bevins slipped on his shoes and tucked his wallet into his back pocket.

The beautiful woman with black flowing hair clutched the covers over her chest. "Call me later, okay? Maybe we can see each other again soon?"

She sounded casual enough, but Bevins recognized the hint of desperation beneath her words. He didn't understand much about women, except that they didn't like being tossed aside; forgotten; used. But it was his nature, no matter how hard he pretended it wasn't. "Sure, I have your number. My job keeps me pretty busy, but I'll call you when I have some free time." He leaned over the bed to kiss her cheek. "I had a lot of fun. Get some sleep."

As he walked out of her bedroom, he felt her stare bore into the back of his head. The anger and disappointment laying just beneath its surface. Some girls were cool about it. Most were not. She was among the latter.

He made his way outside her apartment and walked to his car. The shiny black Ford Mustang was his baby. He loved that car more than anything, except for getting laid.

Bevins drove back to his one-bedroom apartment, which was on the top floor of a complex near the edge of the River-walk. He didn't make nearly enough money to afford the place, or to drive the Mustang, for that matter, but his parents were wealthy. They paid his rent. No one knew it. It wasn't something he was proud of, but things were going to change now. This murder investigation was going to prove to everyone that he was a good detective and he deserved to be there.

They all thought he got the job because of West Point. The letters of recommendation from his father's associates probably helped too. After all, some had been congressmen. No one at the station house understood why he worked there. It was simple. He'd screwed up. Bad. Almost got himself kicked out of the Academy. That part of his resume seemed to have magically disappeared, as if none of it had ever happened. Almost as if he never drove that car into the ditch that killed his friend.

His father insisted the accident need not ruin his life; never mind his dead friend. But any career in Washington just wasn't possible. Bevins knew it, so did his father. And after the other five police departments he'd applied to rejected him, they both knew few options remained. To this day, he had no idea why Abbott agreed to hire him.

Bevins drove into the parking garage and rode the elevator to the top floor of the building. As he made his way along the corridor, he considered that of all his co-workers, Ellis was the only one who hadn't dismissed him because of his age, or because of his arrogance. Yeah, he knew he was an egotistical prick, but now she'd tasked him with helping them on this homicide.

So he would continue to do everything she asked of him, because at the end of it all Rebecca Ellis ran that department, no matter what Sergeant Abbott or Lieutenant Serrano had to say. That place was part of her. It was in her blood. If he wanted to prove himself a worthy homicide detective, he would have to win her over to do it. So grunt work? Sure, no problem. He'd do it. Even if Euan McCallister seemed to relish in handing it over to him. Made no difference. Because if there was one thing no one knew about him, it was that Connor Bevins would step on whoever was in his way to get what he wanted. His father had taught him that.

6

She was late again. Janice Buxton hurried through the shop floor toward the back to punch her time ticket. It was probably the fourth or fifth time in the last month that she'd come in more than fifteen minutes late for her shift. Surely, they would make an exception this time. After all, one of her co-workers was found dead in the woods and the cops had come. It was all anyone had talked about for the past two days. She was devastated.

Janice had been employed at Connex Solutions for nearly ten years. And in all that time, she'd been promoted once. She was convinced it was because she was a woman—and few women worked the floor here—but it was still a job, and she couldn't afford to lose it. Janice stood at the time clock, ready to enter her number, when Wayne Byrd stepped out from the nearby men's room.

"Morning, Wayne."

"Morning, Janice." He glanced at the clock on the wall.

"Yeah, I know I'm late." She pressed the button to clock in and carried on toward the lockers. Janice slipped off her sneakers and tucked them inside the small cubby, then grabbed her work shoes to pull them on. With the hair tie on her wrist, she quickly pulled back her bleached blond hair into a tight bun.

"Hey."

She spun around and noticed Wayne now stood behind her. "Yeah?"

"Did the cops talk to you the other day? You know, about Terry?" he asked.

"Only briefly. I didn't think they would, but then as they were leaving the female cop stopped me in the hall. Why? They talk to you?"

He shrugged. "Yeah. Only 'cause Harry knew me and Terry worked the same line."

She looked down. "I'm sorry he's gone. But at least he didn't have a family, I guess. No kids."

"I suppose so," Byrd replied. "I wonder what's going to happen now."

"What do you mean?" Janice secured the back brace around her midsection. The job took its toll on her body. That, along with the extra twenty pounds she carried.

"I mean, I wonder if they're going to figure out what happened to him. Last I heard, they couldn't find his truck or anything. That's crazy, right?" he asked.

"Yeah, it is." She closed the locker door. "I'd better get out on the line. Harry's going to have my head. I'm late already."

"Sure. See you later," he replied.

Janice walked out to the shop floor and carried on toward her station. She switched on the machine and poured the resin into the tank. Moments later, the line moved, and she pulled the levers. She wondered why Wayne had asked her about Terry. He hardly talked to her at all, except on the rare occasion when they were in the break room together and it was someone's birthday. Had he known about the two of them? While it hadn't been a big secret, neither of them were very open about their private lives, but Terry often had a big mouth. Maybe he let slip one day that they'd gone out for a while and Wayne got curious. The bigger problem was that she hadn't mentioned it to the cops.

"Janice, you're late again."

She spun around and saw Harry looming behind her, pushing up his eyeglasses. "I know. I'm so sorry. My car—"

"Everyone here drives cars, Janice, and they manage to get in on time."

She nodded. "It won't happen again, Harry. I promise."

"I'll hold you to it, Janice. You know I will." He started away.

She watched him leave. "Oh, I know you will, Harry."

OFFICER TRIGGS, who worked in Patrol, arrived at the detectives' bullpen. Ellis noticed him march straight for her.

"Detective Ellis."

"Hey, Triggs, what's going on?" She liked Triggs. He'd been there when the trouble with Carter had brewed a few months' back and she recalled how he'd made sure the situation at the pawnshop hadn't escalated. And when it came to Carter, that was no easy task.

"The guys at Impound called me just now," Triggs continued.

McCallister, who was at his desk, drew his attention to him.

"Detective Bevins ran a motor vehicle records check for a 2015 GMC pickup truck," Triggs added.

"Yes, he did. It's for a case we're working," she replied. "Why?"

"You won't believe this, but the impound lot has it."

Ellis drew back in surprise. "What?"

"Yeah, I know, it's crazy. But listen, go down there and see for yourself. I told them I'd come and talk to you. I don't know all the details."

She got up from her desk. "We'll go right now. Thank you."

"Anytime, Detective." Triggs turned on his heel and glanced at Bevins, who was at his desk. "You should see Ellis. It's about that vehicle you were after."

Bevins walked toward the others with his palms upturned. "What's going on now?"

"Triggs just said our impound lot has Satchel's pickup," Ellis replied. "When you ran the BMV check, they got pinged. The truck is here. We need to get down there now." She wasted no time and carried on to the first floor.

Bevins shook his head. "Son of a bitch."

"No time for questions, just move." McCallister brushed past him.

The impound lot was around the corner and Ellis waited for the others to catch up. When they arrived, she carried on through the rows of impounded vehicles and reached the building. "They had the vehicle and didn't notify anyone?"

"We don't know how long they've had it," McCallister said. "Our guy went AWOL sometime in December."

She stood at the kiosk's window and peered inside at the officer. "You have a 2015 GMC pickup truck?"

"Detectives." The officer pulled his feet from the desk and stood. "What are you looking for?"

"The GMC truck," Ellis replied. "Triggs said you got pinged from a BMV search that Detective Bevins conducted. Why are we just now hearing about this?"

The officer raised his hands in defense. "I don't know. I was off for a few days. But look, no point in getting bent out of

shape, all right? If it's here, I'll find it and I'll take you to it."
He typed on his keyboard. "A 2015 GMC truck, all right. Here
we go. Yep. It's here. I'll get the keys." He grabbed the keys
from a box mounted on the back wall and walked out of the
kiosk. "What's the deal with this truck anyway?"

"It belongs to a suspected murder victim," Ellis replied.

He turned sheepish. "That would explain your anger.
Follow me. I'll take you to it." The officer walked through the
lot. "According to the file, this thing's been here for months.
Owner never claimed it."

"That's because he's dead," Ellis replied. "Do we have a
record of when he was contacted?"

"Of course. It'll be in the file. I'll give you everything I
have."

"There could be evidence inside the truck, right?" Bevins
asked.

"If there was, it's probably boxed up and in the back," the
officer said. "We clean out the vehicles in case they're broken
into and the owners come back and find their things are
missing."

"So it's been cleaned out and sitting here for months."
McCallister rubbed his forehead. "Any evidence there may
have been inside it is now contaminated."

"Look, now, I get you're all upset over this, but let's keep
one thing in mind," the officer began. "If a car is found to
have been abandoned, we make every attempt to contact the
owner. If the owner never shows, then eventually it goes to
auction, or back to the bank. Now, we only just got notified
you were looking for this car when Detective Bevins ran a
check. So, we're only doing our jobs. Just be grateful we didn't
auction it off yet."

As angry as she was, he was right. It was the procedure
that needed to be fixed, not the cops doing the work. "You're

right. I apologize," Ellis replied. "The good news is that we have it and that's better than nothing."

"This is it, right here." He inserted the key and unlocked the door.

"Can you move it into the shop?" Ellis asked. "We need to sweep it."

"Yes, I can do that. Give me a few minutes and I'll have it brought inside for you," he replied.

"Thank you." She stepped away from the truck and examined it while the officer prepared to move it. "I don't see any damage to the exterior."

"There'll be a record of where it was found," Bevins said. "We should take a look at it."

"Absolutely," McCallister replied. "Could've been found at his apartment, and since he'd abandoned that, they might've figured he'd abandoned his car too."

"Why wouldn't they suspect something might've happened to the guy?" Bevins went on. "He doesn't show up for work. He doesn't return home. His truck was left—somewhere. Why wouldn't anyone think that was suspicious?"

"There must be an explanation," Ellis said. "Because you're right. Anyone on the outside would look at the scenario and be suspicious. So, maybe someone was able to explain it away. Maybe he was seeing someone."

"And that person hasn't come forward since he vanished?" McCallister asked.

Ellis pondered the question when the officer started the truck. She stepped away so he could reverse out of the spot. "Best-case scenario now is that we find evidence as to what happened to Terry Satchel. And if we're really lucky, we'll find DNA."

WHEN THE WHISTLE blew for lunch, Janice shut off the machine. That was when the overhead speakers sounded.

"We'd like everyone to come together in the cafeteria for a special announcement."

She looked at her co-workers, who'd shut down their equipment and were making their way to the lunchroom. As she followed, she tapped a man on his shoulder. "Hey, Steve, you know what this is about?"

"No clue, but I hope there's cake," he replied.

Janice shrugged and continued toward the back. As she reached the cafeteria, everyone filed inside. Looking out over the sea of people, she noticed Harry step up to the front, where a podium had been placed. "What is going on?"

Another co-worker nudged her arm. "Don't know, but there better be some damn food because I'm starving. I'll bet they'll make this part of our lunch hour too."

Janice chuckled. "I'm sure they will."

"Listen up, everyone." Harry waved his hand in the air to garner their attention. "Come on, guys, eyes up here, please." He waited a moment while the scattered conversations died down. "Thank you all for being here. First of all, I know it's been a tough few days, with learning about our friend and co-worker Terry Satchel. I want you to know that management truly appreciate your cooperation with the police. I know they're doing their best to figure out what happened."

Janice closed her eyes for a moment.

"However"—Harry turned to an older man, who stood next to him—"it is for a much happier occasion I've called you all in here. As many of you know, Mark Owens has worked here for the past fifteen years. He's been an exemplary member of this company and a good friend to many of you. We've all heard Mark's stories of fishing with his kids. Catching the biggest cod you ever did see. And we were all so proud when Mark's daughter, Megan, got married and moved to Portland." Harry turned back to the crowd. "So, today is a bittersweet day. Mostly for us, because I'll bet Mark's been looking forward to this day a long time." He patted the man's back. "Mark has decided to retire from Connex."

Janice darted a gaze at her co-workers. "Retire?"

Steve leaned in and whispered in her ear. "I didn't know he was considering retiring. Man's only fifty years old."

Staffers cleared a path, as two people rolled in a large cake on top of a metal table with candles that burned brightly. Janice noticed the words written on it. "Happy Retirement, Mark."

Harry looked on. "So, as a thank you for your years of hard work, not only did we get you this stellar cake but we'd also like to offer you this." He handed him a box. "Go on, open it."

Mark opened the box and pulled out a gold watch. "Well, this is something. Thank you so much." The wrinkles around his eyes deepened as he smiled, and he peered out over his co-workers. "And thanks to all my amazing friends." A sudden raspy cough erupted from him. He grabbed his handkerchief and quickly wiped his lips. "Sorry about that. This truly has been a wonderful time in my life, and I will miss you all."

Harry patted him on the back again. "Well, all right. And thank you, Mark." He turned to the crowd and raised his hands as if preparing to conduct an orchestra. "On three... one, two...For he's a jolly good fellow..."

It took a moment for the rest of the crowd to join in the song, but Janice remained quiet. She'd known Mark pretty well. Even talked to him in the past couple weeks, catching up with him about his family. He never said a word about retiring. And looking at him now, his hair thinning, his cheeks gaunt, the man wasn't well. What had he not told her?

Steve nudged her arm. "Come on, Janice. You gotta join in."

"Right. Sure." She smiled and began to sing.

THE TRUCK WAS PARKED inside the garage bay. It was now Forensics' job to sweep it for evidence that might point to whatever happened to Terry Satchel. Ellis gathered with McCallister and Bevins, as they awaited the tech's arrival. A moment later, he appeared. Ellis smiled and offered a greeting. "Seavers. Didn't think I'd be seeing you so soon."

"Detective Ellis. Neither did I. How you been?"

"Doing all right." She turned to McCallister. "You remember Euan McCallister?"

"I do. Good to see you again, sir." Seavers shook his hand before turning to Bevins. "And I know this guy."

"How's it going, man?" Bevins nodded. "Haven't seen you since that carjacking last month."

"I know. So, they got you working a homicide, huh?"

"How'd you guess?" Bevins asked.

"Because you're paired up with this one over here." He thumbed to Ellis. "She's the go-to when it comes to the hard cases."

"Yes, sir." Bevins returned a half-smile.

Seavers turned back. "So, Ellis, tell me what's going on with this truck. We're looking for prints?"

"Prints, fibers, blood, anything you can find. This was our victim's truck, and here's the kicker—the man's been dead in the woods for what we think was probably months. Turns out, Bangor PD was called by City Forest officials to have the truck towed off the side of the road near their trails back when this went down."

Seavers raised a brow. "They didn't think that maybe the car belonged to someone inside the forest?"

She shrugged. "It'd been there a while. They assumed it was abandoned."

"I see." He slipped on a pair of gloves and opened the driver's side door. "Well, let me take a quick peek inside."

Ellis set her hand on Bevins' shoulder. "Why don't you go see if they boxed up anything that was found inside the truck?"

"Sure thing." He started back.

McCallister stepped toward the truck. "This was towed out of the preserve part of the forest, from what the report read."

"Where they allow hunting," Ellis cut in. "And, according to the report, it appeared to have been there several days."

Seavers glimpsed inside the truck. "Do we know if they searched for him in the woods? I mean, you see an abandoned vehicle, you have to think it belonged to someone."

"It's possible they looked around at the time," Ellis said. "But depending on when, we could've had a big storm. Snow probably covered the ground. If they looked, it's likely he was buried under the snow."

"It's plausible," McCallister replied. "Still doesn't pass the smell test, if you ask me."

"That's why I'm here, Detective," Seavers replied. "Give me a couple of days and I'll have some answers for you. I hope."

"Thanks. I appreciate it. We'll check on Bevins to see if they found anything inside the vehicle." She continued on with McCallister beside her, when her phone rang. "Detective Ellis, Bangor PD," she answered.

"Yes, Detective, you were at Connex Solutions the other day talking to some people."

She stopped cold and grabbed McCallister's arm to halt him. "Yes, ma'am."

"Well, you talked to me for a few minutes. My name is Janice Buxton."

"Yes, of course. Mrs. Buxton."

"It's Ms., but anyway, I was wondering if I might come talk to you."

She eyed McCallister. "Of course. Would you like me to come back down to your workplace?"

"Oh, uh, no, ma'am. I'd prefer to speak someplace else. Someplace where we might have some privacy, if that's okay."

"Yes, of course. There's a quiet café not far from the police station. We could go there, unless that's too far out of your way. I'm open to suggestions, Ms. Buxton."

"Okay, well, how about, uh—there's a small restaurant about a mile or so from my house. I couldn't meet until after my shift, but I'm off at six o'clock, so I could be there by about seven. If that's too late—"

Ellis raised her hand. "No. No, ma'am. It's not too late at all. Why don't you text me the address and we'll come see you this evening?"

"We?" Janice asked.

"I'd like to bring my partner, if you're okay with that. I believe you met him. Detective McCallister?"

"Yeah, of course. I remember him. Okay, that'll be fine. I'll send you the address now. Thank you, Detective."

"Thank you, Ms. Buxton." Ellis lowered the phone.

"What was that?" McCallister asked.

She turned to him with mild surprise. "Janice Buxton. We talked to her briefly the other day. Probably in her mid-forties. Dyed blond hair, a little thick around the middle."

"I think I remember her." McCallister clutched his hips. "If I recall, she didn't have much to say about Satchel."

"Which is why I'm surprised to hear from her now. She

wants to meet us tonight. Strange how we're getting calls from these people now. Almost like they didn't feel free to speak to us at the plant." Her phone pinged with the incoming message. Ellis opened the text. "This is where she wants us to go."

McCallister glanced at the address. "Okay. We can do that."

7

I n a strip mall located next to a small community was a
restaurant called the Rusty Spoon. Ellis double-
checked the address Janice Buxton had sent her and
eyed the place. "I think this is it."

McCallister opened his car door. "I see a couple of cars
here. I hope one of them is hers and that she didn't get cold
feet." He stepped out and waited for Ellis to join him. "First
Scott Littleton wants to pull us aside to talk, and now this
woman. And then we have Wayne Byrd, who seemed afraid
of his own shadow when we met him. What do you suppose
that means?"

"I'm really hoping we're about to find out," she replied.

McCallister opened the door to the restaurant. "Ladies
first."

Ellis nodded her appreciation and walked inside. She
surveyed the rows of rustic booths and tables under the lights
of farmhouse-style pendants. A hand waved at them ahead.
"There she is, over there."

"I see her," McCallister replied. "She called you. Better for
you to take the lead here."

Ellis walked toward a booth near the back. "Ms. Buxton?"

Janice pointed to the opposite bench. "Detectives. Have a seat."

"Thank you." Ellis slipped inside the booth and shuffled toward the window when McCallister moved in next to her.

Only moments passed before a server appeared and smiled at them. "Evening. Can I get you folks something to drink while you look at the menus?" He placed the menus on the table.

"We won't be eating dinner," Janice said. "But I will take a Coke."

"Yes, ma'am." He looked at the detectives. "And for you two?"

"Water for me, thanks," Ellis replied.

"Same for me too." McCallister nodded.

The server appeared annoyed at the skimpy order and turned to leave.

"Thank you for meeting with me," Janice began.

"Yes, ma'am," Ellis replied. "I can't tell you how much we appreciate the call. When we met the other day, you hadn't seemed to know much about Terry Satchel."

Janice canvassed the area. "Well, I knew him all right. Probably better than most. I was dating him—sort of."

Ellis raised a brow. "Sort of? What does that mean, exactly?"

"It means we went out a few times. People at work didn't know about it. Not that it was some big secret. We just didn't say anything."

"Did you break it off?" McCallister asked.

"His disappearing is what broke it off." Janice eyed the server when he returned with drinks. "Thank you." She took a sip from her glass of Coke. After he left, she continued. "We weren't serious or anything. Honestly, Terry had a lot of animosity toward the company, and he struggled to keep it from consuming him."

"Why did he dislike it?" Ellis cut in. "Was it his boss? Higher ups?"

"Look, here's the thing." Janice set her eyes on them. "Terry was a bit of a conspiracy theorist. About a lot of things, but about Connex in particular. But you know, he said he knew things and tried to pull me in with him, and then...that was it. I never heard from him again."

"What did he know?" Ellis asked.

Janice stared at her Coke for a moment, appearing hesitant. "Listen, what I do know is that Terry didn't hunt. In fact, he wasn't much of an outdoorsman at all. So when you said he was found in the woods, it didn't jibe with what I knew about him."

"What did you do after he disappeared?" Ellis pressed on. "Were you concerned about his safety? Did you speak to either your bosses or anyone else about it?"

Janice played with her straw. "No, I didn't say anything. I just kept my head down, not knowing what to do. I'd called him several times but never got an answer. I just figured he'd had enough and decided it was time to go. After a while, I went to his apartment and the manager said Terry had left his place untouched. Then I talked to Human Resources and all they could tell me was that Terry decided to quit. That was that."

McCallister rested his forearms on the table. "Ms. Buxton, I don't think you would've called us here if you didn't have something more to say on the subject of Terry Satchel's death. If you know more, you can tell us. No one has to know that you talked to us at all."

Janice glanced around again. "Talk to Mark Owens. He's set to retire soon. Despite Terry's flaws, he was, at heart, a good man. He wanted to do the right thing. I'm not sure he knew how, though. He got in over his head." She shuffled out of the booth and grabbed her jacket. "I should go."

Ellis raised her hand. "Ms. Buxton, wait."

Janice turned back.

"What are you afraid to tell us?"

She donned a timorous smile. "I've told you what I can. The rest is up to you."

JANICE RETURNED TO HER HOUSE, regretting telling the cops anything, but it was done now. The months of confusion, thinking Terry just up and quit. Now she knew the truth, going back to work at the plant would be a mistake. "I can't stay here," she told herself. But maybe once she was clear of Bangor, she could leave the cops with the final pieces of the puzzle of what Terry believed he had learned.

Janice hurried to her bedroom and tossed a duffel bag onto the bed. The few clothes she owned hung in her closet and she clutched an armful of hangers, then shoved the items into the bag.

She glanced at the desk that rested under her bedroom window. "The emails." Several printed sheets of paper rested on top of the printer and she walked over and grabbed them. Her laptop was open and she deleted the printed emails from her computer, along with the files that were attached.

A call rang through on her phone, which lay on the bed. The number was unknown. "Damn it." She ignored the call and continued packing, throwing in her toiletries next. The overstuffed bag resisted until she pushed on it with her knee, finally zipping it.

Janice slung it over her shoulder and carried on into the

living room, surveying her small home. "Time to go." She stepped outside into the brisk night air and walked to her car.

Inside, Janice turned the engine and shoved the papers into her glove box. She drove out of the neighborhood, heading straight toward the highway. "I should've kept my mouth shut," she repeated over and over, glancing into the rearview mirror. But she had cared for Terry and, knowing he was dead, after months of speculation, she almost wondered why she wasn't dead too. Maybe they hadn't known what Terry had told her. But with the cops on the case, how long would it be before they figured it out? "They'll know soon enough."

Janice entered the freeway on-ramp and merged westbound. She checked the time on her phone. She could be in Vermont by midnight. An old friend lived there who could help. Her phone rang again and again, the caller ID unknown. This time, she answered the call.

"Yeah."

"Don't do it, Janice. You can stay here. I can help you. Whatever cockamamie story Terry spouted off wasn't true. You have to know that."

"Why are you calling me? What do you know?" she asked.

"I know you're scared. You don't have to be."

"Did you do it?"

"Janice—"

"Don't call me again." She ended the call and then it hit her. "Son of a bitch." Janice slammed her palm against the steering wheel. "My laptop." For a moment, she considered turning around and going back for it, but after that call, it was too risky. "No. Don't. You deleted everything. Just leave it."

As Janice gained miles between herself and Bangor, the knot in her gut loosened. Once she was in Vermont, she'd call that detective and tell her what she had. Tell her about the call earlier. Maybe then she would be safe and she could go back home.

Mesmerized by the tedium of the darkened highway, it wasn't until headlights in the rearview mirror blinded her that she was drawn back . She squinted for a better look and her face deadpanned. "How did you find me?"

ALONG THE HIGHWAY, headed back to the center of the city, tall streetlamps lined both sides of the lanes. Ellis drove on while her headlights captured the mist that swirled in the air. "Another name," she began. "What does Mark Owens have to do with anything?"

"I suppose we'll have to find out." McCallister was quiet for a moment. "Hey, you want to grab some dinner? I was actually pretty hungry earlier, but you know..."

"I could eat. I'll have to stop in to see Hank later, but I think he enjoys my late-night drop-ins. Gives him an excuse to stay up."

"I have no doubt he appreciates your visits," he added. "And the fact that you lean on him sometimes for advice makes him feel useful. You're a good daughter."

"He was a great detective. I do lean on him. He makes me better." She glimpsed the contour of his face in the muted light. "How about Indian?"

"What's that?"

"For dinner. I haven't had a good curry in a long time," Ellis added. "Unless you don't like—"

"Fine by me. I do eat more than clam chowder and lobster rolls."

Ellis laughed. "Don't get me started on Boston's lobster rolls. They can't hold a candle to a proper Maine one!"

"Oh really? Someday I'll take you to a spot in Westchester. Best damn lobster rolls in the state."

"All right." She eyed him. "Then I'll take you to a place I know of that has the best Maine lobster rolls. We'll see who wins out."

He tapped his hand on his arm rest. "It's a date."

Ellis felt mild heat rise on her cheeks but shook it off. She drove down State Street just north of the Penobscot River. Several restaurants and shops lined either side. "This is it." The small parking lot fronted Masala Bites, a popular spot for Indian fare, and Ellis's only spot when she wanted a curry.

They walked inside the restaurant with scant light and soft music. In hindsight, Ellis now recalled the place was a little too much on the romantic side.

A host approached. "Table for two?"

"Yes, please," McCallister said.

"Right this way."

Ellis followed the host, as he led them through the restaurant. This suddenly felt very much like a date and, with McCallister beside her, the feeling was more than a little unsettling.

An undeniable attraction existed between them, but so far neither had acknowledged it. Ellis had the kind of baggage that made it hard for her to get close to anyone, even her ex-husband, which was one of the reasons why he was her ex. And she'd only been on a handful of dates since her divorce two years ago. Mostly, they'd been blind dates Piper had set up. Each one ended in disaster. And McCallister was her partner. Getting involved in a relationship with a partner never ended well. She'd heard plenty of stories about that.

"Here you are." The server showed them to a cozy table near the back window.

"Thank you." Ellis grabbed her chair to pull it out, just as McCallister stepped in to do the same. "I got it. Thanks."

He stepped away, wearing disappointment.

Ellis hadn't wanted this to feel like a date. This was just the two of them grabbing a bite to eat, like they often did.

When they sat down, the server handed them menus. "I'll be back with waters."

After he fell out of earshot, McCallister began, "Just so we're clear, what I said before about a date—I didn't mean—"

"No, I get it. I didn't think you did." Ellis picked up the menu. "So the chicken tikka is really good here."

He held up his menu. "Sounds good."

It was several minutes into the meal before Ellis pushed away whatever insecurities she felt about this dinner and returned to the case at hand. "Tomorrow, we track down Mark Owens and talk to him, for whatever that's worth."

"And by that point, we'll have access to not only Satchel's personnel records but his phone and banking records too. That'll open some doors for us."

"I'll keep a fire lit under Dr. Rivera as well. We need an official cause of death in addition to a time of death. Then we can work our way backward," Ellis added.

McCallister swallowed down a bite of his chicken. "You weren't kidding. This food is delicious."

She smiled. "Told you."

He wiped his lips with a napkin. "How are things going with your dad, given what's happened with your brother?"

Ellis raised her shoulder. "Hank managed to get Carter transferred to a rehab facility. That's supposed to happen in the next few days. He'll serve out the rest of his sentence there."

"Wow. Do you think it'll help him? Your brother, I mean."

"Long term? I doubt it. It never has before. We've been down this road, but Hank won't give up, so I either get on board or the ship sails without me. I won't abandon my dad, so I guess I'm with him. I'll do what I can to keep in Hank's good graces and see to it he takes care of himself."

"Sure, I get that." McCallister sipped on his glass of iced tea. "But who makes sure you're taking care of yourself?"

———————

ELLIS ARRIVED home after a quick call in the car to Hank. It had gotten too late to stop by. As she walked inside, she flipped on the living-room light and set down her bag on the nearby dining chair.

She made her way to the kitchen. Inside the refrigerator, a nice cold beer called out to her. Her thoughts turned to Piper and the man who had almost attacked her.

She'd struck out returning to the bar where it happened. It had been a long shot, but she had to start somewhere. Now, however, it was time to step it up. She had his name, or at least the name he'd given Piper.

Ellis grabbed her laptop and logged into the Bangor PD database. She entered the name "Tom Sutton." No fewer than fifty "Tom Suttons" were returned. "Damn it." Piper had only given her a vague description and so the best she could do was to narrow down the names to locations. Bangor was a good start. "Show me who you are."

Her phone rang on the side table, and she answered it. "Bryce, hey, what's up?"

"Hey, Becca. I'm not calling at a bad time, am I?" he asked.

"No. I just got home a few minutes ago. Everything okay? Are you at the station?"

"No, no, I'm home. Fletch and I had to answer a robbery call today, so it's been a long one."

She felt his hesitation. "What's going on, Bryce?"

"Uh, nothing. I wanted to see how things were going with you on the Satchel case. How's Connor doing with all that?"

"So far so good. He's doing what I need and hanging in there. Why do you ask?" she continued.

"No reason. Just making conversation. I needed to hear a friendly voice, that's all."

"Oh." Ellis uncurled her legs and sat upright on the sofa. "Why is that? Did something happen today? On the call, or something with Fletch?"

"No, nothing like that. I figured we hadn't had a chance to catch up like we used to, so I thought I'd call to see how you were doing," Pelletier replied. "Listen, I didn't mean to bother you, really—"

"You're not bothering me. Hey, you know what? Mind if I ask you a favor?"

"Sure, anything."

"I'm working on something...let's say it's unofficial. Can you help me out with it?"

"Of course. I'm all ears," he replied.

"I'm trying to find a guy. His name is Tom Sutton." Ellis took a drink from her bottle of beer. "I entered the name in the database, and it returned a whole lot of Tom Suttons. Think you can help me filter through them?"

"Yeah, absolutely. You mentioned this was unofficial. Can I ask who this guy is? I mean, we do have some limitations," Pelletier continued.

"I understand that, and this is legit. I don't know exactly who he is, but I will tell you that he's not a good guy. So I'm trying to figure out just how bad he is."

"Then I'll do what I can to help."

Ellis heard the enthusiasm in his tone. "Thank you, Bryce. It means a lot and I'll keep it above board. Make sure we're not going places we shouldn't be."

WHEN PELLETIER ENDED the call with Ellis, he felt lighter. She needed him and he was happy to oblige. It seemed that over the past couple of months—well, really since Euan McCallister—they'd grown distant. And after years of being close friends, it hurt. In fact, it hurt like hell. But now, maybe she was back, and he could help her with whatever this was.

And Euan McCallister...sure, he was handsome and tall, but Bryce knew he had secrets. They all knew. What he couldn't let happen was for McCallister to pretend to be someone he wasn't. The guy was all right, but no one leaves a big city police department for a squad like theirs without a reason. So, he would help out Becca with this Tom Sutton thing. And maybe if he gave her what she needed, he'd find the confidence to tell her how he felt. Because if McCallister got the chance to do that first, he would regret it for the rest of his life.

He set down his phone on the coffee table and walked to his kitchen. Pelletier lived in a small two-bedroom cottage in an older neighborhood on the north end of town. After leaving Portland PD, and coming to Bangor, his life had changed dramatically. He hardly spoke to his family. They were angry he'd left. But what choice was there? His mom was dead. He needed to start fresh. And he was damn good at his job.

When he met Becca, he knew he'd made the right choice. She was funny with a sardonic wit that, on her, had been endearing. She was beautiful and had the best smile. And right away, they clicked. The kind of connection he'd never before experienced.

While he'd had a few girlfriends, none were serious, and he wasn't exactly a chick magnet in any case. The girls always told him his best feature were his blue eyes. He'd gone out on a few dates, but they never amounted to much, but maybe that was his fault. He'd had eyes for Becca almost since Day One.

Pelletier grabbed a bottle of beer from his fridge and twisted off the cap. He took a long swig, then grabbed his laptop and returned to the sofa. It was getting late, just past ten o'clock, but he wanted to get a jump on this favor she'd asked.

He logged into the system. "Tom Sutton. Okay, Tom, who the hell are you, and why is Becca looking for you?"

8

Inside the station, as eight a.m. arrived, the harried pace had already begun. Bangor wasn't a big city, but there was no shortage of crime committed on any given day. It was what had always driven Ellis to become the woman she had. Of course, Hank and her past had played a part, whether she could admit it or not. And now she was already at her desk, ready to learn more about Mark Owens and why Janice Buxton insisted they talk to him.

A call arrived on her cell phone, and she answered. "Seavers, you have news for me?"

"Why don't you and McCallister come down here? I'd like to show you something."

"You got it. I'll find him and we'll head down shortly." She ended the call and looked at McCallister's desk. He hadn't made it in yet, which raised her curiosity. She grabbed her phone again and was about to press his contact number when she noticed his approach. "Hey, you have a minute?"

"I just got in. Can I check my emails first?" He dropped his bag to the floor beside his desk and sat down.

"Can that wait? Seavers just called me. He wants to show

us something. Come on. Your emails can wait." She started ahead.

"Okay." McCallister quickened his pace to catch up to her. "How was the rest of your night? Did you go see your dad?"

"No, I ended up just calling him on my way home. I'll stop by tonight." She glanced at him. "What about you? How was the rest of your night?"

He shrugged. "Uneventful, but thanks for asking. So, he didn't say what it was he wanted to show us?"

"No. Seavers does have a flair for the dramatic. I think he might have wanted to be a detective at one time, so he likes to stay involved, which I don't mind. He's the best, as far as I'm concerned."

"He came through for us on the Claire Allen case, so you don't need to convince me." McCallister reached the door to the shop and held it open for her.

She walked through with a nod. "Thanks."

"You got it." He followed her inside.

Ellis spotted the white GMC still on the epoxy-coated concrete floor—its doors open, the tailgate down and the hood up. She continued on until noticing Seavers at his desk inside a small glass-enclosed office.

The two locked eyes and he stepped out. "Detectives. Thanks for coming down." He continued toward the vehicle. "We're almost finished with our sweep, and I did find something I thought you'd both be interested in."

"Great. What'd you find?" Ellis asked.

Seavers stopped at the truck and eyed them. "Have you progressed much on the case?"

"Some," she answered. "I was about to check in with the medical examiner when you called me."

He turned back to the vehicle. "When we checked for prints, we were able to pull a couple of different sets. I've run them through the database, but I didn't get any hits."

"We knew Satchel didn't have a record," McCallister replied. "But no match on the other prints?"

"No, sir." Seavers walked to the passenger side. "But here's why I brought you both down here. As we checked for prints, fibers, blood, and what have you, I pulled up the seat. There's a small storage area back here and that was when I saw this."

Ellis walked over to glance inside the cab of the truck. "What is it?"

"Right here, on the back of this bench seat." He aimed an index finger at it. "Burns."

She examined it. "Doesn't look like cigarette burns."

"That's because it isn't." Seavers turned to them. "These appear to be chemical burns."

"Chemical burns?" McCallister focused on Ellis. "Like the burns found in Satchel's throat and stomach lining?"

"Could be." She eyed Seavers again. "Can you identify the source?"

"I'm going to cut around the burn and see if any residue remains on the surrounding fabric. Give me the rest of today. I'll see if I can get some answers," he replied.

"Keep us posted." Ellis turned on her heel and started on toward the exit. When McCallister caught up, she eyed him. "Sounds like whatever Satchel was forced to drink, he ended up carting in his own truck and spilled some of it. And now we have multiple prints, which could mean that whoever killed him was with him on the drive to the forest. So then I guess the question remains, was this person a friend or foe?"

Her phone rang in her pocket, and she noted the caller ID. "It's about time." She answered. "Dr. Rivera, I was just getting ready to contact you." She placed the call on speaker. "You have something for us?"

"I'm still writing the preliminary report, but if you'd like to come in, I'm happy to go over some results with you. Mind you, I don't have bloodwork back yet. I know you're awaiting those as well. But as you know—"

"It takes a while, I understand," she replied. "I'll gather my team and we'll be there inside an hour. See you then." She ended the call. "Let's grab Bevins and we'll head out now."

WHILE ELLIS DROVE TOWARD AUGUSTA, she glanced into the rearview mirror at Bevins. "How far have you gotten on the phone records? Do we know who Satchel last spoke to and when?"

"I haven't received them from the cell phone provider. They said it would be another day or two before I could get them," he replied.

"Okay. Something you should know is that those guys are never in a hurry. And especially not when it comes to the police." She pressed on, "If you don't get them by tomorrow, we get a subpoena. They won't want the hassle and they'll move quickly."

"Yeah, okay. I didn't—"

"It's okay. This is how you figure it out. Without a phone or a computer that belonged to our victim, we're relying on a lot of outside resources to come through. Usually, they need a good shove in the right direction."

"Got it. Thanks," Bevins replied.

"We're here." Ellis turned into the parking lot of the Office of the Chief Medical Examiner. "Let's hope whatever he has will help move us forward." She jumped out of the driver's side and headed into a biting wind. The day had turned cold and served as a reminder that spring hadn't quite finished clawing its way out of the snow.

Inside, Ellis reached the front desk, but before she spoke,

the man who stood behind it recognized her. "You and your partners can go on back, Detective Ellis. Dr. Rivera is expecting you."

"Thank you." She waved on McCallister and Bevins and pushed through the double doors that led into the long corridor. Rivera's office was the third door on the right and he spotted her through his window. When he waved at her, she and the others walked inside. "Good morning, Dr. Rivera. You remember Detectives McCallister and Bevins."

"Morning, everyone. All right. Let me go through the findings with you." He put on his reading glasses and opened his computer. "I'll send it to this screen behind you and you can take a look."

Ellis turned around and eyed the monitor.

"First, let's go over the physical findings," Rivera began. "I have determined the cause of death was the blow to the head, secondary was the chemical ingestion. The tox screen, when it comes back, will indicate just exactly what those chemicals were. The blow to the head appears to have been from a fall."

Ellis examined the image on the screen. "Did someone push him?"

Rivera displayed the next screen. "I found defensive wounds on his hands and arms. He tried to fight off his attacker, so it's safe to say someone else was involved here, especially when you consider the use of the chemicals." He pointed the mouse at Satchel's left forearm. "Burn marks. Those are from chemical spills. And I will also say this: the orange vest he wore was placed on him after the fact. There were no signs of the chemicals on that vest, as there had been on his shirt."

"Someone put him in that vest after he died?" McCallister cut in.

"Yes, sir. It was probably done to make it appear the victim had simply wandered into the woods, hunting, or hiking possibly, and then died from exposure. I estimate the victim died between December third and December eighth." Rivera set his sights on them. "Detectives, Terry Satchel was, without a doubt, murdered."

THEY RETURNED to the station and Ellis walked into the bullpen with Bevins keeping pace. "Get on the phone with the cell phone provider. I don't care what you have to do, get those phone records now."

"I'm on it." Bevins retreated to his desk.

She continued on when Lewis called out to her.

"Becca?"

"Yeah?" She turned back and headed toward her. "Hey, Gabby, what's going on?"

"You look like your hair's on fire. Anything I can step in and help with?"

"No, not just yet." She raised her index finger. "Actually, I take that back. I need to know more about the victim. I could use your expertise. I didn't get a chance to run that social media search. Can you head that up for me? Looking into Reddit blogs, chat rooms, anything like that, to give me a sense of who he was. All I know right now is that chemicals were poured down his throat; we don't even know what chemical yet, not until the labs come back. So I'm looking for a reason to tie him to some cause, whatever it may be. He has to have been into something."

"All right then," Lewis began. "I got you. I'll get on it now."

Ellis lay her hand on Lewis's desk. "Thanks, Gabby. I'm not taking you away from anything?"

"I'm playing the waiting game, same as you are right now. I got time. It won't take much of it."

"Thanks a lot. I appreciate it." Ellis walked back to her

desk and raised the lid of her laptop. She glanced at McCallister. "What was this guy involved with to make someone go through the trouble of staging him the way they did?"

"Can't say, but Mark Owens might know. You want me to put that call into him now?"

"That's a good idea. I'll reach out to Buxton and let her know what the ME found. It might help her to open up more than she did last night. We need information and I know she has it."

"She's scared," McCallister cut in. "And she might have a good reason to be."

Ellis made the call and waited for the line to answer. "Come on, Ms. Buxton. Pick up." It continued to ring until going to voicemail. "Damn it." She waited for the message to finish before beginning, "Ms. Buxton, this is Detective Ellis. Please call me back. I have some information about your friend I think you should know. You have my number." She ended the call.

McCallister glanced at her. "I hope she's not going off-grid. This woman probably knew Satchel better than anyone else. We need her."

"If she's feeling the way Wayne Byrd felt, then we may not hear from her again," Ellis added. "He seemed concerned about people listening in on our conversation the other day at the bar. Like he was being watched."

"Maybe he was." He appeared to consider an idea. "Listen, we could head back to the plant and talk to Mark Owens. Maybe we'll see Buxton, just to confirm she hasn't gone dark. And now that we have the subpoena for Satchel's personnel files, we can kill two birds."

Ellis pulled on her jacket. "Let me track down Buxton first. I'll let you know how it goes."

After Ellis left, McCallister walked to Bevins' desk. "Any luck with the cell phone provider?"

He looked up. "They're promising I'll get the records by tomorrow. They say that's the best they can do, even with the subpoena."

"Good." He shoved his hands in his pockets. "What about banking? You must've gotten his account details?"

Bevins checked the files on his desk. "Yes, that was how I tracked down the phone carrier." He retrieved the file. "I haven't had a chance to take a deep dive yet because we ran off to the ME's office."

McCallister pulled out a chair and sat down next to him. "Let's do that now."

Bevins opened the file and pulled out the reports. "He banked at Bangor Credit Union and I was able to get the past six months' worth of statements." He set them out on his desk. "This is the most recent statement."

McCallister grabbed the report. "What about recent transactions? Do they have anything not shown on this statement?"

"Not that I'm aware of." Bevins grabbed the previous month. "These go from October to December. These are from January to current."

"Those are the ones we're interested in. When do you show was the last time he accessed his money?" McCallister asked.

Bevins thumbed through the most recent statement. "Here in March"—he paused a moment and creased his brow —"Nothing."

McCallister checked the statement from December. "It looks like the last time he accessed money was a few days before the doc says he died. So if no one else tried to get to his funds, then it doesn't help us much."

"Okay, so where does that leave us?" Bevins asked.

McCallister tilted his head. "I just can't believe no one came looking for this guy. Buxton apparently dated him, yet she wasn't concerned enough about him to go to the police when he vanished."

"Do we need to look harder at this Wayne Byrd guy? Didn't he have some kind of argument with the vic?"

"He did, and he seemed paranoid when we talked to him," McCallister replied. "So, I don't know, maybe it's worth a second look."

"I can do that," Bevins jumped in. "Let me take the reins. You and Ellis got your hands full, working other angles. I can manage this."

McCallister eyed him. "Look, man, I know you're trying to make a good impression with the sarge and I get that. But you have to handle these things with kid gloves. People get freaked out when the cops talk to them, especially more than once. I don't want to scare this guy."

"I do know what I'm doing. I am a detective, same as you. I might not have your years of experience, but I got this, all right? I got it."

He eyed Bevins. "Okay. Run down Byrd again—away from Connex—and see where it goes. But do not let on that we know exactly what happened to Satchel, you hear me? We're still waiting on forensics, as far as he's concerned. Get him to talk about the culture at the company. How management handles guys like Satchel. Shift the focus to management. I have a feeling this could be a situation where Satchel opened his mouth one too many times and someone didn't like it."

"I got it. I'll take care of it." Bevins grabbed his things. "I'll get hold of him. I can do this."

"Then do it." He started back to his desk just as Lewis called out to him.

"Euan, I got something for you," she said.

He turned on his heel and walked to her desk. "What is it?"

She held out a sheet of paper. "Becca asked me to find Satchel's social media intel."

"And did you?" He took the paper.

She raised her brow and crossed her arms. "Of course I did."

———

ELLIS ARRIVED at the Connex building and peered between her wiper blades as they cleared the rain from the windshield. The drizzle continued to fall as it had since this morning. Buxton drove a four-door black Toyota and Ellis had the plate number in front of her. "Okay, Ms. Buxton, let's see if you're here."

She drove through the large parking lot of the facility that employed roughly 300 people, checking every mid-sized black sedan in the lot. "All right, no dice. So, are you at home?" Ellis pulled out of the lot and double-checked the woman's home address in the file. Finding her was critical, because if Buxton was gone, she would have to think twice about reaching out to Mark Owens.

She returned to the highway and started in the direction of the home, located at the west end of the city. Double-checking the address, she made a right turn. The neighborhood was middle-class. Homes looked to have been built in the early 2000s. Nice, but not too nice.

"This is it here, I believe." Ellis slowed to a crawl as she checked the numbers on the front doors of the homes. "Here we go." She stopped alongside the curb and glanced at the empty driveway. Ellis jumped out and slipped on her weatherproof jacket, then started toward the front door.

The modest home had white siding with gray trim on the

door and shutters. Looked fairly well kept. The yard was only just beginning to come back, as the weather warmed. The front porch had a white railing and an evergreen hedgerow planted in front of it.

Ellis knocked on the storm door and the metal frame rattled. She waited a moment, then rang the doorbell. "Ms. Buxton, it's Detective Ellis." She continued to wait and retrieved her phone, dialing the woman's number again. She heard the voicemail pick up and ended the call. "Damn it." She rang the bell again. "Ms. Buxton?"

Several minutes went by before Ellis turned out toward the street, glancing along it as though she might see Buxton pull up into her driveway at any moment. But it appeared she wasn't home, and she wasn't at work. "So where are you?"

9

D etective Gabby Lewis was the person everyone relied on when it came to pretty much all things cyber-related. She was a brilliant detective, who got her start in Chicago. It was a hell of a proving ground. But she'd been in Bangor with the police department going on three years. For her, it was the best move she'd ever made. Now, her teenage sons were away from the worst parts of that city; however, she knew she could never be far from crime and violence. It was her job. And when it came to tracking down people online, she knew exactly how to do it.

McCallister viewed the file Lewis had handed over. "I've heard of Reddit, but what's a subreddit?"

She sat next to him at his desk. "A subreddit is a forum—a topic, you could say, where people join in these forums and discuss certain subjects. This one here, your boy Satchel was heavily involved in."

"How did you find him?" McCallister asked.

"A simple search. Most people don't get that cute with their usernames. The younger ones do, but this guy was what, in his late thirties?"

"Early forties," he replied.

"Makes sense. So you just go into the search bar of the Reddit site and type in the username. It took me a dozen tries, but I figured it was a variation on his name in some form, and it was. So that's what popped up. Now, there could be more than one of these usernames, and he might not be your guy, but I think I'm right on this one." She pointed to the file. "He talks about the city, the area, and his job, so I figured he's the guy you're looking at."

McCallister nodded. "I think this is him. Did you find any other social media?"

"No, I didn't, which is a little strange. Someone who's familiar enough with the Reddit community likely has other social media accounts. If he does, he's not using anywhere close to his own name, so I struck out."

"No, this is perfect, Gabby, thank you. And is this the latest on this forum?" He examined it again. "It doesn't appear he's been active, which of course tracks, considering we know when he died."

"Well, there you go," she replied. "It's not active because he's dead, I assume." She stood from the chair. "I hope that helps. It's not much, but if you and Ellis need anything, just ask."

ELLIS RETURNED to the bullpen and noticed McCallister at his desk. She walked on and set down her bag when he seemed to notice her arrival.

"Oh, good. You're back. Gabby managed to dig up digital dirt on our guy and I was just getting into it."

She glanced at Lewis, who was at her desk. "You found something already?"

"I did. Went over with Euan, but I'm happy to catch you up."

"I'll take a look. No need to take up more of your time. Thanks, as always." She continued back to her desk. "Well, no sign of Janice Buxton. She's not at work. Not at home. Tried calling another couple of times and got her voicemail."

"Damn," McCallister cut in. "Do you think we scared her off?"

"Maybe. I'm tempted to reach out to Connex's HR department and ask if she took time off."

"It's worth a shot," he replied.

"So Gabby uncovered some social media posts?"

"Better than that." McCallister handed over the report. "She found him on a subreddit. I don't know if you're familiar—"

"I am," she cut in.

"Oh, okay, good. Then you'll see that he was part of a forum. Take a look at the topic."

Ellis searched for the primary post. "What?" She shot him a look. "This is about people who blew the whistle on their employers."

He raised a brow. "Interesting, right? Someone in management could be looking to hide something. Satchel found out, and it got him killed."

"What the hell could someone be hiding that was big enough to kill him for?" she asked.

"Depends on how big and how high up the ladder it went, would be my guess."

"Okay, so where does that lead us?" She considered her own question. "We start looking at his boss? His boss's boss? Still, murdering an employee...Whatever he knew had to have been big. Really big. I'd like to know what that was."

"Buxton might have answers for us," McCallister added. "Whenever you do catch up with her again, we tell her what we found. See if she'll crack. If she dated him, then he must've mentioned what was going on in his life."

"If we can get her to take my calls." She picked up the phone. "Let me touch base with their HR department. Maybe you can hunt down any corporate complaints lodged against the company. Civil or criminal lawsuits."

"I can do that." He returned to his laptop. "What about Owens? Any luck with that?"

"I'm holding off until we track down Buxton. Something about these guys, Buxton, and now maybe Byrd, going dark concerns me and I'm not sure I want to bring in anyone else just yet." She waited on the line when it was finally answered. "Yes, good afternoon. This is Detective Ellis, Bangor PD. I'd like to speak with someone in your HR department, please. A manager would be preferable." She nodded. "I'll hold." Ellis waited only moments before the call was answered.

"This is Ginney, the HR manager. How can I help you, Detective?"

"Ginney, hi, thanks for taking my call. Listen, as you know, we're working hard on figuring out what happened to your former employee, Terry Satchel."

"Yes, I'm aware."

"To that end, we did get a subpoena for Satchel's personnel records, which I'll send over shortly, but I also need to get in contact with Janice Buxton. We found something in Terry's belongings that suggested the two may have gone out once or twice in the past year. I'd like to clarify that with her."

"Janice didn't show up for work today, I'm afraid," Ginney replied.

"Did she call in sick?" Ellis asked.

"No, ma'am. No call, or email. No text to her immediate supervisor. She has been known to arrive late for work on occasion, even been written up for it. But to not show up altogether is unusual for her. Did you try her at home?"

"I did. She may have been there, but I didn't get an answer. Maybe she'd gone out for a while. So, nothing at all from her?" Ellis glanced at McCallister, who'd tuned in to the conversation.

"Again, no, ma'am. But I'm sure she'll be in tomorrow and, given all that's happened, her supervisor will probably cut her some slack. If she does show, I'll be sure she's made aware of your attempt to contact her. And I'll be on the lookout for that subpoena."

"Yes, thank you. Goodbye." Ellis ended the call and eyed McCallister. "She didn't show for work. Didn't call in sick. They got nothing from her."

BEVINS TRAILED the man in khaki pants and dark blue Oxford inside the Connex manufacturing facility. "What is it that you make around here?"

Harry, the middle-aged man with thinning hair and black eyeglasses, glanced over his shoulder. "Parts for machinery. Mostly O-rings and other types of rubber sealants. Ship them all over the world. We're the largest manufacturing facility in the northeast."

Bevins nodded as he surveyed the floor, where people went about their jobs. "Cool."

"Yeah, cool." Harry pursed his lips before heading down another section of the shop. "Byrd works down here. I can do without him for a few minutes, but you need to talk to him longer than that, let me know, yeah? Causes us a backup on the line, if you know what I mean."

"I'll keep it brief," Bevins replied.

"Thanks." He gestured ahead. "That's Byrd. Hey,

Wayne?" When he didn't reply, Harry turned back to Bevins. "Can't hear me with his earplugs in." The man stepped closer. "Wayne? The cops are here to talk to you again."

Byrd turned around and pulled out his earplugs. "What's going on?"

Bevins held out his badge. "Bangor PD. Can I talk to you a minute, sir? It's about your buddy, Satchel."

Byrd glanced at his boss. "First of all, he wasn't my buddy. But yeah, I can talk."

"Ten minutes," the boss said.

"Yes, sir." Byrd started toward the back.

"Thank you." Bevins followed him. "Appreciate you taking the time, man."

Byrd walked into the break room and noticed it was empty. "What the hell? I told you people I didn't want to talk to you again. And here? Are you kidding me?"

Bevins suddenly recalled he was to arrange to meet Byrd outside the facility. His heart pounded in his chest. "I'm so sorry, sir. I—"

"Damn it." Byrd kept his eyes fixed on the entrance. "What do you want?"

"Right, uh, I'll make this quick." Bevins cleared his throat. "Do you know what sort of chemicals are used here? I ask because, well, Mr. Satchel had been exposed."

Byrd shrugged. "We're all exposed. What's that got to do with anything?"

"Can you tell me if Satchel had reason to be in direct contact with chemicals in his job? In other words, would there ever be a reason he might carry them in his truck?"

Byrd pulled back. "Are you serious? You have any idea how much trouble he would've been in for that?"

"No, sir, I don't, actually. What would he be doing with them?"

"Shit." Byrd pushed his hand through his light brown hair. "The man wasn't right about some things."

"Such as?" Bevins pressed on.

"Hell, I don't know." He appeared to think on it a moment. "Okay, well, there was this one time. Terry gets bent out of shape about something the boss said. Starts bending my ear about it. I finally told him, 'Man, you don't like it here, you can always leave.' Well, Terry didn't like that I said that, and he just goes off, you know? Starts saying stuff like, 'You ever wonder why people around here retire all the time?' And I was like, 'cause they're old and they don't want to work anymore.' He's like, 'No.'" Byrd swatted his hand. "I don't know. Shit like that happened all the time. It was just Terry. Dude should've quit a long time ago. Would've saved us all a lot of heartache."

"I see."

Byrd noticed an employee walk inside. "I gotta go, man. And I'm warning you, don't come for me again."

Just as Byrd began to leave, Bevins reached for his arm. "Hang on." He lowered his tone. "Listen, if you think of anything else, contact me here on this app." He held up his phone. "I'll send you my username. It's the safest way to communicate."

Byrd grabbed his phone from his pocket and noticed the invite. "Fine. But I don't have anything more to say to you or any other cops."

DETECTIVE BRYCE PELLETIER was in his car when the call came in. "Detective Pelletier."

"Hey, man, it's Otero."

Pelletier smiled. "Tony? What's up, man? It's been a long time. What's going on?"

"Too long, my friend. How's Bangor PD treating you?"

"Good. Great, actually. And you? Still happy there in Portland?" he asked.

"It's not the same without you, bro. I got no one to bitch about when the captain tells me to rewrite my reports."

"That's because you failed English class, dude." Pelletier laughed. "No, it's good to hear from you. It really is. I do miss it there sometimes, but you..."

"I know, brother. I know you had family issues. I'm sorry for that. But hey, I didn't call just because, as much as I might've wanted to."

"Okay, what's going on?" he asked. "I'm sitting here in my car, getting ready to grab some lunch."

"Listen, uh, we got a call a couple hours ago, earlier this morning. Accident on the 95, on the outskirts of town."

"Okay." His heart raced for a moment as he considered his brothers and sisters. "Is it my family?"

"No, man. Sorry. No, it's not them. But it is someone who lives in Bangor. Figured I'd call you so we can arrange to notify the woman's next of kin. She didn't survive the accident. Single car. One occupant. No other vehicles involved."

"Oh, okay. Yeah, I can coordinate that. What's the name of the victim?"

"Janice Buxton. Forty-five years old. I can shoot over the address too."

"How about you email me the file? I'll run back into the station and get started on it."

"Sure thing. Thanks, man. Hey, you take care, all right? And you ever want to come back here, you know Captain would be good with that."

"I appreciate it, Tony. Thanks. I'll keep an eye out for the file." Pelletier ended the call and pressed the ignition on his 2020 silver Chevy Impala. The engine roared to life, and he started back toward the station.

The call from his old friend and co-worker reminded him how much he missed Portland, and his family. But his life was here now, and the choice he'd made was a choice he would stick to. Even if he never told Becca his true feelings, he would stay here because she was here.

He soon arrived at the station and entered the lobby, continuing into the back corridor to find the sergeant who ran the day shift. Pelletier spotted the officer ahead and knocked on the door frame. "Sergeant Moss?"

Thirty-three-year-old Devin Moss was the day shift sergeant after having been recently promoted from the patrol unit. With a head full of thick brown hair and a prominent nose, he eyed the detective. "Hey, Pelletier. What are you doing down here in the dungeon, huh? Getting tired of your ivory tower?"

Pelletier smiled and walked in. "Thought I'd come visit the peasants. Nah, man. It's good to see you."

"You, too. What's going on?" Moss asked.

"I got a call from a buddy in Portland. There was a vehicular accident on the 95 this morning. One fatality. She lives here. I've got the file."

Moss nodded. "Send it over. And your friend's contact. We'll coordinate with Portland PD to get the family notified and get her back home."

Pelletier swiped open his phone. "Okay, I'm forwarding it to you now. Let me know if you need any help, but those are good guys up there."

"You used to work for them back in the day, right?" the sergeant asked.

"I did."

Moss glanced at his phone. "I just got the file. I'll handle it and let you know if we need anything. Take care, man."

"You, too, and thanks." Pelletier returned to the hall and reached the staircase. He climbed up to the second floor and toward the bullpen. Ellis was at her desk, and he'd wanted to talk to her about the favor she'd asked. Thing was, he hadn't had a chance to get too far yet and since this was supposed to be off-book, well, maybe it was best not to bring it up in front of McCallister. But as he returned to his desk, he noticed her approach. "Oh, hey."

She placed her hand on his shoulder. "Any chance you've been able to look into that thing we talked about?"

"I got a start, but I'd planned on working on it still today. I actually just got back from talking to Sergeant Moss downstairs. A former co-worker and friend in Portland had a highway fatality for a woman who lived here. He called me and sent over the file. I walked it to Moss for his guys to run on. So, I'm back and can set aside some time to dig into that situation a little."

"That'd be great. Thank you so much, Bryce. I owe you."

As she started to leave, he called out. "Hey, you have time for dinner this week or weekend? We haven't been able to hang out in a while."

"I know. That's on me." She turned back to him. "Euan and I are right in the middle of this murder investigation, but I'll see if I can set aside a few hours to catch up."

"That'd be great. I'll see what I can come up with and get back to you when I have something."

10

A cursory review of the Connex Solutions corporation exposed troubling and unexpected details. Substantial fines had been levied against the company decades ago. Ellis read on while alarm bells rang in her head. "What happened here?"

McCallister took notice from his desk. "Find something interesting?"

She turned her laptop so he could view the screen. "Take a look. Connex received multiple fines extending into the hundreds of thousands of dollars over an illegal discharge of chemical waste."

McCallister eyed the online document. "It's a manufacturing facility and that was back in the nineties. I think you'd be hard-pressed to find a plant that hadn't received fines."

"Okay, maybe I can buy that," Ellis began. "But that brings to mind Satchel. What if he found fresh evidence the company had gone back to its old ways?" Her phone rang on her desk, but the caller ID was unknown. She answered the call. "Detective Ellis."

"What the hell are you trying to do to me, huh?"

She drew in her brow and placed the call on speaker. "I'm sorry, who is this?"

"You think I'm stupid enough to say my name over the phone? I told you people I didn't want to talk again and what the hell did you just do?"

"I'm not sure I understand you, sir," Ellis continued.

"No? Then allow me to make myself crystal-clear. Stay the hell away from me. You got that?" The call ended.

McCallister narrowed his gaze. "Who was that?"

"I'm pretty sure it was Wayne Byrd." Ellis's eye was drawn ahead, as Bevins arrived. She raised her hand to catch his attention. "Connor, join us." As he neared, she noticed hesitation on his face.

With his hands in his pockets, he nodded. "Hey."

"I take it you found Wayne Byrd?" McCallister asked.

"Yeah, I did. He opened up a little more, but I'm not sure how useful—"

"Connor, I just got a call from him," Ellis shot back. "Why did you go back to Connex? Byrd was already set against talking to us and to go there—"

"What the hell were you thinking?" McCallister cut in.

Ellis raised her hand. "All right. What's done is done." She focused on Bevins again. "You said he opened up, so tell us what happened." She stood from her desk. "Actually, we need to brief the sarge about our status. We'll lay everything out on the table for him."

She carried on into the hall, toward Abbott's office. Not only had this situation with Connor raised the stakes, so too had her discovery of past misdeeds by Connex Solutions. They reached his office door and Ellis peeked inside. "Sarge, you have a minute? We'd like to brief you on the Satchel investigation."

Abbott raised his eyes to her and removed his reading glasses. "All right. Come in."

Ellis took a seat and Bevins sat beside her. McCallister leaned against the door after he closed it.

"The gang's all here," Abbott said. "So, let's hear it. Where do things currently stand?"

"A couple of things first, sir," Ellis began. "Connex Solutions has a history. They've been heavily fined in the past for illegal waste disposal. I think that's a significant lead on our Satchel murder. The man had some kind of deadly chemical poured into him. That's no coincidence."

"And secondly, sir"—Bevins raised his index finger—"I screwed up. I may have jeopardized a witness. I went to his workplace rather than tracking him down outside of it. I wasn't thinking. Now, he's probably afraid of some kind of retribution."

"And he won't talk again," Abbott said.

"It's unlikely," Ellis replied. "I think we need to shift our energies into the company. They broke the rules before—"

"And given what Mr. Byrd did say to me," Bevins interrupted, "it could be the reason Satchel was killed. He said Satchel had made a big stink to him about how the company lied, and asked Byrd if he ever wondered why everyone kept retiring." He shrugged. "Nothing specific, but it sounds like the guy believed Connex was doing shady things. And since he's dead now…"

McCallister moved away from the door. "Gabby found social media posts through a forum known as Reddit that suggested Satchel was seeking information on whistleblower protections. Possibly looking to speak to people who had gone through it."

Abbott set his gaze on him. "Whistleblower. Clearly, it wouldn't be the first time." He hesitated a moment, shifting his gaze between the detectives. "Something you ought to know about Connex. Back in the day, Lieutenant Serrano and

Detective Hank Ellis tackled a case that involved the people over there."

Ellis straightened in her chair. "What? Why are we just hearing about this?"

"Frankly," Abbott began, "your connection to Connex has been a recent development. Last I knew, you were searching for an ID on your victim. Now you have one and you know where he worked, I'm telling you the company has had run-ins with the law in the past. You want details? Ask your dad. Or better yet, ask the lieutenant. That said, where do we stand as of now? How are you making progress on this?"

"A former girlfriend, Janice Buxton, reached out to us," Ellis continued. "She mentioned we needed to talk to another employee named Mark Owens. He's set to retire soon, according to Buxton. I've made a few attempts to reach out to her again, but she's not answering my calls."

McCallister nodded. "We're planning on going back to her house—"

"Sorry, did you say Buxton?" Abbott cut in.

"Yes, sir. Janice Buxton. Forty-five, works at Connex," Ellis replied.

Abbott returned his glasses to his face and typed on his keyboard. "Hang on a second. I was copied on an email earlier, just about an hour ago from Bryce."

Ellis cocked her head. "What's Bryce got to do with this?"

"I'm about to tell you," Abbott replied. "Here it is. He forwarded a case file he received from Portland PD this morning. A fatality on Highway 95. Single car accident. Those fellas up there ID'd the woman and learned she lived here." He removed his glasses and eyed Ellis. "The victim's name is Janice Buxton."

ANOTHER TRIP to the medical examiner's office to wait for the arrival of Janice Buxton's body. Ellis began to feel like this was a bad omen. "Thanks for running down here with me. You didn't have to."

Pelletier shrugged. "I know I didn't have to. But it was my friend who contacted me and it's starting to look like this case of yours is snowballing."

"Tell me about it. Then Abbott springs on me that my dad got tangled up on an investigation with this company years ago." She noticed Dr. Rivera appear from behind the double doors and raised her hand. "Hey, Doc."

"Detective Ellis, I didn't think I'd be seeing you so soon."

"Me either. We'd like to see Ms. Buxton please. Her sister has authorized it," Ellis replied.

"Okay. You know the drill. Follow me back and you can take a look."

She and Pelletier entered the autopsy room, and Ellis headed toward the table where the body lay. "I've been here too many times, Dr. Rivera. I'd like to not have to come back anytime soon. Oh, and I think you already know Detective Pelletier?"

"It has been a while, but yes." Rivera nodded. "Good to see you again." He pulled down the sheet that covered the woman's body. "This is Janice Buxton. Forty-five years old. Heavy smoker—"

"How do you know that?" Pelletier asked.

"I won't know for certain until the autopsy, but I'm basing that on years of recognizing the signs. Her heavily lined lips. Yellowed fingers. She is aged much older than her chronological years, so I'm surmising that she was a heavy smoker."

Ellis approached the body. "Her airbag deployed."

"Yes, it did," Rivera replied. "The burns on her face and other markings suggest the impact. She wore a seat belt."

"How did she die, then?" Pelletier asked.

"Most likely, internal bleeding." He pointed his index finger at her torso. "You can see bruising in the abdomen." He walked to his desk and retrieved a file. "I don't know if either of you have seen these photos."

"Of her car?" Ellis asked.

"Yes." Rivera returned and handed her the file. "As you can see, the impact was substantial. She must have traveled at excessive speeds."

"Oh, man, you can hardly tell it's a car," Pelletier said.

"And it was just her." Ellis looked at the doctor. "I need to know if she was impaired. The tox screen—"

"I can get a blood alcohol content fairly quickly. If there were any drugs in her system, that will take more time."

"Then get me the BAC as soon as you can," Ellis said. "Although, I suspect I already know what the results will show."

Rivera creased his brow. "How's that?"

"She's the friend and former girlfriend of Terry Satchel."

Rivera's face wore sudden recognition. "I see. Then I'll do what I can to push this as well as Satchel's tox screen. I'll try to get that before the end of day tomorrow."

SERGEANT MOSS STOOD at the door of Buxton's home. The woman's sister, Joan, was beside him, while McCallister and Bevins stood nearby. Moss turned to Joan. "You have the key?"

"Yes, sir." She unlocked the front door and stepped inside the dark living room. The curtains on the front window were drawn, so she pulled them open to let in what light remained of the day. With the living room illuminated, the emptiness seemed to amplify the loss of her sister and Joan's knees buckled.

Moss grabbed hold to steady her. "Ma'am, you don't have to wait in here if you don't want to."

"No, she was my sister." Joan stood on her own again, smoothing down her soft pink blouse. "I need to be here. Just, please, do what you must to find out what really happened to Janice. I know my sister. She would never speed along the highway unless she had a very good reason."

"We'll work to find that reason, ma'am." Moss glanced back at the detectives. "You two ready?"

McCallister started inside while Bevins trailed. He surveyed the living room. "Joan, is this how your sister usually kept her home?"

"Yes, sir. She was always a very neat person."

"Okay." McCallister walked on toward the hall. "Connor, let's check her bedroom. We're going to look for whether any of her clothes are gone, toiletries—"

"Got it. You want to know if she planned to leave," he replied.

"And if she had, and no one found a suitcase in the car... the alarms start ringing." McCallister arrived at the bedroom and noticed the desk. "Hey, there's a laptop in here," he called out to Bevins.

Bevins walked inside and glanced at the closet. "Looks like some clothes are missing, too."

McCallister turned around. "It does look like she packed a few things, but not a lot. Let's ask Joan about that." They headed into the living room, where the sister stood in tears. "Joan?" McCallister set his hand on her shoulder. "Did Janice mention she was planning on taking a trip?"

"No, sir." Joan cleared her throat. "She doesn't get a lot of vacation time from her work, so she doesn't travel much. And even if she did plan on taking time off, she wouldn't have had the money to go far for very long."

"But she would've told you?" he pressed on.

"Yes, sir. Absolutely." Joan regarded him with swollen eyes. "Did someone make her leave?"

"I don't know, but that's what we're trying to find out." He glanced up a moment. "Did she ever mention someone named Terry Satchel?"

"Terry? Yes. He came over for dinner once with my husband and me. A sort of double date, you could say."

"Was that the only time you met him?" McCallister continued.

"It was. They didn't go out for long. Janice said he had too much baggage, but she never told me what that baggage was."

McCallister and Bevins traded glances. "Did she mention that Terry was dead?"

Joan placed her hand on her chest. "What? No. No, I had no idea. Are you sure? When?"

"His body was found in City Forest several days ago, but it appears he died back in December."

"Oh my God." She stumbled back. "I don't know why Janice wouldn't have told me about that."

Bevins stepped toward her. "Sergeant Moss indicated Janice's cell phone was busted in the wreck. But we noticed her laptop on her desk. It would be good for us to be able to get inside that."

"It is surprising she didn't take it with her. Do you know her password, by chance?" McCallister asked.

"No, but I have a pretty good idea of what it was. Janice wasn't much for cyber security. In fact, I'm pretty sure she only used a couple of passwords, and I know what they are. I can try to get into the laptop for you."

Bevins retreated to grab the laptop and hurried back, setting it down on the coffee table. "Here you go."

Joan turned it on and sat down on her sister's couch to log in. "Like I said, Janice wasn't that concerned about people getting access to online details. In fact, I'm not sure she did much of anything online. She wasn't into social media. I know she didn't have Facebook."

While Joan attempted to access Janice's computer, McCallister answered a call that rang through. "Hey, where are you?"

"We're leaving Augusta now," Ellis said. "Rivera believes Buxton died from internal bleeding sustained in the crash. You should've seen the car, Euan. It was hardly recognizable. She must have been traveling eighty-five, ninety miles per hour to do that kind of damage. I asked him to rush a BAC to determine whether she was impaired. Tox screen will tell us more. If she wasn't impaired, then something happened to make her crash."

"Right, okay," McCallister replied. "We're here at her home with her sister. She's trying to get into the laptop we found on a desk."

"How's the sister doing?" Ellis asked.

McCallister glanced at Joan. "About as you'd expect. We're almost finished here, so we'll meet you back at the station." He ended the call and looked to Bevins. "Let's finish taking photos and bring the laptop once she's able to unlock it for us. Becca and Bryce are heading back from the ME's office now." He walked toward Joan and sat down next to her. "I want to thank you for helping us today. I know none of this is easy and you're doing an amazing job of holding it together. We're working with the medical examiner to determine your sister's cause of death, but his preliminary findings suggest she passed away from internal bleeding due to the wreck. There is more to come, so we'll keep you posted at every chance."

Joan turned the screen toward him. "I got in. Please, Detective. Janice wasn't a reckless driver. She never did a single reckless thing in her life. This so-called accident? I promise you, it isn't one."

THE STATION HOUSE came into view and McCallister turned into the parking lot. He glanced around for Ellis' Chevy. "Looks like we beat them here." He stepped out and waited a moment for Bevins to catch up before he continued toward the entrance. "What do you think so far?"

"About the case?" Bevins shrugged. "I have my theories."

"Care to share them?"

He scratched his smooth chin and appeared to consider the question. "All right. So, it seems like, after talking to the dude—Wayne Byrd—no one really liked Satchel. That he was always complaining about something with his job. So I'm like, you know, maybe Byrd had a beef with the guy, even if he didn't admit to it. Maybe someone else there did too."

"So you don't subscribe to the idea it could be a higher-up? A manager who had something to hide?"

"But like what?" He walked inside. "I understand this company did things back in the day, screwing with the environment and stuff, but they didn't kill anyone then. Why would things be different now, assuming they're up to their old tricks again."

"You have a point." McCallister headed toward the staircase. "But then what about Janice Buxton? She didn't have beef with anyone, by the sounds of it. We don't know if her accident was actually an accident, but if it wasn't, who would want her dead and why?"

"I guess I don't really know." He turned to McCallister. "This isn't like my other cases."

"No, sir. Homicide never is." They climbed up to the second floor. "Robbery, carjackings, domestic incidents.

These are things that leave a more obvious trail. People are generally motivated by money in most robberies. Homicide? Finding motivation is the hardest part of the case. That's what we need to find out. We need to know why Satchel was murdered and now, as it appears, why Buxton was killed too."

"Hey, can I ask you something?" Bevins pressed on.

"Sure." He reached the landing and stopped to square up with him.

"Do I come off as an asshole?"

McCallister grinned. "Sometimes, man. Sometimes."

Bevins looked away. "Yeah, I get that. Becca, she always backs me up. I don't know why, you know? It's just her way, I guess."

"She sees your potential. Becca's smart and she can smell bullshit a mile away, but underneath that, if she sees the real person"—he raised his shoulder—"she'll cut you a break. Problem is, I don't know where the line is."

"What do you mean?" Bevins asked. "What line?"

"Her line in the sand. I don't know how far she's willing to cut someone slack before they've crossed that line."

Bevins scoffed. "Well, shit, I don't think I want to find that out."

McCallister glanced at him. "Neither do I."

Pelletier had been mostly quiet on their return from Augusta. He was happy to be involved with Ellis on this case. "It's strange how this connected, right?"

Ellis grunted. "It's strange. If you hadn't copied Abbott on that email, I bet we wouldn't have made the link for days, maybe longer. I'm glad you still have friends at Portland PD."

"Yeah, me too." Pelletier fiddled with the buttons on the

car door. "Listen...so I know we've been friends for a long time."

"Uh-huh," she added. "We've been great friends."

"I think so, too, Becca. And I'm so glad you asked me to help with this other thing you're working on..."

"Right, speaking of...do you have some time to jump back on that today?"

"Of course. What's it about, anyway?"

Ellis appeared reluctant. "I wasn't going to say anything until I knew more, but since you're helping, you should know too. The other night, Piper called me."

"Oh, how's she doing?"

"Okay, but the reason she called was because she barely escaped an attack on her outside a bar."

"Oh my God. I'm so sorry." He narrowed his gaze. "Is this Tom Sutton guy—is he the one..."

"That was the name he gave her. I don't know if it's his real name, which is why I asked for your help. Piper didn't want to call the cops because she'd been drinking and was about to get into her car."

"But she was almost attacked," Pelletier said.

"That's what I said, but you know what she's like."

"I remember," he replied. "Jeez, I'm so sorry that happened to her. So you want to find him to press charges?"

"Press charges, maybe," she added. "Or maybe I'll just see what kind of man he is on my own."

He wore a sideways glance. "What are you planning to do if you find him?"

11

Piano music played throughout the upscale restaurant as the sun dipped below the horizon, its rays reflecting off the Penobscot River. The bar on the second floor was where Harry Carver waited. This wasn't his type of place, but it was exactly the type the man he was set to meet preferred.

And that man seemed to be running late. The troubling situation that swirled around Terry Satchel appeared to have taken a turn for the worse and if they didn't get a handle on it, bad things would happen.

"Sorry, I was delayed."

Harry turned around. "I don't mind if you're late, as long as you've come up with a solution."

Goyer sat down next to him. "This isn't going to be like it was in ninety-eight."

"No?" Harry asked. "Because I was there. I know what went down. It feels like someone is working against us and the last thing we need is Hank Ellis's daughter catching wind of what happened then. There won't be a chance in hell we'll be able to defend ourselves."

Goyer sipped on his whiskey neat, which had just arrived. "I've figured a way we can hold her off for a while until we can get to the bottom of what's happening."

"Is that so?" Harry raised his finger at the bartender. "I'll have the same as this one." He nodded in Goyer's direction.

"Yes, sir. Coming right up." The barman fell out of earshot.

"We're going to tie them up in mounds of red tape," Goyer replied. "We've done this by the book and can't afford the bad publicity that comes along with Satchel's death." He turned to Harry. "You just make sure none of this points back to Connex. The company won't survive the scrutiny a second time."

MOST OF THE cops frequented the Waterfront Bar. It just so happened to be a stone's throw away from the station and made for an easy trip. As night fell, Ellis joined her co-workers for a drink. While the occasion was infrequent, it offered her an opportunity to unload the day and connect with the people who meant so much to her.

They sat at a long table to accommodate all of them, including Fletch. The short but fierce twenty-seven-year-old had made detective a year ago, after spending four years as a traffic cop.

Ellis raised her bottle of beer. "Glad you could join us tonight, Fletch."

"Hey, you know I try not to miss team outings. How's that case you're working on?"

"Complicated." Ellis smiled.

"Aren't they all?" Fletch glanced over at Bevins, who was in conversation with McCallister. "And him? How's he doing?"

"We had some backlash with a witness, and I don't know how that's going to pan out, but otherwise, he's been doing a good job. Not complaining about the grunt work. So, we'll see," Ellis replied.

"Don't fool yourself, Becca." Fletch took a sip of beer. "Connor will do what it takes to get what he wants. And if he wants to take the lead on the next homicide, he knows he'll have to have you on his side."

Ellis glanced down at her beer. "That's not true."

"No?" She tilted her head. "Come on. You know Abbott and Serrano look to you as the leader of our band of detectives." She raised a preemptive hand. "I'm not saying it's a bad thing. You were practically raised in that station house. I'm just saying, given the history they shared with Hank, well..."

Ellis chewed on her lower lip. "I didn't realize you thought that way. Does everyone see it like that?"

"There's a pecking order in our department, Becca. You should be flattered. Abbott and Serrano look to you. Don't knock it. Hell, I'd be happy to be in your shoes."

"Yeah, well, I have a feeling someday I'll be working for you," Ellis replied. "Not the other way around."

"Next round's on me." McCallister got up and walked to the bar, but not before glancing at Ellis.

She raised her nearly empty bottle.

Fletch appeared to notice the exchange. "You two seem to be getting along well. Abbott must see the chemistry, too."

"He's good at what he does. I can't complain."

Fletch set her sights on McCallister while he placed the order at the bar. "He's not bad to look at either."

Ellis laughed. "No, he's not."

She turned back to Ellis. "I think he's made it clear that he has a thing for you."

"I don't think so." Her cheeks flushed as she glanced away.

McCallister returned and set down a bottle of beer in front of Ellis. "Here you go."

"Thanks," she replied.

"Anytime." McCallister handed out the other drinks.

As his back was turned, Fletch nudged her. "Guess that look was no big deal, huh?"

ELLIS KNOCKED on Hank's front door before opening it. "Dad? It's just me." She continued inside and noticed him in his usual spot, his recliner. "Hey, it's not too late, is it?" She checked the time on her phone, and it showed 9 p.m.

"No, come on in, kiddo," he replied. "How's the gang? You said you'd gone out for a beer." He sat up in his chair and pressed the TV remote to mute the volume.

"I did, yeah. It was nice. We try to get out together at least once a month, so it was good. Everyone's doing well and they send their best." She sat down on the sofa across from him. "How you feeling?"

"I'm fine."

She returned an uncertain gaze.

"Really, I'm fine," he added. "More importantly, how's your case going?"

She grumbled under her breath.

"That good, huh?" Hank replied. "Tell me about it. Maybe there's something I can do to help."

Truth be told, Hank had proven an excellent resource for Ellis on multiple occasions. There was a reason he had a stellar reputation.

"A woman who'd come to us, Euan and me, to talk about the murder of her friend, well, she's dead. Died in a car accident in Portland. A single car accident."

Hank's brow raised. "Is that so?"

"Yep. So now we're working on getting a BAC on her, and of course a tox screen, just to rule out whether she was impaired."

"What's your gut telling you?" Hank asked.

"That the car accident was no accident. That someone ran her off the road because they knew she'd talked to the cops. Now she's dead."

"What do you plan on doing about that, kid?"

She noticed the corner of Hank's mouth turn down. "Dad?"

"I asked…" he trailed off, slurring his words.

Ellis jumped from the sofa and rushed toward him. "Dad, I think you're having a stroke." She snatched her phone from the coffee table and dialed 911. "This is Bangor PD Detective Rebecca Ellis. I think my father's having a stroke."

"What's the address, Detective?" the operator asked.

"2749 Buckroe Avenue. Hurry. Please." The call ended and she looked at Hank. "It's okay, Dad. Help's coming. Just hang on."

"Aspirin," he muttered.

"I can't give you aspirin. I don't know what kind of stroke this is, and it could make things worse." She glanced at the window with drawn sheer curtains. "Come on. Hurry up!"

Minutes later, the sirens sounded, and the lights flashed through the curtains. "Oh, thank God. Hold on, Dad. They're here."

"I'm fine," he slurred.

"No, you're not." She hurried to the door and opened it to see the paramedics. "In the living room. Go!"

The pair of EMTs rushed to find Hank on his recliner. One of them turned back to Ellis. "How long has he been like this?"

"We were talking and he was fine. Then he started slurring his words. It's been twenty, maybe twenty-five minutes tops."

"Are you his next of kin?" the medic asked.

"Yes. I'm his daughter."

"Is he on any medication?"

"Uh, yeah, uh, blood pressure medicine," she replied.

"Do you give consent to administer tPA?"

Her gaze narrowed. "What is it?"

"It's our best shot at stopping, possibly reversing, the effects of the stroke, even if we don't know whether this is ischemic. There is risk of cerebral hemorrhage, but it is rare."

"Jesus." Ellis placed her hand on her forehead and paced a small circle.

"Ma'am. We don't have time."

"Yeah, okay. Do it."

He turned back to his partner. "Administer tPA now. Get the IV in and we load him up."

Ellis grabbed Hank's hand. "Dad, it'll be okay. You'll be okay." Her eyes reddened when he tried to smile, but paralysis seemed to have taken hold.

As they loaded Hank onto the stretcher, Ellis trailed them. "I'm coming with you."

The EMT looked at her. "You're Bangor PD?"

"Yes, sir."

He gestured to the truck. "Get in."

INSIDE THE HOSPITAL ROOM, Ellis waited for Hank to return after a slew of tests. She walked a circle with her arms folded, considering whether to call anyone. Carter should've been at the top of the list, but in her current state, speaking to him now would only upset her more.

The notion that she could lose her father terrified her. As

much as she believed herself to be independent, Hank had been her sounding board, her mentor, and the one person on whom she could totally rely.

Ellis spun around when the door opened, as the attendants rolled Hank in on a gurney. She captured the eyes of the nurse. "How is he?"

"The doctor will be in in a moment to speak with you, Ms. Ellis," she replied.

This wasn't good. And to look at Hank now was to see him in a state she'd never witnessed before. Eyes closed, wires and tubes connected to him. His vulnerability and fragility were on full display.

While they returned Hank to the bed and checked his vitals, she caught sight of the doctor.

"Ms. Ellis?" he asked.

"Yes, sir. I'm Hank's daughter. Is he going to be okay?" She glanced back at Hank.

The doctor continued inside and waited for the nurse to clear the room. He appeared to examine Hank for a moment, leaving Ellis to think the worst.

"Please, tell me he'll be okay," she pleaded.

He regarded her with apparent indifference, a detachment that was surely a form of defense doctors developed over time. "Ms. Ellis, you told the EMT your father was on blood pressure medication."

"That's right." She waited for him to elaborate.

"His blood pressure was dangerously high, and that is what caused the stroke," he continued.

"You're saying he stopped taking his meds? That's not possible. I visit him almost daily and I ask him all the time about that. My dad wouldn't lie to me."

"Then you should speak to him about that." He eyed Hank a moment, who remained asleep. "He must continue to take the medication, or the next time I'm not sure he'll survive."

ELLIS REMAINED at Hank's bedside for the entire night. He hadn't awakened once. As daybreak came, she was roused by an incoming text from McCallister. She rubbed her eyes and unfurled her body from the uncomfortable side chair. On standing, she stretched tall and walked the few steps to Hank's bed. "You're awake."

"Been awake for a little bit," Hank said. "Didn't want to disturb you."

"That should be the least of your concerns, Dad. How are you feeling? You're looking better."

"All right." He sounded anything but all right. His voice was gruff and weak, and he struggled to keep his eyes open.

"Dad, the doctor said you suffered a stroke. He says you'll be okay, but..." Her eyes welled. "Your blood pressure was through the roof and that was what caused it." She reached for his hand. "I don't understand how that could happen, Dad. You have pills to control that. Had you missed a few?"

"What do you mean?" Hank asked. "Of course not. I take them every day."

Her lips trembled. "No, you haven't. You couldn't have been. Had you been feeling off before I came over last night?"

He shrugged.

"Did your doctor change your medication? The dosage, maybe?"

"They're the same ones I always take, Becca. I don't know what you're talking about."

She grew exasperated. "You can't mess around with that kind of stuff, Dad. This is serious, okay? I don't want to lose you too."

Hank placed his hand over hers. "I'm not going anywhere,

kid. I'll be fine. You have more important things to worry about than me."

"No, I don't," she insisted.

He glanced at her phone as it buzzed. "You sure about that? Go on. Take the call."

She looked at the caller ID. "Yeah, okay. I'll be right back." Ellis answered the line as she walked out of Hank's room. "Euan, hey. Sorry I didn't answer your text."

"You okay? I thought we were getting an early start today," he replied.

"Yeah, sorry, uh, Hank had a stroke last night—"

"What? Oh my God. Is he okay?"

"Yeah, yeah, he's going to be fine. I'm here with him at the hospital. I was with him when it happened."

"Thank God for that," McCallister added. "You want me to come down? Can I do anything to help?"

"No, no, I'm good." She turned back to Hank's door. "I can come in. I just need to check with the doctor first to make sure Hank doesn't need anything else."

"Becca, take the day off. I can handle the case. Bevins and I will keep things moving."

"No, it's fine, but I do need to make a quick stop at Dad's house and then I'll be in. Really, it's okay. I'll see you soon." She ended the call and returned inside.

"Your partner's wondering where you're at, I'll bet," Hank said.

"I didn't get a chance to let him know when this all happened last night."

"Did you call your brother?" he continued.

"No, Dad. I didn't get the chance." Ellis felt the sting of her harsh tone. "Sorry, I-I didn't mean...I'll call and tell him soon."

"All right. Just do me a favor, kid? Go to work. Do your job and solve your case."

AFTER REASSURING words from the doctor, Ellis took her leave with the promise she would return as soon as possible. The guilt of the decision weighed on her, but Hank was right. She needed to do her job. But first, it was time to learn whether Hank had been less than forthcoming regarding his blood pressure medication. She refused to believe he'd outright lied about it, but it was possible Hank thought he'd taken his pills when he hadn't. If that was the case, her visits would have to become more frequent because she had a snowball's chance in hell of getting Hank to agree to a daily visit from a nurse.

She arrived at Hank's home and stepped inside. The house felt cold, so she walked to the thermostat and checked the temperature. "Jeez, Dad. Sixty-two. Really?" He kept the heat on a timer, and it wasn't set to kick on again until tonight.

Ellis continued into the hall, toward her father's bedroom. The primary bathroom was adjacent and was where Hank kept his medications. She'd told him a hundred times it was better to keep them in the kitchen on the counter to serve as a reminder every time he went to the fridge for a beer.

She opened his medicine cabinet and examined the three bottles of pills he took daily, recognizing the prescription for blood pressure. The bottle was half-empty. "Maybe you were taking them." Ellis opened the cap and poured a few pills into her hand. She then examined the bottle and read the description. They always put a brief description of the contents so that people can double check the pharmacy gave them the right medication. And as she read the description and looked again at the pills, her expression fell. "What the hell?"

ELLIS WALKED INTO THE BULLPEN, and it became evident McCallister hadn't mentioned to anyone what had happened. It was the kindest thing he could've done. And as she headed to her desk, his eyes drew up and captured hers.

"Hey, how you holding up?" he asked.

"Me? Fine."

"And Hank?" he asked quietly.

"He'll be okay. Thanks for asking and thanks for not telling the others," she replied.

McCallister raised his shoulder. "Not my place. So, listen, we have a couple irons in the fire that need to be addressed. The tox screen on Satchel. The BAC for Buxton, and we still have to talk to the guy she mentioned, Mark Owens."

Ellis pulled out her desk chair to sit down. "I'll follow up with Rivera on where we're at with the labs. If you want to figure out how to get in touch with Owens and not raise any flags in the process—"

"On it." He returned to his work.

She picked up the phone. "Dr. Rivera, please. Thanks. I'll hold."

A moment later, Rivera picked up. "Detective Ellis, I know why you're calling, and I do have the information we discussed yesterday—"

"Actually, I have something I was hoping you could help me with, unrelated to the case," she said.

"Of course, what is it?"

"I-uh-I found some pills in a bottle that I don't think are the right medication. There's a chance the pharmacy got it wrong, but I'd like to ask whether you might be able to tell me what the pills were?"

"Well, Detective, I'm not a pharmacist, but if you want to send me an image of the pills, I can make a couple of calls and get them identified for you. But why don't you just go back to the pharmacy and ask?"

"The pills aren't in my name. I'd appreciate your help. I'll send over a picture when we're finished here. How long do you think it might take?"

"Not long. I'm sure I can get an answer for you within the hour," Rivera replied. "In the meantime, would you like to go over the results I do have?"

"Yes, thank you. I'm going to put you on speaker and grab my partner," she replied.

"All right."

"Hang on, Doc." She turned to McCallister. "You want to listen in?"

"Sure." He pulled his chair close to her desk.

Ellis pressed the speaker on her phone. "All right, Doctor, go ahead."

"Okay, good morning to you both. We'll start with Mr. Satchel. As initially discussed, he ingested chemicals that produced postmortem burns throughout his organs. The toxicology report came back. Mr. Satchel was shown to have trace elements of benzene in his system. As well as TCE, or trichloroethylene."

"What are those exactly, Doctor?" Ellis asked.

"Benzene is found in solvents used in the manufacturing of rubber, resins, plastics, a whole host of products. And unfortunately it dissipates from the body rapidly. In fact, it was only in the small amount of blood found in the thoracic cavity that I was able to find those trace amounts.

"However, that isn't what caused the burns. TCE caused the most significant organ damage." Rivera paused a moment. "By the grace of God, this man was not alive when this happened. In addition to extreme convulsions and vomiting, the inhalation of the benzene would've caused asphyxiation as well."

Ellis closed her eyes a moment. "And those chemicals would likely be used in a manufacturing facility?"

"Yes, most definitely."

"Okay, Doc," McCallister continued. "What about Buxton's blood alcohol? Did you find evidence of drugs or alcohol in her system at the time of the accident?"

"No, Detective. I did rush her toxicology and it revealed NSAIDS, such as ibuprofen, in her system. It also showed high levels of cotinine, which essentially is a byproduct of nicotine after it enters the blood stream. BAC was below the legal limit."

"So she was a heavy smoker," Ellis said. "But that's it? Some over-the-counter pain meds and nicotine."

"Yes, ma'am."

McCallister eyed Ellis. "Now we wait for Moss to determine the cause of the accident, and whether it was likely someone had run her off the road."

"What happens next, Dr. Rivera?" Ellis asked.

"I'll perform the autopsy on Buxton. I don't know what more I can do for you on Satchel, Detectives. I will list his death as a homicide."

"Okay. Thank you, Doctor. Keep us updated. Goodbye." Ellis ended the call. "I don't know what part Mark Owens has to play in this, but given that Buxton mentioned his name, I'd put forward that his life could be in danger."

12

Bevins approached Ellis at her desk sporting confidence like it was a Prada suit. He set down the report and bared his teeth in a wide smile. She'd come to expect the behavior, of course, but her level of tolerance at present was low. Hank's pills weighed on her mind as she awaited a response from Dr. Rivera. And now two Connex employees were dead, both having perished in painful and horrific ways. "What is this?"

Bevins jutted his chin. "The results from Computer Forensics. Brown's analysis of Janice Buxton's laptop. Her email revealed that she'd been in contact with Satchel days before his murder. And, in fact, had sent several more emails after the event. Apparently, unaware he was gone."

"What did the emails say?" Ellis thumbed through the report while McCallister stepped in. "Here they are. This one dated November thirtieth says, 'You better be sure of what you think you know, Terry. You go back to management with something you can't prove, they'll fire you. I'm your friend, always...' And then she goes on to talking about their brief romantic relationship."

"Proof?" McCallister drew in his brow. "Proof of what?"

Ellis set her sights on Bevins. "Did she call him before or after his death?"

"He didn't have a landline and, as you know, I've managed to track down his cell phone provider through the banking records. I don't have those records yet, but they've been promised for today. I'll follow up ASAP."

"Okay. Keep on them." Ellis returned to the report. "So all we have at the moment are these emails, which are good, but..." She continued to review them and came across another. "This was later on in early December, so we know he was still alive as of December third. She tells him to quit while he's ahead. 'Don't keep pushing them, Terry. You know what they'll do. Send what you have to the cops. Let them deal with this.' And that's it. No reply."

"He was probably killed shortly after that," McCallister said. "But what did he have, and where is it now? We searched the storage unit and came up with nothing."

"But we didn't know what we were looking for," Ellis added. "If he had evidence of wrongdoing on behalf of Connex, that's what we need to focus our efforts on finding."

"Where does Mark Owens fit in this scenario?" Bevins asked.

Ellis tilted her head. "I don't know, and I'll be honest, I'm a little hesitant to reach out."

SCOOTER LITTLETON CAUGHT sight of Harry on the phone in his office. The shop foreman soon hung up and stepped out onto the floor. His face appeared cloaked in grief. "If everyone could shut down for a minute. Shut down, please. Thank you." The workers silenced and the machines stopped. "Why don't you all gather around? Come on over."

Soft whispers scattered among them as they drew close. Roughly fifty workers stood in a semi-circle around him.

"Thanks for that." Harry wiped his nose with the back of his hand. "Uh, listen, I have some upsetting news. I just got off the phone with Mr. Goyer. He received a call late last night from the Bangor police. I'm sorry to say that our good friend and co-worker Janice Buxton was killed in a car crash last night."

Chatter immediately spread among them.

Harry raised his hands. "Settle down. Settle down, so I can get through this." He cleared his throat. "Janice was driving along the 95, heading into the Portland metro area, when she, uh, drove off the shoulder of the highway and wrapped her car around a tree. She was the only person in the accident. No one else was involved, no one else was injured."

"She just wrecked her car and was by herself?" Littleton asked.

"I'm afraid so, Scooter. I don't know all the details. The cops don't know all the details, but they are working on finding out just what happened. Whether Janice had blown a tire and she lost control, or what have you, I just don't know."

"What was she doing in Portland?" Byrd asked.

"Couldn't tell you, Wayne. She didn't show up for work yesterday, as you all know. But I was going to give her some slack after what's been going on with the cops finding Terry and all that. So, I don't know what she was doing there or why. I just figured you all would want to know, as I'm sure you'll hear about it soon enough. Take a few minutes for yourselves. Get a drink of water. We'll start back up in ten minutes." Harry walked back into his office.

Littleton scratched his head and turned to his co-workers. "What the hell is going on around here? First Terry and now Janice?"

"You know they were seeing each other for a while, right?" Byrd cut in. "Seems a little to coincidental, don't you think?"

"What are you saying, man?" another asked.

More workers moved in around Byrd, as it appeared their curiosity piqued.

"I'm just saying, it's weird," Byrd continued. "Terry had his issues. I'll be the first to admit that. But Janice? She hardly ever talked to anyone. Kept to herself, mostly."

Littleton set a suspicious gaze on Byrd and glanced at the others, as if looking for consensus. "We all know you had words with Terry before he disappeared. What was that all about? Did Janice know?"

"Man, I've already talked to the cops about that, all right? You know as well as I do, Terry rubbed me the wrong way. He did that to a lot of people."

WHEN SATCHEL'S apartment manager unlocked his former tenant's storage unit and rolled up the door, Ellis walked inside. "Thank you. Per the warrant, we'll load up anything we believe pertains to the investigation. Anything that even remotely looks like it's out of place."

"Yes, ma'am. I'll leave you to it. Hope you find something this time." He returned to his truck.

Ellis surveyed the concrete room and turned to the patrol officers who'd come to assist. "We'll tag the boxes and haul them into Evidence. Better move before the rain comes." She stepped aside and waved McCallister along. "I'm not taking any chances this time. We leave nothing behind. None of this seemed important days ago, but all that's changed now."

"I agree, and it's time to find Mark Owens. But I don't

want to go in blind. Let's have Bevins run a background check. We'll find out where he lives and go from there," McCallister said. "No point risking making more waves for him, at Connex especially, but for us too. We've seen where that got us last time. We could be the ones responsible for Buxton's death." He stepped away to make the call.

Way to pack on the guilt on a day she already felt like shit about Hank. But McCallister was right. Buxton didn't die in an accident. Someone knew she'd talked to them and made her go away. Her phone rang in her pocket, and she noted the caller ID. "Dr. Rivera."

"Detective Ellis, I have some answers for you, pertaining to the pills you sent."

"Yes, sir. I'm listening." Her pulse quickened.

"They're a placebo."

She blinked hard, as if she hadn't understood his answer. "I'm sorry—a placebo?"

"Yes, ma'am," Rivera continued. "A sugar pill, whatever you want to call it. Those pills were not blood pressure medication and it's highly unlikely any licensed pharmacist would've made such a grossly negligent mistake." He paused a moment. "Pardon me for asking, but I assume these pills were for a family member?"

"Uh, yes, sir, they were."

"And something happened to bring your attention to this," he pressed on.

"You could say that. Listen, thank you so much for doing this, Dr. Rivera. I'll take it from here. Goodbye." She stared off into the distance, paralyzed with questions that swarmed in her head. Had this been done on purpose? If the doctor was right and a mistake like that was inconceivable, then what other conclusion could be drawn?

She hadn't even begun to think about questioning Hank

on his involvement with Connex all those years ago. Abbott was so matter-of-fact on the subject that it hadn't seemed important at all, but was it possible? If so, how?

Ellis covered her mouth as fear and anger vied for position in her heart. "It's not possible. Why?" she whispered.

McCallister approached her with apparent restraint. "Hey, is everything okay?"

She swallowed hard and replied flatly, "Everything's fine."

"The hell it is." He reached out for her hand. "Becca, what's wrong? Talk to me. Did you find something inside?"

"No, um…" Ellis hardened her gaze. "I think they got to Hank."

JUMPING to conclusions was never something Ellis succumbed to, and this could be no different. The signs were there, but the idea still seemed outlandish and such a risk that it bordered on the ridiculous. What would have been the point of it? So, she suppressed the urge to take that leap, and forced herself to consider the ramifications.

She and McCallister had left the storage unit and were on their way to visit Mark Owens at his home. He may yet hold answers as to why Buxton would mention his name.

The two-story vinyl-clad home sat on a large plot of land surrounded by newly emerging greenery. Ellis stepped out of her Tahoe.

McCallister climbed down from the passenger seat and headed toward her. Only he knew about Hank's stroke and now this latest suspicion. How long she could keep it a secret remained to be seen. "Looks like he got himself a new car for retirement." She pointed toward the driveway. "Still has temporary plates on it."

McCallister joined her. "Nice retirement gift. That Lincoln would've set him back, what, fifty, sixty grand?"

"At least," she replied.

They walked along the driveway and stepped up the slightly raised porch toward the front door.

"I have no idea if he's heard about Janice Buxton," Ellis began. "We'll have to approach this with caution."

"Couldn't agree more," McCallister said.

She knocked on the walnut-stained solid wood door.

After a few moments, footfalls approached and the deadbolt unlatched. The door opened and a man stood on the other side.

Ellis displayed her badge. "Good afternoon, are you Mr. Owens?"

"Who are you?" Owens appeared as though he'd only just awakened, though it had already reached midday.

"Sorry, I'm Detective Ellis. This is my partner, Detective McCallister. We'd like to talk to you about Terry Satchel and Janice Buxton." She noticed his gaunt cheeks and baggy clothes.

He cast a suspicious eye before opening the door a little farther. "Come in."

"Thank you, sir." Ellis stepped inside and observed the home's interior. Slightly outdated brown sofas, beige walls. The kitchen screamed 2005, with its dark cherry cabinets and Corian countertops. "You're married, isn't that right, Mr. Owens?"

He closed the door after they entered. "Yes. My wife's out shopping. What is it that you want, Detectives?"

"May we sit somewhere?" Ellis asked.

He waved them over to the living room. "Will this do?"

"Yes, sir. Thank you." She sat down on the sofa and eyed McCallister to join her. "As you are probably aware, Terry Satchel was found dead several days ago in City Forest."

"I'm aware," Owens replied.

"Were you friends with him?" McCallister asked.

"Not particularly. Terry didn't have much in the way of friends. It was his personality. It put off a lot of folks. Me included."

"That's a nice car outside. Looks brand new," McCallister added.

Owens returned a sideways glance. "That's 'cause it is. I figured I'd try to enjoy my retirement. I worked damn hard for Connex for a lot of years. That's not against the law, is it? Treating yourself?"

"No, sir. Of course not," Ellis replied. "It's wonderful you have the means to do that. That's how retirement should be, in my opinion. Of course, I work for the city, our police pension isn't as good as it used to be."

"Uh-huh. Detective Ellis, can you tell me what you all are doing at my house? I don't mean to be rude, but—"

"Sorry, yes of course." She clasped her hands in her lap. "Yesterday, we were informed that another co-worker of yours, Janice Buxton, well, unfortunately she was killed in a car accident. Had you been made aware of that, Mr. Owens?"

He swallowed hard. "Uh, no, ma'am. No, I wasn't aware." He placed his hand over his heart a moment. "A car accident, you say?"

"That's right. She was the only person involved. I suppose that's some consolation," McCallister added.

"I suppose so." Owens set a curious eye on Ellis. "Is that why you're here? Janice was always a good friend, work friend, anyhow."

"We're actually here, Mr. Owens, because Janice suggested we speak to you about Terry and about Connex," she pressed on.

His gaze roamed between the detectives. "I don't understand."

"Mr. Owens, we were hoping you did understand because, you see, we can't, for the life of us, figure out why Janice would mention you," Ellis said. "Unless it had something to do with what happened to Terry Satchel." She watched Owens lick his lips, fidget with his fingers, and cross and uncross his legs as he sat in the chair. "Do you know anything at all about what happened to Terry?"

13

So far, everything had gone to plan. Bevins knew that if he fell in line, and did everything he was asked to do without hesitation, Ellis would tell Abbott that he was ready to handle a homicide as the lead investigator next time. It was all he'd wanted, and it was almost his for the taking.

Ellis wouldn't be the go-to for everything in this department. She was currently the de facto leader of the division, but that was because of her father. Bevins only wanted a slice of the pie for himself; a notch on his belt, so that when the time came, a bigger police department would look on him favorably. His past would no longer hold him back.

His phone rang and he answered the line. "Detective Bevins."

"Detective, this is Julie Miller with Pactel Wireless. I'm calling to let you know that we have been authorized to release the cell phone records of Terrance Satchel. Would you like me to email them to you?"

"Yes, thank you. That's great news. If you have a pen and paper ready, I'll give you the address."

"Go ahead, sir," she replied.

Bevins relayed the email address. "Will you be sending them now?"

"Yes, sir. Give me just a few moments. I'll do it right now and keep you on the line in case I got the email address wrong."

"Great." He waited on the line and heard her type on the keyboard.

"I've just sent them, Detective."

He refreshed his screen. "And there it is. That's awesome, thank you so much. I appreciate your cooperation."

"Anytime, sir. Have a good day."

He ended the call and opened the email. "Thank you, Judge." Several attachments were included but the ones he was most interested in were the history of calls made in November and early December, just before Satchel was killed.

Bevins opened the attachments and briefly scanned the numbers. It would take time to review all of them, but the plan was to cross reference these numbers with employees at Connex to determine who Terry had spoken with during that time. They all knew there was a connection —that Terry had information about his employer—but who had he told?

MARK OWENS REMAINED silent for too long. He hacked a deep and visibly painful cough before he reached for his glass of water.

Several more moments went by before Ellis began, "Mr. Owens? Are you all right?"

He shook his head as though coming out of a dream. "Yes, sorry. I'm not well, actually."

Ellis tilted her head. "I'm very sorry to hear that. Is that why you retired? For health reasons?"

He stood from the living room chair. "I'm sorry, I should go and rest. I have to say that I really don't know why Janice would mention me. I'm terribly sorry about what happened to her, and Terry, believe me, but I just don't know what to tell you."

Ellis got to her feet. "Of course. We don't want to keep you. It's just that, well, it looks as though Terry may have wanted to speak out against Connex in some form. Unfortunately, we have no idea why or what it entailed. And now with Janice gone, too. Well, I guess you could say we were concerned about you."

"Concerned about me?" he asked.

"She'd mentioned you," Ellis went on.

Owens narrowed his gaze. "Are you telling me you think Janice's car accident wasn't an accident? Because that's how you're making it sound, Detective."

"We're trying to cover every possible scenario until we get all the facts," McCallister cut in. "Nothing can be ruled out at this point."

Owens walked ahead to the front door. "Look, I don't know what happened to Terry or Janice, okay? I think it's best you both leave."

Ellis squared up to him when he opened the door. "Mr. Owens, if you know anything, anything at all, we can protect you."

He wrapped his arms over his chest as though a chill had fallen over him. "Protect me? From what? I don't need protection. I'm doing exactly as I'm supposed to, okay? Now, if you don't mind, I really need to rest."

"We'll leave you alone." McCallister started out the door and turned back. "If you change your mind, Mr. Owens." He handed over a card.

"Thank you, but I'm sure I won't. Goodbye."

The door closed and they stood on the porch once again. Ellis turned in the direction of the front yard. "What the hell was that?"

"You mean the part where he said he was doing exactly as he was supposed to? Yeah, I picked up on that too." McCallister started back toward her SUV.

Ellis unlocked the doors and spun around to face the Owens' driveway. "The man buys a brand new sixty-thousand-dollar Lincoln. His wife is out shopping. And yet he has just retired."

McCallister stepped into the passenger seat. "Must've been offered one hell of a good retirement package."

ON THEIR RETURN to the station, Ellis and McCallister arrived at the bullpen where, within moments, Bevins descended on them.

"I've been going through the phone records—" Bevins started.

Ellis raised a finger. "I need a minute. Feel free to get Euan up to speed." She turned on her heel and walked back into the hall. Abbott had told her about the Connex investigation Serrano and her father had worked, so it was time to understand what that entailed and whether it was possible someone held a grudge because of it.

She knocked on the lieutenant's door and heard his voice call out to enter. "Sir?"

"Becca, come in. What can I help you with?" Lieutenant Abe Serrano towered over Ellis by several inches. His thick gray hair made him look a little older than his fifty-seven years, as did the deep-set wrinkles at his cheeks. He knew

Hank well and had been a mentor, even a substitute father, to her at the beginning of her career.

Ellis continued inside, hesitant to tell him about Hank. "Thank you, sir. Um, I thought I should tell you that Hank had a stroke last night."

He gripped the arms of his chair and pulled up straight. "Is he all right? Is he still in the hospital? Why am I just now—"

"Sir, he's fine. They're keeping him in the hospital for a while longer, but he will be okay. I didn't get the chance to speak to you this morning with this case going."

He softened his stance and gestured to the chair. "Sit down, Becca."

She took a seat and shifted in the chair a moment, trying to find the words. "Sir, Sarge mentioned that you and Hank worked a case against Connex Solutions back some years ago."

Serrano drew in his brow. "Ninety-eight, why?"

"Well, Euan, Connor, and I have been working a homicide the past several days and it turned out the victim had worked for Connex. We went to the plant and talked to some people. And then yesterday, we were told another worker there, a Janice Buxton, had been killed in a car accident. This was probably within hours of her speaking to us away from her workplace."

He glanced away. "Jesus."

"And so, you know, the sarge mentioned this case and I thought, well, something else happened and I'm not sure if it's related," Ellis continued.

"What's that?" he asked.

"Hank's stroke. The doctor said it was his blood pressure. It got really high. And the thing is, he takes medication for it." She cleared her throat. "Sorry, sir, this wasn't supposed to be a long story, but what I'm getting at is, after some research, it appears that Hank's medication was wrong."

"What do you mean, wrong?" Serrano continued.

She sighed. "I don't know if it was a mistake, but his blood pressure medicine had been replaced with a placebo, and it appears that is what brought on the stroke. I don't know how long he had been taking the placebo, but my guess is that it was about as long as I've been working this case."

Serrano leaned over his desk. "Am I hearing you right, Becca?"

She held his gaze. "Yes, sir. I think—somehow—someone at Connex hasn't forgotten about your case and they figured out that I'm Hank's daughter. I don't know what to do about this, sir. But I think it was a warning for us to back off."

He leaned back in his chair and pushed a hand through his thick gray mane. "You sure about this, Becca?"

She let loose a nervous laughter. "No, sir. I'm not at all sure." Ellis watched as he appeared to consider the situation.

"Let me take this from here, all right? I'll go see your dad. Does he know about the meds?"

"No, sir. I only just found out an hour or so ago."

He nodded. "Okay. Keep working your investigation. Do not let up. I'll find out what's going on."

Ellis pushed off the chair. "I can't do this if Hank's at risk."

"I know. You let me worry about that."

ELLIS RETURNED TO THE BULLPEN, shaking off the fear that someone had come for Hank because of this investigation. The how and the why were unknown, but she knew he would want her to continue, now more than ever. And without proof, this could still be an innocent mistake that almost cost Hank his life.

Bevins called out to her. "Come on over. We're still going through this."

She joined them at McCallister's desk. "What'd you find?"

"So, as I was saying to Euan, I got the phone records," Bevins continued. "Nothing but a bunch of numbers and I had no idea who they belonged to. But as I started parsing them, I went back down to see Brown in the lab. I asked him to print off all the contacts in Buxton's laptop. He came back with several. That made much easier work of it, and I was able to match the numbers against what was on Satchel's phone records. They didn't all match, of course, but take a look here." He set a file on McCallister's desk. "Out of the contacts that were also on Satchel's records, I looked up the names and ran checks on them."

"And?" Ellis asked, as she scanned the file.

"Several of the names I pulled came back as former Connex employees," Bevins added. "But here's the kicker. Most of them? They're dead. As in, recently dead."

Ellis pulled back her shoulders. "What?"

"That's what I thought," Bevins replied. "Weird, right? So they were alive when Terry contacted them, obviously. But not anymore. And get this, there's no police reports or anything like that. No foul play."

"How did they die, then?" McCallister asked.

Bevins raised his palms. "I don't know. We'd need to pull their death certificates."

"Then that's what we'll do." Ellis noticed her phone ring. "Hang on. I have to take this." She answered as she walked into the hall. "Ellis here."

"Ms. Ellis, this is Lily Emerson. I'm a nurse at Bangor General."

Ellis's heart stopped. "Is my dad okay?"

"The doctor advised me to contact you. Your father, Hank Ellis, has been taken into surgery—"

"What happened? Why?" Her tone turned harsh. "Is he going to be okay? He was fine when I left—"

"Ms. Ellis, it's best if you come down to the hospital right now, ma'am."

Ellis ended the call and hurried back to her desk.

McCallister appeared to keep a close eye. "Hey. Hey, what's wrong? You're white as a sheet."

"I have to go to the hospital. My dad's in surgery."

"Oh my God. Yeah, okay. You want me to drive you?" he asked.

"No. Stay here and work with Bevins on these phone numbers. I'm sorry. I have to leave." She rushed through the bullpen and nearly collided with Pelletier.

"Becca, what's wrong?" he asked.

"Nothing. I have to go." Ellis regretted her blunt response, but there wasn't time to explain, and she hadn't wanted everyone to know, not yet.

Her emotions rose to the surface as she reached her vehicle and climbed inside. From behind the wheel, her chin quivered, and her eyes stung. She pressed the ignition and did her best to hold it together. Driving in this condition wasn't wise, but having McCallister with her in this moment, well, it was just too personal. She wasn't ready to share this with him. Except there was one person.

She pulled out of the parking lot and pressed the call button on her steering wheel. The line rang. She knew Piper was usually busy showing homes, but right now she needed her friend more than anything. "Come on, Piper, please answer. Please." The call went to voicemail. "Hey, it's me. Listen, Dad had a stroke last night. I'll explain later, but I'm headed back to the hospital. They said he had to go in for surgery. If you get this message, come down to Bangor General. Please. Bye."

McCallister held open the window blinds and watched Ellis pull out of the parking lot as Pelletier approached.

"What the hell happened with Becca? Is she okay?" Pelletier asked.

McCallister spun around. "Uh, I think so, yeah." He didn't want to be the one to tell everyone about Hank. It wasn't his place, and now he felt guilty for it. If she'd wanted everyone to know, she would've told them earlier. Now, they all looked at him: Lewis, Fletch, Bevins, Pelletier standing here with that look on his face. Like he was about to lose his best friend, or the woman he loved. The guy didn't hide his feelings well. "You know what, I'm sure she'll call and tell us all what's going on. You know Becca—"

"Yeah, I do," Pelletier cut in. "We all do, so maybe I'll just call and ask her myself." He reached for his phone and dialed her number.

McCallister returned to his desk when it appeared she hadn't answered the line. Pelletier returned his phone to his pocket, and he glanced back. "Nothing?"

"No, she didn't answer." He returned to his desk.

"Man, we have to move on this information, right?" Bevins asked. "Like Becca said? We can't waste time waiting around for her."

"No, I get that," McCallister replied. "Let's get started on those death certs. They'll tell us a lot."

"On it." Bevins turned on his heel.

Meanwhile, McCallister felt the pull to Ellis. He was worried about her. Probably more than he should be. Definitely more than he should be. If Hank didn't make it..."No, don't," he whispered.

When a call came in on his phone, he hoped it was her. Instead he answered, "Moss, yeah, what's up?"

"We have everything from the storage unit you and Ellis requested. It's being transferred to Evidence now. Figured you'd want to be the one to sign off on it."

"Yeah, thanks. I'll be right down." He ended the call and walked ahead, stopping at Bevin's desk. "I have to run down to Evidence. They're bringing in Satchel's things now. I'll see what they have. You keep on those death certs."

"You got it," Bevins replied.

McCallister carried on to the stairs and jogged down to the first floor, where he reached the Evidence room. Sergeant Moss stood at the cage where they kept the guns, drugs, and money. "Hey, Moss. Thanks for the call."

"Yeah, of course. I tried Ellis, but I got her voicemail."

"She had a thing. I'll contact her later and let her know."

"Cool." Moss headed back toward the piles of boxes. "Anyway, here's everything my team pulled out of there. No paperwork left inside the storage unit. I even had them check in the seat cushions of the couches that guy had. And Ellis mentioned something about chemicals or whatever."

"Yeah, did your people find any?" McCallister asked.

"No. There was nothing."

"Okay. I'll stick around here and see to it everything is entered, and then we'll see what we can find."

Moss eyed the stack of boxes. "Have fun, man. There's a lot here."

ELLIS ARRIVED at the hospital and hurried to the administration desk. "They told me my father's gone in for surgery—"

"Who's your father, ma'am?" the woman asked.

"Hank Ellis. He was brought in last night after suffering a stroke."

She looked up the name and eyed Ellis. "Yes, ma'am. He's still in surgery. Dr. Holden is the surgeon. Go on up to the surgical floor, number three. You can check in up there and they'll let the doctor know you're waiting."

"Thank you so much." Ellis headed toward the elevator and rode up to the third floor. Her heart raced and fear squeezed her lungs. The familiar feeling sent her thoughts back to the day it happened when she was twelve. The day she killed her stepfather. Strange how it felt the same now as it had then.

Ellis reached the surgical desk. "I need to speak with Dr. Holden. It's about my father, Hank Ellis. They told me he's in surgery."

The nurse behind the counter checked the computer. "Yes, ma'am. He asked to be alerted when you arrived. I'll send someone to get him." She gestured to the waiting area. "Feel free to take a seat over there."

"Thank you." Ellis didn't feel like sitting. Her nerves refused to relent. Instead, she stood near the chairs and paced.

Several moments passed, though it felt longer, when she caught sight of a man in scrubs from the corner of her eye. Ellis turned to him and waited while he seemed to take forever to reach her.

"Ms. Ellis, I'm Dr. Holden, your father's surgeon." He offered his hand. "I understand you brought your father in last night after he suffered a stroke."

"Yes. He was fine this morning. What happened? Why is he in surgery? Will he be okay?"

Holden held up his hands. "First of all, your father is going to be okay."

Ellis lost her breath and her knees weakened. "Oh, thank God."

"He did suffer another stroke this morning while he was

in for imaging. This one was larger. A blood vessel in his brain ruptured and he suffered a brain bleed. I understand your father had stopped taking his blood pressure medication?"

"I'm working on finding that out, Doctor, but you say he's going to be okay?" she pressed on.

"Yes. The fact he was already here is what saved his life. We were able to treat him immediately. Now, he's being closed up, and I expect him to be in recovery for a few hours. After that, you'll be able to see him."

Ellis considered the next question carefully. "Doctor, will he have permanent damage?"

"The surgery we performed was to relieve the pressure due to the bleed. We accomplished that as well as accelerating his clotting to stop the bleed altogether. So, to answer your question, no, he will not suffer permanent damage, primarily because we were able to intervene quickly."

Her eyes welled as she caught her breath. "That's good news. Very good news. Thank you, Doctor."

"Of course. I will say this—your father must understand the importance of keeping up on his medication. High blood pressure is the leading indicator for this type of stroke."

"I'll see that he does. I promise."

He nodded. "I'll have the nurses let you know when you can see him. Thank you, Ms. Ellis."

"Thank you, Doctor." As he fell out of view, Ellis collapsed onto a chair. She took in deep breaths to calm down.

Every argument they'd had over Carter, over work, over everything; it was all meaningless. She knew that now. Maybe the time had come to stop fighting him over how he dealt with her half-brother. The only thing that mattered now was that he was alive, and he was going to be okay. The root cause gnawed at her, but that would have to be set aside for the moment.

She felt her phone vibrate in her pocket and retrieved it. "Hey, what's going on?" She cleared her throat.

"Is this a bad time?" McCallister asked. "I-I don't mean to interrupt—"

"No, it's fine. My dad, uh, he's going to be okay. It'll take time, but he'll be okay."

His relief was clear. "I'm so glad to hear that, Becca. I truly am. Listen, I don't want you to worry about the case. Connor is pulling the death certs for the people who'd been in contact with Satchel. I'm sitting here in Evidence now getting everything they took from his storage unit logged in—which is the reason I called."

"Okay." She looked up and saw Piper approach. "Hey, I'm going to need to call you back."

"Oh, yeah, sure."

Ellis ended the call and stood on weak knees.

Piper pulled her into a tight embrace. "Oh, honey. I'm so sorry."

14

Hank drifted in and out of sleep for the better part of two hours. Ellis had sat at his side since they'd put him in his room. He'd spoken a few words, knew she was there, but hadn't had the energy to keep his eyes open. Now, as she set her gaze through the hospital room window, the sun had all but disappeared, leaving behind a blueish gray haze atop the horizon.

Piper had gone home only after Ellis insisted multiple times on it. There was still the matter of Tom Sutton, but she couldn't think about that just now. Ellis only had room for Hank and making sure he would survive the night. The doctors seemed confident of that, but after this morning, it wasn't a risk she would take again.

When the knock came on the hospital room door, Ellis expected it to be one of Hank's nurses. "Come in." But when the door opened, it wasn't a nurse who entered.

She turned away from the window. "Euan."

He made his way inside and glanced at Hank. "How is he?"

"Good, thanks for asking. Doctors say he'll fully recover."

"I'm sure that must be a relief. I'm sorry to just drop in. I tried to call, but—"

She grabbed her phone. "I've had it on silent. Sorry about that." She gestured to a hard plastic chair against the back wall. "Take a seat. He's been in and out since they brought him here, so don't worry about disturbing him."

"I really don't want to take up your time with this, so I'll be brief and get out of your hair." He took a seat. "When I called before, I mentioned I was getting the evidence taken from the storage unit logged in."

"Sure, I remember," Ellis replied.

"We finished a little while ago and I thought you should know that we found some recent medical records that indicated Satchel had been diagnosed with Parkinson's."

"He was sick?" she asked.

"He was, yes. But then Connor called my attention to the death certificates he pulled from the people Satchel had been in contact with over the past six months or so. Three, to be precise. All three people died from leukemia."

"That's no coincidence," she replied.

"No, I don't believe it is either. The question then goes to timing. When had these people been diagnosed, and how long had they suffered before succumbing to their disease?"

Ellis shifted in the chair. "And they all worked for Connex."

McCallister turned up his palms. "Yes, although the records were oddly difficult to find. And when he dug a little deeper, it appeared that each of them was fairly well-off, financially."

"You were able to get banking details?" Ellis asked.

"No, but we pulled property records. It turns out that, over time, each of these people sold their homes, modest homes at that, and purchased much larger, much nicer homes in upscale areas. We also found Quit Claim Deeds that indicated those homes, in all three cases, had been signed over shortly thereafter to family members. That's all we have for now."

Ellis considered the implications. "So we have a scant record these people worked for Connex, yet Satchel was in touch with each of them. They all had leukemia, and he'd recently been diagnosed with Parkinson's. This isn't looking good for Connex." Ellis noticed Hank's hand flinch and she jumped to his side. "Dad? Dad, are you awake?"

Hank turned his gaze to her. "Why didn't you mention the name of this place before?"

She took his hand. "The sarge mentioned you and Lieutenant Serrano conducted an investigation at Connex years ago. I was going to ask you about it before—"

Hank expelled a mild cough. "Sounds like they're back at it again."

She glanced at McCallister before returning to Hank. "What do you know about all this, Dad?"

"I know those sons of bitches were dumping toxic waste and getting away with it."

"And your investigation was about that?" she asked. "Seems like that would be OSHA, or even the EPA."

"They were involved too, but our part..." Hank coughed again. "We got calls about employee harassment and intimidation. That's why we were there. And they didn't like it."

Ellis chewed on her lower lip a moment. "Dad, is it possible they would try to send a message to you about this current case?"

He slowly raised his eyes to her. "What kind of message?"

"Your blood pressure medication was wrong. The bottle was filled with a placebo, sugar pills or whatever. That's why you had the stroke, Dad."

"What?" He narrowed his gaze. "What are you saying, Becca? Are you saying someone tried to kill me?"

ELLIS ARRIVED at the station later that morning and climbed the steps to the second floor. A second night at the hospital left her body aching and exhausted. Abbott appeared only feet in front of her and forced her to stop. Based on his expression, he wasn't at all happy.

He blocked her way with his broad stance. "In my office... please." Abbott spun around and walked into the hall.

This could be the result of one of two things. Either Hank had called him about the stroke, which seemed unlikely, or Serrano had told him what happened. Without a word, Ellis carried on behind him.

Abbott entered his office and gestured to the chair. "Sit down, Becca."

"Okay." Ellis took a seat.

He pulled out his chair and dropped onto it. Abbott was quiet a moment before he pulled closer to his desk and leaned over it with his forearms resting on top. "Why didn't you tell me about Hank?"

She turned down her gaze. "Did he call you?"

"As a matter of fact, he did. Called from his hospital bed first thing and told me to make sure you pulled the archived case files on Connex. Imagine my surprise when he said he was set to be discharged in a couple of days."

"It was a family matter, sir," Ellis replied.

"A family matter? I see." Abbott knitted his brow. "You know, Hank's my friend. Why the hell didn't you tell me what was going on?"

"It happened fast," she began. "I got him into the hospital. Next morning, he seemed okay, I came in. The case took over and then I get an emergency call that he'd had another stroke."

Abbott leaned back in his chair. "I will say this, I'm damn

grateful you were there when it happened. God knows how it would've turned out otherwise."

"I'm grateful too."

"Right." He cleared the sentiment from his throat. "Point being, you don't need to be here. Despite what Hank said, you'd be better off spending some time with him. Euan and Connor can run the investigation."

"Believe me, that's what I told him this morning and he practically shoved me out of his room himself. You know what he's like. He doesn't want anyone making a fuss over him." Ellis leaned on her elbows. "We've uncovered some serious allegations against the company Terry Satchel worked for. Not all dissimilar to the original investigation Hank worked on. Sarge, the time to move on this is now, before they realize we know what we know and start destroying evidence. Please...Hank would want me to push through, and I feel like that's what I need to do."

"You are your father's daughter." He appeared to consider the request. "All right. If you and the team think you're getting close to something big, then see that you get what you need to prove it."

"Thank you, sir." Ellis stood and turned to leave.

"One more thing, Becca."

"Yes, sir?" She waited for him to speak.

"When it comes to your dad, remember that you're not an island. You don't have to bear the weight all alone, you understand?"

She looked down a moment. "I do, sir. Thank you." Ellis returned to her desk and noticed McCallister had arrived. "Good morning."

"Morning." He set his eyes on her. "You sure you're ready to be here?"

"Yeah, I'm ready. I'm okay. Hank's doing better this morning, and he doesn't want me sticking around, so, let's keep moving forward on this case."

"What about, you know, his medication? How do we get to the bottom of that?" he asked. "Becca, if someone over at Connex is responsible—"

"I know, Euan." Frustration caught in her chest. "Right now, we have a double homicide to solve. If it's related, we'll find out." She took a seat and surveyed the bullpen. "Where's Connor? He should be in on this discussion."

"He's in Computer Forensics with Brown. They're searching for more details on Buxton's computer."

She nodded. "If Buxton knew about any of this, it would've been relayed to Satchel. The question then becomes, why hadn't she come forward with this information?"

"I would guess because she was afraid and when Satchel turned up dead, she decided it wasn't worth risking her life for," McCallister replied. "Except now Buxton's dead, too."

Bevins appeared in the bullpen and started toward them. He eyed Ellis. "Good. You're both here."

"What did Brown find?" she asked.

"After Satchel's murder, Buxton deleted several files," he continued.

"She was scared." Ellis sighed. "She knew something was wrong when he stopped contacting her."

"That's what I thought too," Bevins added. "In those recovered files, Satchel had sent her reports on chemical exposure and the impact on the health of those exposed."

"What kind of chemicals?" McCallister asked.

"Benzene, TCE, solvents," he said.

"We know Satchel had been recently diagnosed with Parkinson's. His tox screen revealed exposure to benzene and TCE," Ellis continued.

"And benzene, in liquid form, is instantly lethal," Bevins said.

"Exposure to it is also known to cause myeloid leukemia. And, thanks to your work," Ellis continued, "we know some of the people Satchel contacted later died of leukemia."

McCallister raised a shoulder. "So that's it. The reason Mark Owens didn't want to talk to us is because he may have been given a substantial retirement package so that he wouldn't speak about his illness."

"We don't know for certain that he's sick," Ellis said.

McCallister scoffed. "If I were a betting man, I'd stake my life on the fact that he is."

Scooter Littleton started his shift like any other day, but the news of Janice's death had rattled him. Two of his co-workers were dead, and it hadn't looked to him like either death was an accident. And that wasn't his only concern. He'd noticed other things during his tenure that, at the time he picked up on them, hadn't seemed suspicious. But in light of recent events, his perception had changed. Maybe Terry wasn't just mouthing off to anyone who would listen.

He called out to a nearby co-worker. "I'm taking a quick break."

The man removed his earplugs. "Huh?"

"Break time," Littleton said.

"Oh, okay." The man returned a thumbs-up.

Littleton shut down his station and headed toward the south end of the first floor where the cafeteria was located. Inside, he stopped at the coffee station and poured a cup, noticing other employees on their breaks too. The food line was quiet, so he made his way there and grabbed a blueberry muffin and a pot of oatmeal.

With his tray in hand, he sat down at one of the tables. He sipped on his coffee and noticed his co-workers engaged in light-hearted conversation. Odd, considering two people they knew were dead. None of this looked right. Who were these people exchanging banter? No one seemed to give a shit about anything or anyone except what happened in their own pathetic lives. Littleton scoffed. Who was he kidding? He was exactly the same, only now that Janice was gone, he was experiencing an awakening. A tickle in the back of his brain. "Something's not right."

He reached into the front pocket of his jeans and retrieved a card. Printed on the front was the detective's name: Rebecca Ellis. He'd spoken to her about Wayne, insinuating the notion Wayne played a part in Terry's death, and had heard nothing since. But as he flipped the card between his fingers, he pondered whether he should take more action.

With the decision made, Littleton shoved back his chair and shot up. He snatched the tray and headed toward the exit, dropping it into the shoot.

"You all right, Scooter?" one of the men called out.

He stopped and turned back. "No, man. I'm not all right." He continued into the corridor and marched along the shop floor. From the corner of his eye, he glanced into Harry's office. Good thing his boss was busy on a call. Littleton slipped outside and stood at the employee exit, heart racing, hands clammy. "Just make the call."

───────

WHILE MOTIVE for the murder of Terry Satchel came into focus, given the information Bevins helped recover on Buxton's laptop, it was Hank's stroke that consumed Ellis. It seemed impossible to reconcile the two events: the double homicide and her father's stroke. Too much was at stake for second-guesses and speculation. As she returned to her desk, a call rang through on her phone. "Detective Ellis, here."

"Yeah, this is Scooter, uh—Scott Littleton. You came to talk to me the other day about Terry and we talked—"

"Yes, sir, Mr. Littleton. What can I do for you?" she replied.

"Listen, uh, all this stuff happening, you know, with Janice and Terry, I mean it's weird."

"Yes, it is."

"And so, I started thinking about a bunch of other stuff, and well, I can't really go into it. You think I could maybe sit down with you sometime soon?"

"Absolutely." She hunted for a pen and notepad and found them buried on her desk.

It seemed McCallister took notice and stopped what he was doing, turning his attention to her.

"We can meet you anywhere at any time. You tell me what works for you." She waited for a response as silence sounded on the other end of the line. "Mr. Littleton?"

"I'm sitting in my car right now, outside Connex. I told everyone I was taking a break. Detective Ellis, I think something weird is happening here, so I can meet tonight. I'll text you the address. But there's one thing I'm worried about."

"What is it?" she asked.

"Uh, did Janice talk to you too? Like before..."

"Yes, sir. Janice did reach out to us. Terry was her former boyfriend, and she was concerned." Ellis was about to lose him. He was scared to speak out.

"That's what I thought—"

"But I can also tell you that if you're concerned, we can put a plan in place to ensure you're not exposed."

"How's that?" he asked.

"We can set a time and place to meet that no one will know about. You say you're outside in the parking lot?"

"I am."

"Are there security cameras outside?" Ellis asked.

"Yes, ma'am. They're everywhere."

"Okay. Here's what you're going to do. When we're finished here, you'll return inside and make a point to tell your co-workers, and your supervisor, that you have a family issue brewing. I don't know what that is, but you'll have to think of something. And that was the reason you were on the phone in your car."

"You're scaring me, Detective."

She raised her hand. "This is just a precaution. So then when your shift is over, I want you to go to your regular grocery store. You need to pick up a few things. I'll run into you and hand over a note that contains an address. We'll meet there. No one will know any of this. And in fact, after this call, I want you to delete my number from your phone history, you understand?"

"Yes, ma'am, I'll go to the store on Briar and nineteenth."

"Perfect. I won't be in my car. No one will see me. I promise you."

"Okay. Okay then. I'm off at six o'clock."

"All right. Remember to delete the record of this call. Goodbye, Mr. Littleton." She ended the call and looked at McCallister. "He wants to talk, but he's scared."

He raised a brow. "I would be too."

15

Regardless of what Ellis believed had caused Hank's stroke, the best and safest place for him to be was in the hospital. Serrano insisted he would get to the bottom of what happened, yet so far there was no word on his progress. Lack of control was never her strong suit, and neither was waiting for others to do their jobs. But before any meetings with potential witnesses could occur, she would see to Hank first.

Ellis emerged from the hospital and headed into the parking lot. Amid the dusky skies, she strained to find McCallister behind the wheel of the white sedan they'd borrowed to make the appointment with Littleton. The precautionary measure was necessary to protect the man whom she hoped had relevant information on their double homicide. After Janice Buxton, she wasn't taking any more chances.

A signal of acknowledgment as she locked eyes with McCallister, and Ellis carried on through the parking lot. She opened the passenger door and slipped onto the gray cloth seat.

McCallister waited for her to close the door. "How's he doing?"

"Good. Much better, actually. Doctor says he should be able to go home in a couple more days when he's a little stronger. Which, I'll bet you can guess how well that went."

"From what little I know about your dad? Probably not great." He pressed the starter. "It's best Hank stays there for a while, all things considered, but are you sure you want to do this? Connor and I can run this thing with Littleton alone."

"No, he contacted me. I have to follow through. The guy's skittish already," Ellis replied. "Besides, we need Connor to be on the lookout for tails."

"Fair enough." McCallister drove out of the parking lot and headed north toward the plant. "If Littleton has something real, we'll need to keep him safe."

"I agree. At this point, we're done giving Connex Solutions the benefit of the doubt," Ellis replied.

McCallister drove on as the sun fell. "You know, I'll be the first to admit that Connor has done everything by the book and just as we've asked. He screwed up with Byrd, but so far, no damage done."

"The important thing was that he owned up to it," she added. "Kind of surprised me, if I'm honest. But this was what the sarge wanted, so maybe the next time Connor will get the lead. Not that I'm holding my breath for another homicide in our jurisdiction."

"Yeah, well, we all know it's going to happen." He exited off the highway and drove along the main road toward the building. "Do you want to stay back and wait, or go into the parking lot?"

"Let's be safe and avoid their security cameras. There's a building across the street. We'll park there and wait until we see him leave."

"You got it." McCallister drove into the parking lot of the

adjacent building and faced the opposite side of the street. "Should be about ten minutes or so."

Ellis noticed another call ring through on her phone. She answered the line. "Hey, Piper, it's not the best—"

"Becca, I think I'm being followed."

The hairs on her neck stood on end. "What? Where are you?"

"I'm driving home. I'm almost there. I swear, this car's been behind me since I left work."

"Okay. Okay." She raised her hand. "Don't go home. Whatever you do, do not go to your apartment building. Here's what I want you to do. Turn around and go back to your office. You have security in the building, right?"

"Yeah. People are still there. What do I do when I get there?"

"First of all, if you are being followed, I doubt whoever it is will follow you back to work," Ellis continued. "He'll figure out that you know you're being tailed and will leave. But in the event this car does follow you back, I want you to call me again. Park near the front of your office, where people inside can see you. Don't get out of your car. Call me and I'll send a unit, okay? *Don't* get out."

"Okay, I hear you." Piper hesitated a moment. "What if it's that guy?"

"Did you tell him where you worked?" Ellis asked.

"No, I didn't. I told him what I do for a living," she replied. "But he doesn't know where."

"Then maybe this is just a coincidence." Ellis couldn't even swallow that lie. "Look, turn around and go back. And if you can, look to see what kind of car it is. If you can't, don't worry about it."

"I will. Thanks, Becca."

"Just call me when you get back to the office. I want to know he's off your tail."

"Okay. Bye."

Ellis ended the call and closed her eyes.

"What the hell was that all about?" McCallister asked. "Is your friend okay?"

She set eyes on him. "Is it possible it's the same person?"

"What are you talking about?"

Ellis looked out at the plant across the street. "A few days ago, Piper was almost attacked by a guy she met at a bar."

"Jeez." He turned away.

"I didn't think it was anything related to this, but now, after Hank." Ellis hesitated. "What if they're coming after me? Going through the people I care about to get to me?"

"Look, you've got great instincts, but I don't know...seems a hell of a stretch and a seriously dangerous move on their part if you're right. Whoever *they* are. And then we have to wonder why you and not me." He glanced at her. "That said, we've got two bodies, so I'm not sure we can rule it out. If she is being followed, what then?"

"For now?" Ellis began. "I'll get Moss to send a unit to her location. After that, I don't know what to do."

"Heads up." He pointed at the windshield. "There's our boy now. Are you still onboard or do we pull the plug so you can deal with this other issue?"

Ellis spotted Littleton step inside his beige compact truck. "We do this now. I don't want to lose him."

McCallister waited for the truck to leave the parking lot. "What was that address again for the grocery store?"

Ellis retrieved it on a sticky note. "Head south to nineteenth street and then right on Briar."

"Copy that." He drove on for a couple of miles, with Littleton's beige truck well ahead of them.

She pointed ahead. "He's pulling into the grocery store now."

"Got it." McCallister turned in several feet away while

Littleton parked. "I think I should be the one to go in and find him."

"No, it should be me." Ellis unbuckled her seat belt. "I'll be quick. I'll hand him the paper and keep on going right back out again."

"Okay." He shoved the gearshift into Park. "I'll be here. I'll give you five minutes. If you're not out—"

She opened her door. "I will be. Sit tight." Ellis walked out into the night sky and checked her surroundings as she made her way inside the large-chain grocer's. She tracked down Littleton to the bread aisle and when she captured his gaze, Ellis carried on and brushed by him, dropping a slip of paper into the top section of his cart. The doors were straight ahead, and Ellis walked out again, right to the car, where McCallister quickly fired up the engine.

She opened the door and slipped onto the passenger seat of the sedan. "It's done."

He pulled away. "Let's get over there and hope he shows."

Ellis picked up the phone. "Hey, Connor, it's done. Littleton should head over there in a few minutes. Euan and I are leaving now."

"Okay. See you there," Bevins replied before ending the call.

Ellis held her phone in her hands and stared at the screen.

"Call her," McCallister said. "You'll feel better."

"Yeah, okay." She dialed Piper once again. And when the line answered, relief swept through her. "Hey, how are you holding up?"

"Fine. I was followed back to the building, but when I waited in the car at the front, he didn't bother turning in and left. I figured it was safe to go inside. Now, I'm in my office doing some work. Might as well catch up, huh?"

Ellis smiled. "Can't hurt. Listen, I planned on sending a

unit your way, but things have changed. I want you to stay at my place tonight. I expect to be home in about an hour or so. You don't mind hanging out there a while longer?"

"No, I'm still pretty shaken, so I'm happy to stay here where I know no one else can get in and security is just downstairs."

"You know what? I think I'll come pick you up myself," Ellis said. "I don't want to risk you driving alone."

"Becca, you don't have to—"

"No? Seems to me I do. At least until we can figure out if it was the same guy who came at you the other night. I'll call you when I'm headed in your direction. Love you."

"Love you, bye."

THE CLOAK and dagger routine was new to Littleton. He considered himself a regular guy with a regular job. Clocking in, day in, day out. And now he'd just been slipped a piece of paper by a cop, telling him where to go to meet to discuss his friend, who'd been murdered.

"That'll be thirteen dollars and eighty-five cents, sir," the cashier said.

"Right. Okay." He reached into the pocket of his baggy jeans and grabbed his wallet before handing her a twenty.

She handed over the remainder. "Here's your change, sir. Have a nice night."

"Thanks." Littleton grabbed the grocery bag with bread, a six-pack of beer, and a couple candy bars inside. He walked out into the parking lot, checking the area for the cop, but she was nowhere in sight. His compact Toyota pickup was ahead and he pressed the remote to unlock the door before stepping behind the wheel.

The address on the note was a place familiar to him and

so he turned the ignition and drove out onto the road. He kept a close eye on his surroundings and continued toward the highway. Turned out, the cop knew what she was doing and he felt her plan had worked. Revealing what he'd suspected about the company could put him in the line of fire, as it seemed to have done to both Satchel and now, possibly, Janice Buxton. Caution was in order, but for now he seemed to be in the clear.

The highway on-ramp came into view and Littleton veered left to merge. The plan was for him to arrive within twenty minutes of the grocery store, and he was on-track to meet the deadline as his exit was just two miles ahead.

From the corner of his eye, in the driver's side mirror, lights shone brightly. Within seconds, he heard an engine roar and race toward him. "Jeez!" Littleton swerved to avoid the collision with a truck that whizzed by. But his right tires tipped off the edge of the shoulder and he struggled to keep control of the wheel. He felt the shudder when one of his tires went flat. "Damn it!" He drove off the shoulder and slowed to a stop. Ahead, he watched the brake lights from the vehicle that ran him off vanish in the distance. "Asshole!"

McCALLISTER MADE a final right turn and glanced at Ellis. "That's the place. Looks like we beat Littleton here."

Ellis surveyed the grounds. "I don't see Connor yet either."

"I'm sure he'll be along shortly." McCallister pulled into the parking lot of the closed restaurant. Trees surrounded the building, and it appeared the place had been shut for years. No reason for anyone to be here.

"I see headlights," Ellis added. "I think that's Connor there." As the car approached, she continued, "He should know to turn off his lights. We don't need passersby seeing cars in an abandoned restaurant parking lot and giving them an excuse to call the cops."

"Like you said, he's still learning," McCallister replied.

Ellis creased her brow. "He's not slowing down."

"Damn it." McCallister thrust the gear into Drive and slammed on the gas pedal. "That's not Connor. It's not Littleton either. We were followed."

Ellis gripped the armrest. "Go!"

He peeled out of the parking spot and drove around to the back of the building, making his way out the other side. "You see his plates?"

But when gunfire rang out, Ellis ducked into her seat. "Get down!"

"Son of a bitch." McCallister tucked his head low as he tried to drive out onto the main road again.

Ellis grabbed her phone. "Come on! Answer, Connor!"

The line picked up. "Yeah?"

With one eye just above the dash, Ellis ordered, "We've been spotted. Don't come here. Do not come here!"

"What's going on?" Bevins asked.

Another shot was fired.

"Was that a gunshot? What the hell's happening right now?" Bevins demanded.

Ellis dropped her phone as she remained low, peeking her head just above the dash to get a good look at the vehicle. "Who the hell is that?"

"I don't know, but he knows who we are." McCallister spun the tires and reached the main road. "Can you see it? Can you see the car?"

Ellis peeked through the passenger window. "It's an SUV. Uh, gray, I think. Shit, I can't..." Another round echoed in the night air. "Cadillac. It's a Cadi."

"Plates, Becca. I need plates! I can't sit here forever!"

"I'm trying." She squinted. "Gray Cadillac Escalade. I can't see the plates." She slammed her fist on the dash. "He's heading around the back of the building." Ellis reached the floorboard to pick up her phone. "You still there?"

"Are you guys okay?" Bevins asked.

"We're okay. We got away." She looked back at the shrinking building behind them. "Whoever it was knew we were coming."

McCallister returned a stony glare. "Littleton."

16

The lobby of the high-rise building came into view. Ellis opened the car door. "I'll be back in a minute." Still shaken after dodging several bullets only minutes before, Ellis stopped at the entrance and pressed her hand against her chest, working to slow her breathing. She walked inside, where Piper had just exited the elevators. Ellis donned a forced smile and approached.

"You're earlier than you said you'd be," Piper said.

"Things didn't quite go as I thought they would," she replied. "Listen, I've got my partner with me, and we need to head to the station for a little while. I know it's probably the last place you want to be, but I'd feel better if you came with me."

"Sure, I don't mind. I am feeling better, and I could just drive home."

Ellis took her hand and turned around to leave. "On any other day, I'd say you're right. But not today."

"What do you mean?" Piper followed as they exited the lobby and returned outside.

"Forget it. Not important." Ellis arrived at the car and opened the back door.

Piper stopped cold. "This isn't your car."

"I'll explain later. Just get in." Ellis held the door while Piper stepped inside.

From the back seat, she peered at the rearview mirror, where McCallister looked back. "Hi. I'm Piper Dixon. You must be Euan McCallister?" She stretched her arm over the seat.

"That's me. Good to meet you, Piper. I've heard a lot about you." He shook her hand and after Ellis climbed in, he turned the ignition. "Becca told me what you went through tonight. I'm sorry."

"Sounds like your night wasn't much better," she replied.

He glanced at Ellis and thumbed back. "I like her."

THE RIDE back to the station was shrouded in silence. Piper was scared. Ellis was scared for her, for Hank, and for Scott Littleton. Although, questions remained as to just who told Mr. Cadillac where they were headed. When all this was over, she would tell Piper what had happened tonight, but for now it was news that would only upset her.

Ellis's nerves were shot as she climbed upstairs to CID. Her muscles ached and her heart still thumped hard, like she'd just run a marathon. It was one thing to aim a gun at a suspect. It was something else altogether to sidestep a bullet or two.

Piper followed her inside the bullpen and McCallister continued into the hall.

"I'll find Abbott," he said. "You can get her settled."

"Thanks." Ellis led Piper to her desk. "Why don't you wait for me here? I have to take care of something first."

"Hey, you mind if I check out the break room?" Piper asked. "I'm dying of thirst."

"Help yourself." Ellis placed her hand on Piper's shoulder. "I won't be long and then we'll go back to my house."

"Take your time."

Just as Ellis turned around, Bevins marched toward her. "What the hell was that back there? I heard shots. You guys are okay, right?"

Piper's face masked in surprise. "Shots?"

Ellis raised her hand. "It was nothing. Okay, yes, it was something, but nothing you should worry about, Piper, okay?" She set her eyes on Bevins. "You, me, and Euan need to sit down with Abbott. Piper's here for another reason."

Bevins placed his hands on his hips. "This went south pretty damn quick. What about our boy, Littleton?"

"I don't know." She took his arm. "Let's sit down with the sarge."

McCallister waited for them inside Abbott's office. And when Ellis and Bevins entered, she noticed he stood with his arms folded and his gaze at his feet, as though he'd already been reprimanded.

Abbott clenched his jaw as he eyed the detectives. "You mind telling me what the hell happened tonight?"

Ellis stood behind the chair across from Abbott's desk. "I may have trusted the wrong person."

McCallister turned to her. "Littleton was the only one who knew where we were going to meet. It seemed like he was on our side, but I have no other explanation for what happened."

"You'll have to file an incident report," Abbott added. "So where does that leave you with this case? It's getting pretty damn crystal clear these folks aren't messing around."

"Trusting anyone else who works at Connex is too much

of a risk now." Ellis stopped a moment when her phone rang. "Sorry, sir, I don't recognize the number, but—"

"Go on," he replied.

"Detective Ellis," she answered. "What? Hang on." She pressed the speaker button. "Mr. Littleton, are you okay?"

"No. I was run off the road on the way to come meet you. I got your note. Got back into my truck and then headed that way. I was sure no one followed. Then I got onto the highway and some car or truck, I don't know...They just came right up next to me and pushed me off onto the shoulder. I deleted your number, like you said, but thank God I still had your card on me. You gotta get me out of here. My truck's got a flat and I don't have a spare. I'm sitting here hiding in the damn trees freezing my ass off."

"Stay where you are. We'll come to you. Just send me your location." She ended the call. "The Cadillac SUV. It had to have been the same people who came at us."

"Why didn't they try to take out Littleton when they had the chance, then?" McCallister asked.

Abbott aimed a finger at him. "That's the first question I'd ask too."

McCallister looked back at Ellis. "No one knew where we were going. No one but him. Now he's calling, asking you to come get him?"

"He gave me the location of the grocery store when he called earlier today." She rubbed the back of her neck. "What if someone was listening?"

"You're saying his phone is bugged?" McCallister asked.

"I'm saying, if it's a company phone, is it possible someone from the company was listening, followed him, and ran him off the road to scare him?"

McCallister set his hands on his hips. "Then they came after us?"

Ellis closed her eyes and grew frustrated. "I-I don't know

yet. Look, I get what you're saying, but Littleton reached out to me. He asked if Buxton was dead because she talked to us. He was scared. I know what I said, but maybe I'm wrong."

"Why do you think that?" Abbott asked. "Because this Littleton guy told you?"

"Because he called back," she cut in. "What would be the point in getting us out there to help him when, after what just happened, we would bring backup? No chance they'd ambush us again."

"You might have a point," McCallister said. "But if we meet with him, we will have backup ready."

Ellis eyed Abbott again. "What do you think, Sarge? Am I making the wrong call?"

LITTLETON STAYED low and made his way to the edge of the tree line, where several feet of grassy shoulder lay ahead. He craned his neck to see out onto the highway. Aside from the darkness, trees, and cars that streaked by in a blur, it didn't look as though anyone was waiting for him to come into view and take their shot.

He looked at his truck from the safety of the shadowed tree line off the highway. He wasn't going to risk being spotted out there alone. His little pickup leaned with two wheels on the soft earth and two wheels on the paved shoulder. With a flat tire and no spare, calling that detective was his only chance. This couldn't have been a coincidence, running him off the road like that. It was a warning. Someone followed him. Someone who didn't want him to talk to the cops. "I thought I was careful."

It was too late now. Whoever did this had to have followed him from work. "It was because I made the call in my truck." He recalled peering through the windshield, glancing around like some paranoid fool, and they saw it. They saw his face. But who?

There was no going back. He was going to have to tell the cops everything he knew about Terry and about the things he'd seen during his time at Connex. Things that hadn't seemed all that important until people started dying. The detective would protect him. She promised.

Littleton took a step out from the cover of the trees and into the grass. The cops would be there soon, as he'd sent her his location.

A vehicle approached in the distance and appeared to slow. Littleton continued to his truck when he noticed it glide over to the shoulder. "That was fast." He stood near the tailgate and raised a hand to garner the driver's attention. "Just get me the hell out of here." As the vehicle came into view, his face deadpanned. "Oh God."

The passenger window of the truck rolled down. He couldn't be sure, but this didn't look like the cops. Littleton spun around and slipped on the grass. He quickly regained traction and ran back in the direction of the woods. A shot rang out and the bullet whizzed by his ear. He instinctively raised his hands for protection and pushed onward. Another bullet was fired and pierced his back. The searing pain forced him to cry out. He stumbled a few more steps, arching his back as the pain grew unbearable. Blood soaked his shirt and spilled down his spine. His lungs collapsed and he gasped for air before falling to the ground.

The grass cooled his cheek as he lay on his stomach. Atop the soft earth, footsteps neared. "Help me, please," he muttered. The loss of blood weakened him. He struggled for breath from lungs that no longer drew in air. With every bit of strength he had left, Littleton turned his gaze up to a shadow of a man. And a gun. "Please don't."

ELLIS AIMED her index finger toward the highway's shoulder and slowed her speed. "That's his truck, right there."

"I see it," McCallister replied. "But I don't see him." He narrowed his gaze and leaned closer to the passenger window. "He might still be in the woods."

"It's the safest place for him." She rolled to a stop behind his truck and jumped out of her Tahoe. Ellis landed on soft ground and stepped through the long grass. The wind from passing vehicles brushed against her back.

McCallister veered off to the right, while she went straight on. She called out. "Scott? Scott, where are you? It's Detective Ellis. Come out now. You're safe."

"Becca!" McCallister yelled. "Becca, over here!"

She marched through the grass toward him. He wore an expression she'd come to know well.

McCallister glanced down.

Ellis peered at Littleton's body just feet in front of her. She squatted low and placed her fingers on his carotid artery. "No."

"They got to him first."

She let her eyes roam over him. "Finding Satchel set this off. Everyone who knew him and came to us is dead. Why?"

McCallister closed his eyes a moment. "Maybe there's more at stake than we know."

"With now three dead, what else could possibly..." She stopped cold and turned her gaze toward the disabled truck.

"What is it?" he asked.

Ellis pondered her theory and finally returned her attention to McCallister. "We know the company has a history of illegalities, but murder? That was never among them. People would've been sent to prison. The place probably would've been shut down. So I think there's another reason behind these murders."

McCallister tilted his head. "What about the employees who've died of illnesses? Who appeared to receive large payouts to keep quiet? That all ties in with a company head willing to go to extremes to shut down any question as to their culpability like in years past."

"You're right. It does." Ellis turned up her palms. "But what if one isn't tied to the other?"

WITH THE KEYS in her hand, Ellis unlocked the door of her home and ushered Piper inside. "I'm sorry you had to wait so long at the station."

"It's okay, Becca. I can't believe all you've gone through tonight." She set down her bag and turned to her friend. "Is this what it's always like for you?"

Ellis donned a weary grin. "No, thank God. I'm feeling like I'm at a loss. Two people now dead because of me. Another was already dead."

"No, don't say that. You're doing your job."

Ellis secured the door and walked toward her kitchen. "They went after Satchel's friends. Whoever did this thought they knew something and planned to tell us. So they were killed. We thought the guy set us up, and now he's dead." She opened the fridge and grabbed two bottles of water. Ellis handed over one of them. "Here."

"Thanks," Piper replied. "So, what are you and your partners going to do?"

Ellis walked toward the sofa and sat down. "Our only card is to find a way to get a search warrant on the plant. And if we do that, we can pretty much kiss goodbye to any evidence because it would be destroyed before we could see it."

Piper joined her. "I honestly had no idea this was the kind of shit you had to deal with."

"Well, like I said, it's not always like this. If it was, I don't think I'd be able to do the job." She sipped on her water. "And now we have to figure out who followed you tonight."

"It had to be him. It makes sense he'd be a stalker." Piper scoffed. "It's just my luck."

"Even so, it's dangerous and we can't ignore it. I have Bryce helping me out with that. He should have answers soon. I haven't seen him since earlier, but I'm not going to let this fall by the wayside, Piper. I won't."

Lieutenant Abe Serrano entered the lobby of the hospital and approached the administration desk. "Excuse me, I'm looking for Hank Ellis. Can you tell me what room he's in?" The fifty-seven-year-old in charge of the Criminal Investigation Division at Bangor PD had been a friend and co-worker of Hank's for a long time. Too many years to remember.

"Are you family?" the security guard asked.

Serrano retrieved his badge and held it up for the man. "Hank's an old friend of mine. Used to work together."

"Of course. Yes, sir. He's in 308. Third floor, surgical unit."

"Thanks." He returned his badge to his pocket and walked with a long stride toward the elevators. He rode up to the third floor and entered the hall in search of the room. As he reached 308, he knocked. "Hank, you awake, buddy?" He heard a mumble and pushed open the door. He saw a smile on Hank's face. "Hey there, old friend."

"Becca told you?" Hank pursed his lips. "I didn't want her to worry anyone at the station. I'm fine, as you can see."

"To be honest, man, you kind of look like shit."

Hank chuckled and quickly coughed, as he ran out of breath.

"Now calm down," Serrano said. "Don't want you having another damn stroke. And just so you know, your girl was worried, all right? I will say this, she's just like you. Keeps her entire life locked up in a little box and shoved at the back of a closet shelf."

"I guess I'm glad you came. It's nice to see your old wrinkly face," Hank replied.

"My wrinkly face?" He scoffed. "You taken a look in the mirror lately, my friend?" Serrano laughed and placed his hand on Hank's arm. "Seriously, though, how you feeling?"

"I'm all right. Doc says I can go home day after tomorrow. But I'm supposed to take it easy for a while after that. Watch what I eat, blah, blah, blah."

"Well, you better listen to all that blah, blah, blah, you hear me? These doctors know what they're doing." Serrano sat down. "So, listen, I would've come to see you anyway, but uh, there is something I need to tell you."

Hank furrowed his brow. "I'll bet I already know."

Serrano crossed his spindly legs and rested his arms in his lap. "Connex Solutions."

Hank turned down his lips. "Becca gave me the rundown yesterday. Even thinks they tampered with my meds that landed me here."

"She mentioned that," Serrano replied.

"I don't know what to make of it. Doesn't sound like what we dealt with, though. Our case involved some of their management harassing workers 'cause they lodged complaints."

Serrano nodded. "That's right. Their employees were getting reprimanded for speaking out on safety issues and such. But uh, this does feel different. Worse, if I'm being honest."

"So this isn't a whistleblower case?" Hank asked.

"That whistleblower is dead and so are two other folks now. One just tonight. I'm sorry to say Becca got into a tussle with some folks with guns earlier this evening." Serrano raised his hands. "She's fine. She's a well-trained detective and so is her partner. They got themselves out of the situation."

Hank's expression hardened. "Funny how Becca didn't mention all this."

"No doubt she didn't want to worry you. And she was right to hold back. But here's the thing. We both knew what we were up against when we tried to get in Connex's way last time. Years went by and I assumed they'd cleaned up their act, got new management, whatever, 'cause nothing new ever came out of there. Until now. So either they did clean up and went back to their old ways—"

"Or they never stopped and somehow found a way to silence those who would otherwise speak out," Hank replied.

"That is how it appears."

Hank seemed to think on the matter. "You remember the name of the old manager who came to us?"

"No, but I'm sure it's in the file. You think that son of a bitch is still running things?" Serrano asked.

"Got no idea. He offered valuable intel. Wasn't enough, but maybe there's more now. After all, if I recall, he owes us big time."

17

The deeper Detective Bryce Pelletier dug into Tom Sutton, the more obvious it became that this was not the man's real identity. Made sense. Attackers probably wouldn't offer up their actual names. So all he had to go off was the description Ellis had given him. And that was based on Piper's description at a time when she had been somewhat intoxicated.

Rather than go back to Ellis empty-handed, Pelletier would take another approach. People like Sutton were predators. Ellis knew this and she'd already mentioned she'd gone back to the bar where it happened to find anyone who'd seen the man recently. She struck out. But this was his chance to make another attempt. Predators often return to the place where prey is abundant. Pelletier figured he would come back and make another attempt.

It struck eleven o'clock as he arrived at the darkly opulent, sleek and pretentious cocktail bar where it had happened, and the place was still busy. He understood why Ellis came back here. She would've been an obvious target for Sutton. Pelletier—not so much. But he could observe.

He pulled out a stool at the shiny bar, blue LED lights tucked on the shelves of the liquor wall. Familiar with this particular night spot, Pelletier dressed for the occasion. Dark suit jacket, black shirt and tie. A stark contrast to his light hair and blue eyes, and it detracted from his slightly pudgy midsection. Some men—McCallister in particular—were dark and mysterious, while others, like Pelletier, were boyish and appeared harmless. But Pelletier carried a gun and was well trained in physical combat. He was anything but harmless.

The clamor of the crowd soon became nothing more than a drone of white noise while he focused on any man who might fit Piper's description. He knew the odds were slim of finding Sutton here at this moment, but he had nothing else. He needed to do this to prove to Ellis he would always have her back and be there when she needed him.

"Can I get you anything, buddy?"

Pelletier's attention was drawn back to the bartender. "A Coke, please. Thanks."

"You got it." He grabbed a glass and pulled the lever of the tap to fill it up. He dropped in a cherry and snatched a cocktail napkin from a nearby stack before setting it down in front of Pelletier. "You want to start a tab, sir?"

He looked at the drink and retrieved his wallet. "No, thanks."

"That'll be seven-fifty, please."

"Here you go, thanks." Pelletier set a ten on the table and kept his hand flat on the bill a moment. "Were you working here last Tuesday?"

"No, sir." The barman pointed a finger toward the other end of the bar. "He was."

"Thanks." Pelletier released the bill. "Keep the change." He got up from the stool and walked to the other end of the bar, where several people vied for the barman's attention to place their orders. He was going to try another approach in hopes of learning more, so he waited until the man had cleared his backlog and then Pelletier finally garnered his attention. "Excuse me?"

The harried barman leaned over with a hand cupped around his ear. "What'll it be?"

Pelletier leaned in. "Do you know Piper Dixon?"

The man pulled back and eyed him. "Why are you asking?"

"Look, I'll be honest with you, she's a friend of mine and I'm a cop. Piper was in here last Tuesday. Someone followed her out. It scared her." He left out the part where she was almost attacked and barely escaped. "She comes here sometimes. Thought, if you knew her, you might know who she was with that night. Can you help me out?"

The bartender eyed him again. "You're a cop?"

"Yes, sir. You want to see my badge?"

He waved his hand and glanced around as if those in the bar might bolt if they knew a cop was in there. "Yeah, I know Piper. Long, dark hair. Well dressed. Sexy as hell."

Pelletier smiled. "That's her. Who was she with on Tuesday? You see her with anyone?"

The barman looked down a moment, as if thinking on the question, before returning his attention. "I saw her with some dude."

"Do you know who he was?"

"I served him. I remember because he paid with cash. Most people don't."

So no receipt of payment. "Did you hear a name?"

"Yep. Guy comes in here a lot. Usually leaves with a different girl each time. Lucky, I guess," the barman replied.

"Sure. Lucky. His name?"

"Tom."

Pelletier sighed. "Okay. Thanks, man, I appreciate the help." He turned away.

"Wait," the bartender said. "Hang on. I think I do have something." He raised a finger and then walked to the back.

Pelletier waited a moment until he returned.

"Guy left a business card for me once. Said his company was setting up some event and asked if I could bartend for him." He handed over the card. "Nothing ever came of it, but I stuck the card inside my locker. Forgot about it until now, actually."

Pelletier eyed the card. "Tom Lazaro." He donned a tight-lipped grin and eyed the bartender. "Thanks, man. You don't know how much I appreciate this."

"Piper's a good person. If this guy did something to her, well, you know who he is now. I don't want anyone in my bar pulling shit like that, so you're doing me a favor."

Pelletier nodded and turned to leave. As he arrived at his car, he checked the time. He had a name and where this guy worked. Ellis would want to know.

He drove toward her house and made the call.

"Hey, Becca. Is this a bad time?"

"No, not at all. Is everything okay?" she asked.

"You mind if I stop by? I have some news for you."

"Uh, yeah, that's fine. Piper's here. She's staying with me tonight."

"Oh, okay, great. Well, this involves her too. I'll see you in about ten minutes," he replied.

"See you then."

The drive along the quiet road toward her house gave him time to come up with a plan. Getting Ellis the information on the creep who came after Piper was a priority, but after that, maybe he could pull her aside. This was where his personality got in his way. He was the kind of man who waited for what he wanted rather than going after it. At least, in his personal life. His life as a cop was markedly different.

He turned onto her street and parked in front of her house. The lights were on when most others in the neighborhood were off. He stepped out of his car and headed toward the front door that opened as he neared.

"Hey."

Ellis stood on the other side. It had been a long time since he'd seen her in something other than a suit. She wore an oversized cardigan with a T-shirt and leggings underneath. Her short blond hair was tucked behind her ears and curled up slightly at her jawline. Beautiful as always.

"Hey. How's Piper doing?" he asked.

She stepped aside. "Good. Come in." Ellis closed the door behind him. "You look nice. What's the occasion?"

He'd forgotten that he'd worn a suit and while the jacket was in his car, he still had on a dress shirt. "Oh, yeah, I was out earlier. Listen, I need to talk to you about Tom Sutton. I have news."

Piper appeared from the hallway. "Bryce, hey. Long time, no see." She approached him and offered an embrace. "You look great. Wow."

Now he felt slightly embarrassed by the attention. "Thanks. I was out earlier and needed to stop by and talk to Becca." He didn't know whether Ellis had mentioned to Piper that he was helping her. "I hope you don't mind I came here to talk shop with her for a few minutes."

"No, I don't mind at all. I was about to get ready for bed anyway. I'll let you talk." She spun around and started into the hallway again.

When Pelletier believed she was out of earshot, he looked to Ellis and retrieved the business card.

She glanced at it. "What's this?"

"That is Tom Sutton."

Ellis turned up her gaze and her eyes widened. "It is? Are you sure?"

He nodded. "I'm sure. The reason I'm dressed up is because I went to the bar and talked to the bartender who worked that night. He recalled seeing Piper there with a guy he knew to be that guy right there." He pointed to the card. "That's Sutton, Becca. That's who went after Piper."

She shook her head. "Oh my God. You found him. Thank you so much, Bryce. I mean, this is amazing. I didn't get anywhere when I went. And you-you come back here with his business card."

Pelletier shrugged. "I got lucky the bartender was there. That's all."

"To hell with that. You did your job, and I can't thank you enough," she replied.

"Listen, Becca, there's something I've been meaning to say for a while now, and well, we haven't spent time together lately like we used to—"

She tilted her head. "What is it, Bryce?"

He cleared his throat and looked around, ensuring they were alone. "I know we work together and it's probably a bad idea, but I'd like to ask you out. I've wanted to ask for a long time, but it never seemed the right time. It probably isn't now either, but I know I'd regret not asking you...so, what do you think?"

McCALLISTER KEYED the lock of his apartment door and stepped inside. He turned on the lights and set down his keys and laptop bag. The case had taken a dark turn, with three people now dead and the idea that Ellis's family and friends were getting dragged in. What was worse was that the two of them had narrowly escaped a barrage of bullets tonight. That didn't happen every day. It changed the scope of the investigation.

They didn't know who exactly was behind the murders or their recent attack. He knew what he wanted to do next but wasn't sure if he would get the buy-off from Ellis. Although, after their last case together, she'd proved she had the capacity to bend the rules. And that was what was called for now.

His phone rang, as he retrieved a bottle of beer from the refrigerator. He answered the call and continued into his living room. "McCallister here."

"Detective Euan McCallister, formerly with Boston PD?" the woman on the line asked.

"Yes. Who is this?" He slowly sat down.

"Detective, this is Holly Andrews, *Boston Globe*. Is this a bad time?"

"The *Boston Globe*?" he asked.

"Yes, sir. I'm an online columnist. I apologize for the late hour, but I tried to reach you earlier. Can I ask you a few questions about the death of Taylor Briggs, Detective?"

McCallister rubbed his forehead. "It's very late, ma'am, so I'd appreciate it if you contacted me inside of business hours. Thank you—"

"Wait!" she cut in. "Detective, when you shot the boy, did you know he was carrying a toy gun?"

"You'll have to call back another time, Ms. Andrews. Good night." He ended the call and set down his phone, staring at it like it was possessed. "What the hell?" Why was this reporter calling and asking questions now? He had been cleared of wrongdoing. The gun was an exact replica of a 9-millimeter. He hadn't known the boy was so young. He looked like an adult. "Stop."

This was how it started. The spiraling thoughts that took him to that dark place again. The reporters had hounded him after it happened. Protests erupted, though they had been short-lived. It was no surprise, then, when it became clear he needed to transfer out of that department. And he'd ended up here, in Bangor. But somehow this reporter had decided to dig it up again. If it was given new life in the papers, on social media, chances were good he'd have to leave Bangor, too. No one here knew what he'd done, except for Sergeant Abbott and Lieutenant Serrano. If he didn't find a way to stop this before it started, they would have no choice. And the last thing he wanted was to leave Bangor, because that would mean leaving Becca.

PELLETIER LEFT the question hanging in the air, hovering overhead like an ominous cloud that threatened to unleash a downpour. Ellis stood frozen, unable to answer him. Hank was in the hospital, Piper had been followed, and she and McCallister had been shot at only hours earlier. He wanted to do this now?

"Becca, I'm sorry. I know you have a lot going on right now." He shoved his hands in his pockets. "I shouldn't have come."

"Bryce," she cut in. "You are one of my closest friends. You know that—"

"Friends," he said.

"Just give me a chance, here, okay?" She wore a tight-lipped grin and her eyes held compassion. "What you did tonight for Piper—that was amazing. Not that I'm surprised because you're a great detective. But—"

He nodded. "It's okay, I should go."

"But." She placed her hands on his shoulders. "I don't know how I feel about you, if you want me to be honest. It's not something I've considered because, well, I hadn't known you considered it. I will say that now probably isn't the right time to sit down and talk this through. But you've given me something to think about. And I haven't thought about a future with anyone in a very long time." She held his gaze. "Can you give me time? It's probably not fair for me to ask you—"

"Yes, of course I can, Becca. I figured if I didn't tell you, then I would regret it someday. Look, if you don't feel the same, it changes nothing. I promise you. We will still be good friends and I'll be okay with that." He gripped the door handle before turning back to her. "Just know we're both adults and I can handle the truth."

Ellis raised on her toes to kiss his cheek. "Okay, Bryce." She stood there a moment while he opened the door to step out. "As far as this business card is concerned, I can't thank you enough. This means everything to me."

"Good night, Becca."

"Good night." She closed the door and turned to see Piper with her arms crossed.

"Sorry. I'm super nosy. You know this about me," Piper replied. "I only caught the last part of that."

"Then you heard all you needed to hear." She glanced at the business card and tucked it into her pocket. "You feel like a cup of tea? I think I could use one."

18

Lieutenant Serrano was a hands-off kind of leader. He let his people do what they needed to do and, so far, that strategy had worked well for him. He hadn't always been that way. One only needed to ask Hank Ellis about that. But he'd learned as time went on. Now, however, it seemed he was about to get involved in a current investigation that brought back unpleasant memories. But when his people were in danger, when his friend was in danger, the choice was no longer his to make.

He arrived at the café and spotted the old man at one of the tables. He remembered the face. The dark-rimmed eyeglasses. The thin lips. The pointed chin. Yeah, this was Paul Peck. An unforgettable name that went along with the unforgettable face.

"Mr. Peck." Serrano arrived at the table and pulled out a chair. "It's been a long time, sir."

Peck raised his gaze to meet him. "Detective Serrano. A long time, indeed."

"It's Lieutenant now."

"Oh, I see. Moved up in the ranks. Good for you. I, myself,

retired ten years ago." Peck sipped on the mug of coffee in front of him. "You're the one who called this little rendezvous, so tell me, Lieutenant, why am I here?"

Serrano garnered the attention of a server. "Can I get a coffee, please? Black."

The young man nodded. "Right away, sir."

Serrano returned his attention to Peck. "I'm here to talk to you about Connex."

Peck wore a smirk. "Retired from that place years ago. You know that."

"I do know that, which is why I'm here. It looks as though your former employer might be up to their old tricks again. I'd like to ask if you'd heard anything about that."

"You think I keep in touch with those people who nearly killed me?" Peck asked.

"We never could find proof of that, though, could we?" Serrano eyed the server as he approached. "Thank you, son. You can set it down. Appreciate it."

"Sure."

After the kid fell out of earshot, Serrano continued, "I got three dead bodies. One who'd been dead for months found in City Forest. The other, killed in an unfortunate car accident only days ago, and another last night. Shot in the back while he was on the ground." He sipped on the coffee and returned a sour face. "All three worked for Connex. Two were current employees, the first one, guy took off months earlier, only to find out he was actually murdered."

"Sorry, Lieutenant, but what's this got to do with me? You see I'm an old man now. Retired." Peck shrugged. "Not sure how I can help you. Frankly, you should've pushed your DA harder on the original investigation."

"You think I didn't?" Serrano asked. "I pushed harder for that than anything in my entire life. DA insisted we didn't have the evidence to convict the entire Board of Directors, or any one of them, for that matter."

Peck raised his chin. "Where's that other detective who worked with you? I can't recall his name."

"Ellis. He's long since retired. Like you, I suppose," Serrano replied. "So to answer your question, I'd like to ask for your old files again. The ones you kept. I need to know if this is the same situation, or something different. And I need names. I don't know who's running the operation there now, but if any one of them was there back in the day, then I'll know who to focus in on."

"Are you sure you want to go down that road again, Lieutenant? Seems to me, if I recall correctly, it led you down a dangerous path. One I only escaped from by the skin of my teeth."

"My people are involved in this one. I won't put them in any more danger. That means I need to understand who has the most to lose at Connex and why this would be happening now." Serrano sipped on his coffee again. "So, will you help me one more time?"

IT HAD BEEN NEARLY impossible to find sleep the previous night. Ellis was plagued with thoughts of the investigation. The fact she had been a target of someone's shooting practice, along with McCallister. Then there was Hank—oh, and better not forget the situation with Piper. A situation that was closer to resolution, thanks to her good friend Pelletier, who, by the way, had expressed his feelings for her. So sleep wasn't in the cards.

Ellis arrived in the bullpen and caught sight of Pelletier at his desk. "Morning."

"Morning, Becca," he replied.

Okay, that wasn't so bad. No awkwardness. And she'd been honest with him last night. She really hadn't thought of him in that way before and so the idea needed to sink in.

As she arrived at her desk, McCallister walked in behind her. She glanced back. "I was thinking about what happened last night—"

"Same here." He set down his things and pulled out his desk chair. "They can't keep everyone quiet because sooner or later someone's going to the press."

"I agree. Murdering everyone is going to catch up to them," she replied. "So, here's what I'd like to do."

But before she continued, Seavers hurried toward them. "Good, you're both here," he said.

Ellis narrowed her gaze. "What's going on?"

He set down a file folder on her desk. "I found this, shoved into the glove box in Buxton's car. It was folded over and tucked way in the back, almost as if she'd wanted to keep it hidden. And then I looked at it and knew that was exactly what she'd wanted."

McCallister peered over her shoulder at the file. "What is it?"

She began to examine the papers. "These are emails from Satchel."

"Yep," Seavers said. "I don't know exactly what you two are dealing with in this case, but I will say that just on glancing at those papers, as a guy who knows nothing about this thing, you got yourself a situation. I'd say, enough that it's possible Janice Buxton was forced into that wreck."

"Do you have proof of that yet?" McCallister asked him.

"We found a nail in one of her tires. It burst when she was driving, and because her speed clocked in at almost 90 miles per hour I'm going to say that a blowout at that speed would be nearly impossible to survive given the terrain of where she crashed."

Ellis continued to read the papers and looked at McCallister. "He's telling her he has proof that Connex is killing people."

"When were they sent?" McCallister asked.

Ellis checked the date. "Days before his death." She nodded at Seavers. "This is what we needed."

"What did he have and did he have it in his possession when he died?" McCallister replied.

"I can't say, but she must've been skeptical because why not tell us about these when we met with her? She printed them out and took them for a reason," Ellis continued. "Was she taking them to someone for safekeeping? Had she planned to give them to us later?"

"When she was far enough away that they couldn't find her," McCallister added.

It was then that Bevins arrived and headed their way. "Hey, what's going on? Am I late for a meeting?"

"No," Ellis said. "Seavers just brought these to us." She handed him the papers. "Has Brown finished with Buxton's laptop? Do we know if he found anything else?"

"He's finished getting what he could get from it," Bevins replied. "I was still working on contacting the families of those who died that Satchel had been in contact with. In fact, I got a call from two of the spouses. They want to talk."

McCallister eyed him. "They do? Well, shit. Let's go talk to them." He looked back at Ellis. "If they tell us what they know, these emails Buxton printed might start to make more sense. They could give us enough to get a warrant on the facility."

———

THE DETECTIVES ARRIVED at the home of former employee,

now deceased, Monty Trevino. He was survived by his wife, Helen, who opened the door on their arrival.

"Good morning, Mrs. Trevino, I'm Detective Ellis. I believe you spoke to Detective Bevins." She gestured toward him. "This is Detective McCallister. May we come in and speak to you about your husband?"

"Yes, of course." The older woman of about sixty stepped aside and closed the door behind them. The petite widow had short, silvery hair and was dressed in casual pants and a button-down blouse with a beige cardigan over the top. "I apologize, the house isn't as clean as I'd prefer to keep it. My grandson was with me a few days ago, and it takes me several days to recover from a visit with that young boy."

"Yes, ma'am." McCallister smiled. "You have a lovely home."

"Thank you, sir. Please come in. May I offer you a drink? I have coffee and tea," she replied.

"No, thank you, Mrs. Trevino," Ellis replied.

"It's Helen." She shuffled into the living room. "All right then. We can speak in here, if you'd like."

Ellis noticed the nice décor. Well decorated, well furnished. "You do keep a lovely home, Helen."

"Thank you, Detective. Please sit down, won't you?" She ushered them to the living room and took a seat on an elegant, cream-colored tufted chair.

"Mrs. Trevino, uh, Helen," Bevins began. "When we spoke on the phone, I mentioned that we had been curious about Connex Solutions, where your husband worked. What can you tell us about his former employer?"

She straightened her back and shoulders. "Well, Monty would still be alive if it weren't for them. They said I wasn't allowed to talk about it. But I thought if the police were calling on me, then they must know something. And so I thought, well, thank you Lord for that, because I don't want to keep quiet anymore." She wiped away a tear. "Monty deserved better."

"Who's they, Helen?" Ellis asked.

"Monty's bosses. Their bosses. When he retired, they made him sign this agreement not to speak about anything that went on in that place."

"A non-disclosure agreement?" McCallister asked.

She pointed to him. "Yes. Yes, that was what they called it. I call it a payoff because that's what they did." Helen looked at Ellis. "I don't care what happens to me anymore, Detective. My Monty is gone and no amount of money in this world is going to bring him back."

"Are you saying the company offered your husband, what, like a retirement package?" Ellis asked.

"No, ma'am. I'm saying they offered him money to keep him quiet about the fact they use these damn chemicals to make whatever it is they make over there. Monty and a whole lot of other people had to work around those chemicals. Monty got sick. They told him an early retirement was the best thing for him. That they'd set us up with college funds for our grandchildren. And so he took it on the condition he said nothing about it. Not to anyone. Not to anyone except me. And now I'm telling you."

———

ELLIS TOOK a drink of her iced tea as the detectives sat down in a restaurant for lunch. "Connex was offering a hefty pension package to keep these people quiet. Sounds a lot like what they did with Mark Owens. They signed NDAs, got a lot of money for their families, then died shortly after."

"Who would agree to that, though?" Bevins asked. "Knowing the company was intentionally exposing them to dangerous chemicals?"

McCallister drew a glass of water to his lips. "Money can do that to people. Make all the bad stuff disappear. Especially if the money they offered would see to it the families were well cared for after the fact. Which is why, I suspect, the others on your list refused to talk to us. They don't want to jeopardize their arrangements."

"That's why they've gotten away with it," Ellis continued. "Until now. I assume they offered something similar to Terry Satchel and he refused."

"Fair guess," McCallister said. "So he started gathering evidence, talked to Buxton about it. Now they're both dead."

"Do we think Littleton had figured out what was happening too? And that's why he wanted to meet?" Bevins asked.

"It's possible, but unfortunately we don't get to find out," Ellis replied. "I still can't shake the idea there's something else at play. Here we have these families. They get a payout. Their loved one dies, presumably from chemical exposure. But so far, only Terry Satchel seemed to put up a fight."

"Which was why they killed him," McCallister said.

"I'm not so sure." Ellis raised her index finger. "If he was already sick, and he wanted to talk, why wouldn't he have just gone to the press? Instead, he gets on the wrong side of, apparently, most people he worked with, and then winds up dead. And then you have to think, if the man was sick, why not let nature take its course, so Connex could keep its hands clean? Because murder?" She shook her head. "If you're looking for attention from cops, that'll do it."

———

SERRANO STEPPED into the doorway of Hank's hospital room and noticed him cautiously sitting up in his hospital bed. His feet dangled below, as he attempted to lower himself onto the ground under his own weight. He held the handle of the bed and slid off the edge, landing on his feet. An IV pole was next to him, and he took hold of it. As he started to shuffle along the floor in anti-slip socks, Serrano walked inside.

"Hey, look at you. Up and about already." He approached him. "You need a hand?"

"No, I have to do this. Sons of bitches won't let me out of here till I can walk on my own, so that's what I'm trying to do."

"All right. How about I walk with you? Make sure you don't end up on your ass in front of all those nurses out there."

"Suit yourself." Hank started on again toward the door. "I take it you heard from our former friend?"

"I tracked him down. He was reluctant, but I got him to see reason," Serrano replied.

"What did that cost you?"

He helped Hank through the doorway and into the wide corridor. "Nothing I can't afford."

"What about Becca and the others investigating them?" Hank continued.

"The old man agreed to step in and talk to a few people there he thinks might have an inside track on the situation. Once he gets details for us, we'll find the evidence we need to press charges. My concern is for my people, and you, Hank. I don't know how we prove what Becca suspects, but I'll find a way. Now, I don't know what she has planned for next steps, but I'll have to intervene to see to it she doesn't put herself or the others at greater risk than they are already in."

Hank squared up to Serrano. "That old man owes us. We know it. He knows it. He has to do more to nip this in the bud right now. I won't risk my girl's life on a case that should've ended with us."

19

W hile daylight burned, and nothing but conjecture flourished, only one idea sprang to mind for Detective Rebecca Ellis. With Hank still in the hospital, she had to understand the extent of the original Connex investigation. And when Lieutenant Serrano entered his office, she would learn how all this was tied to her current triple homicide. More importantly, whether it could be related to what happened to Hank.

"Thank you for walking us through this, sir." Ellis took a seat while her partners joined in the briefing. "We need to know the kind of people we're dealing with, and how much influence they have in this city."

Serrano sipped on his late afternoon coffee as he appeared to think how best to begin. "As you know, Becca, this was a case your father and I worked back in ninety-eight. However, things appear to be different this time around. And not in a good way. Three dead and you all are now in their crosshairs. I don't take it well when my people are used for target practice, so as far as I'm concerned, that's the bigger problem."

"What happened in ninety-eight, Lieutenant?" McCallister asked.

"We ended up getting a warrant to search the property. Several complaints had been lodged by the employees about retribution, physical threats for speaking out against the company. Those complaints led to an investigation into their books, which uncovered a host of irregularities. So we got our broader warrant, but we were too late. Everything magically disappeared on us. No paperwork, no evidence. Nothing."

"They destroyed it all," Ellis said.

"We're certain they did. Now, this was a different situation, in that employees had complained that the company wasn't doing things by the rules; they would call them out and get fired. Bangor PD got involved after threats were made to a former employee. He came to us. Point is, I can see where this thing is headed because I've been there."

"No disrespect, Lieutenant, but this is a triple homicide," Ellis continued. "We were targeted, and I still can't be certain those people aren't the reason Hank is in the hospital. They've upped the stakes, sir. This can no longer stand."

"I couldn't agree more," he replied. "Which is why you're in here now. I'm gonna ask you three to take a step back."

"What?" Ellis shot a look at McCallister. "Why would we do that?"

"Because I have someone who owes me." Serrano raised his hands. "This is only temporary. He'll get us the proof we need and then we move forward with making arrests."

"Who is this person, and how do you know he can get his hands on the evidence we need?" Bevins asked. "Sir, look, we are piecing this together. We know what killed Terry Satchel. We know Buxton's car was basically sabotaged, forcing her into that wreck. And we have a body with multiple shots in the back sitting at the ME's office. This goes far beyond complaints or even EPA violations." He circled the office.

"We've talked to a couple families who've come forward about their loved ones who worked there and got sick. We're closing in now—"

"I have no doubt you are," Serrano cut in. "But this is a way to get what we need without putting any of you in harm's way. I'm asking you—no, I'm ordering you—to step aside so that I can finish what I started."

"The thing is, sir," McCallister pleaded, "none of us knows how they got to Scott Littleton last night. We were careful. Connor was on watch for tails. We made sure our contact with him went unnoticed. And yet, they knew. Sir, I have to respectfully disagree with your decision. Connor's right, we are getting close. Let us do what you couldn't. Let us see this through. They came after us. Doesn't that mean something?"

"I appreciate your passion, Euan, I do. But—"

Bevins glanced at his phone and stepped forward. "I'm sorry to interrupt, but I just got something everyone needs to see."

Ellis turned to him. "What is it?"

Bevins showed her the screen. "When I first met with Wayne Byrd, I told him to contact me through an encrypted app. I gave him my username and told him it was the best way to communicate without anyone finding out."

"Smart," Ellis replied. "I didn't think to do that with Littleton."

"Well, Byrd just contacted me. He's scared, now that Littleton is dead. Everyone in the plant is scared, according to him." Bevins looked at Serrano. "I can work with this, sir. He's on the inside."

"You think I'm willing to put another man's life at risk? You say this man is scared, well, hell, he should be. No." Serrano turned down his lips. "There are higher-ups in play now. My contact can get inside that circle and help gather the evidence we need." He looked at Ellis. "Maybe even proof of how Hank's medication was swapped out. So, we stick to the original plan. This is how we run this, for now."

ELLIS PERCHED on the edge of her desk, staring at the floor, discouraged by Serrano's move. "He wants to send someone in there when Wayne Byrd sounds willing to talk. We knew he'd been holding back. And now with Littleton gone, he's ready to come forward."

"Serrano doesn't want the risk," McCallister began. "And I'm not sure I do either. We're o-for-three right now."

Bevins walked in a tight circle. "The last thing we need is another dead body, so I get that, but I don't like this, Becca. They're pulling us off this case. Can't you talk to Hank and ask him to get Serrano to see reason?"

"They worked this case together," she began. "I know my dad. He'll work with his former partner to see it to the end. But the game has changed since they were in it. This isn't about threats made to employees. This is about three employees being murdered, and the attempted murder of my father."

Bevins set his gaze on her. "That'll be even harder to prove."

"I'm aware, but we only need to find proof that one of those murders was committed by someone inside Connex." Ellis peered at her colleagues. "The way we do that is by proving they forced the chemicals into Satchel's throat. The other murders? These guys are smart. A hired gun probably came after us and pulled the trigger on Littleton. Someone we could never trace back to Connex. Buxton? It would be nearly impossible to prove someone put a nail in her tire. She could've picked it up from anywhere. But Satchel?" Ellis shook her head. "Those chemicals track right back to Connex. That's how we get them."

McCallister sat in his chair, one leg crossed over his knee. "You're right. Serrano is looking at the bigger picture, which is to take down the operation. I get that. But our goal is to solve the murders. We know what was happening there. Now it's time to find out who made the move, or who ordered the move against Satchel."

Ellis pushed off the edge of her desk. "We start at the bottom."

McCallister raised his chin. "Who's at the bottom?"

"Satchel's supervisor, Harry Carver. In fact, we start looking into every one of those in the chain of command from the bottom to the top. I want to know financial records. I want to see who owns stock in the company. Anything that points to someone who stood to lose everything if Satchel opened his mouth to the media."

"Byrd wants to help," Bevins added. "Do we follow this path, or let the boss take the lead?"

Ellis surveyed the bullpen and noticed Lewis working at her desk. Pelletier was out in the field, and Fletch had just walked in. She returned her attention. "We have some control over the information we need. SEC filings, public stock records. We start there. As far as Byrd is concerned, all he needs to do is give us names. Who's in charge of the material purchases, particularly the chemicals. Who keeps watch over them. How they're tracked. Someone managed to get them out of the plant and into our victim. That's who we have to find. Whatever Serrano's guy has in mind, we'll let that play out. But we get the names, and we follow the breadcrumbs."

Bevins nodded. "I'll get back with Byrd and have him get that for us. It's an easy ask. Then I'll start pulling the public records."

"I can step in with that too," McCallister said. "The quicker we get them, the better off Byrd will be."

Wayne Byrd prepared to close out his station for the day. The machines had to be cleaned and recalibrated. Excess waste put in the recycler. Any finished parts left unboxed would be placed in the bin for the next day.

It had been hours and he still hadn't received a message from the detective.

"I'm closing up," Byrd called out to the rest of the line. He stepped away and headed toward the lockers to gather his things when his phone signaled a message had arrived. Byrd stopped and cast around his gaze before retrieving it from his pocket. His heart jumped into his throat on reading that the notification was from the encrypted app.

He continued toward the locker room and, after ensuring no one was around, he opened the message and read it. His brow knitted as he double-checked his surroundings again. "Names? That's it? Easy enough."

Byrd closed his locker door and started back onto the floor. Several of his co-workers had either cleared out for the day or were in the process, paying little attention to him. He peered at Harry's office and noticed he had begun to pack up as well. He knew Harry turned in his daily reports to the guys upstairs at the end of the day, so he would wait it out. And after a few minutes, Harry did as Byrd predicted. Staying out of view, he waited for his boss to disappear upstairs.

Now was the time. Byrd walked inside the office and straight to the row of filing cabinets along the back wall. Open orders, filled orders, returns, supplies. All of it was there. Byrd poked his head out the doorway, making sure Harry hadn't started back. The coast was still clear, so he retreated inside again to look at the files. The only drawers that were locked were the two on the bottom. Could've been employee records, but there was no way to be sure. As he rifled through the materials file folders, he grabbed his phone and snapped photos of the purchase orders and who had authorized them. This would be enough to give the cops. Byrd quickly closed the drawer, returning to Harry's doorway as though he'd been there the entire time. He spotted his supervisor descend the metal staircase.

Harry brushed by him as he returned inside. "What are you doing here, Wayne? I thought you went home."

"I was on my way. Thought I'd stop in and see how things were going."

Harry stood at his desk and raised a brow. "What things?"

Byrd shrugged. "Well, you know, the cops and all that."

"It's under control and nothing you should be worried about. Good night, Wayne."

Byrd raised a finger to speak, but thought better of it. "Good night, Harry."

THE PATHS of Lieutenant Serrano and Detective Ellis diverged on this particular investigation. Hers was to learn who tried to kill her father. While McCallister and Bevins homed in on proof of Satchel's murder, Hank was her sole concern.

Now, as they gathered at the bar at the end of the shift, it was time to get down to business. She eyed Bevins, who sat across from her in the booth. "Byrd sent you pictures?"

"Several," Bevins replied.

McCallister, who sat beside Ellis, aimed a finger at him. "You said the chemicals listed on the purchase orders were the same as those found in Satchel's system?"

"That's right, so we know they're kept onsite," Bevins

continued. "What we didn't get from Byrd was who had the opportunity and the access to take the chemicals and shove them down Satchel's throat. I'll ask him about that. We do know these files were kept in Harry Carver's office and he approved the purchases." Bevins tossed back a swig of beer. "I've gone through the papers we found in Satchel's storage unit. Buxton's emails, frankly, were more compelling than anything I came across in Satchel's things."

Ellis raised her index finger. "The chemicals had been spilled inside his own truck, meaning either he got them, as possible evidence, or someone else did to use against him."

"Chemicals alone wouldn't be enough to kill someone over. Everyone knows they use them in manufacturing. What we need to know is who took them. That's where the problem lies. Someone has to keep track of that." McCallister leaned in over his elbows. "There's another possibility."

"What's that?" Bevins asked.

"Something set off this chain of events, and we haven't found it yet," McCallister continued.

Ellis lifted her gaze. "Something Satchel may have shown to someone—maybe his killer—as proof he planned to use it against Connex? The proof he alluded to in the emails to Buxton. But no such evidence was found in his belongings." She considered another possibility. "What if he had it on him?"

"Rivera would've found anything on the body," McCallister replied.

"Yes, but what if he tried to get rid of it?" she continued. "The snow fell quickly after he died. It's gone now. What about going there and looking for evidence? We know where he parked, where his body was found. Unless he ran through the entire forest, we aren't talking about a big area."

"He was smart to have found proof about what his company was doing, at least according to Buxton's emails,"

McCallister added. "He had to be smart enough to keep that information hidden."

Ellis nodded. "You didn't find anything in Buxton's place or a clue on her messages to Terry. This is our shot, while Serrano does whatever he needs to do. But I will say this—no way someone at the top of the ladder killed Satchel. Those kinds of people don't get their hands dirty."

"I agree," McCallister said. "He would've been on the bottom rung for sure. Someone who could easily take the fall and be left with no way to fight it." He appeared to consider her proposal. "We could go back there now and see what we find. CSI didn't sweep it."

Bevins eyed them. "No one did."

INSIDE CITY FOREST, the shade of the trees protected the ground. In the hazy sky, Ellis and her partners traversed the rugged off-trail grounds with flashlights. Police tape marked where the body of Terry Satchel had been found only a week earlier, after spending a long, cold winter encased in snow. A staged hunting accident, as it seemed. But a lot had happened since that assumption. Two more dead, and now they were exploring the area for whatever Satchel might have hidden when he seemingly fled for his life through these same woods.

Ellis trained her light on the exact location. "He was found over here. You can still see the indentation in the mud."

McCallister and Bevins stopped next to her, staring at the shape that had been created by Satchel's body.

"We start here and venture out in a radial pattern." McCallister aimed his flashlight toward the road where Satchel's truck had been found. "We know he parked there, so let's keep the search area tight. He probably didn't have the time to go far from this spot before he was captured."

"What makes you think he ran?" Bevins asked.

"His truck, for one," McCallister replied. "I think he came here to hide from whoever was chasing him. Must've believed he could wait it out, but they found him."

"Let's consider this had been an amicable event, and by that I mean Satchel came out here voluntarily, having no idea the intent of his killer," Ellis said. "Things go bad, he makes a run for it. One thing is certain, we need to get going before we lose all light."

She started toward the northeast, out of the preserve and into the City Forest. With each step, she aimed her flashlight on the ground and carried on over the soft earth, downed twigs, and branches. She peered over her shoulder and saw two other beams of light moving through the trees as darkness settled in. When another light flashed in the distance, she stopped cold. "Hey," she whispered. "Over here."

She heard Bevins and McCallister approach but could no longer see them. They'd killed the lights and headed her way. On their return, she continued, "I saw another light up ahead."

"Shh!" McCallister placed his index finger over his lips.

"Who is it?" Bevins asked.

"Split up. Find cover." McCallister stepped with caution to the nearest tree and stood behind it.

Ellis moved several feet away, each twig and dried leaf crunching underfoot. She reached another tree and steadied herself behind it. All three prepared for the possible ambush. Her heart pounded in her ears. If they could just get back to her car. Who had followed them and how many were in their ranks?

She glanced at McCallister. "We need to get out of here."

He peered beyond her, toward the edge of the preserve. "I

don't know if we'll make it to the Tahoe. Best for you to go, then Connor. I'll provide cover."

"No way. We go together," she shot back.

"That's not how this works," McCallister insisted. "Go. Connor follows."

Her jaw clenched as she glanced at Bevins. Neither had been in this situation before, but at least Bevins had military training. The one time she'd appreciated his West Point schooling. She would have to rely on her police academy training from years ago. "Fine."

Ellis took a step out from behind the tree. She gave a final nod to McCallister and darted out into the open and toward the parking lot. A shot rang out and she instinctively raised her arm and crouched low.

Another bullet whizzed by, only this one was much closer. McCallister returned fire.

The terrain was jagged, and she twisted her ankle as her foot slipped on a boulder. "Shit." Ellis heard another shot, and she fired back into the unknown.

Lights flashed and bullets whizzed, some striking the trees, others heading aimlessly into the darkness.

"Go, go, go!" McCallister shouted to Bevins, as he hurried toward Ellis.

She heard their steps amid the gunfire. Her white Tahoe came into view, and so did a set of headlights in front of her. Ellis stopped feet from her SUV just as she heard the engine of the other vehicle revving.

"Becca, run!" McCallister called out to her, as he caught up. He fired on the beams of light radiating from the running vehicle only feet ahead.

Bevins hurried to catch up to them.

Ellis was on the soft shoulder and ran away from the headlights, away from the blasts of light that flew past her. She heard the steps behind her and more gunfire. Ahead of her was only darkness. She wasn't familiar with the trails but when a sign ahead pointed left, she veered off the roadway to seek cover once again.

Soon, she heard McCallister and Bevins follow. "Over here." When they reached her and the gunshots ceased, she turned to them, shaking and out of breath. "Anyone have any suggestions on how we get the hell out of here?"

20

Lieutenant Serrano waited at the front desk near the entrance to the station. He spotted the old man approach, then the glass doors opened as he entered. The sun had disappeared, and the streetlamps flickered on. He outstretched his hand. "Thank you for coming down, Mr. Peck."

"I said I'd do what I could to help, so here I am," he replied.

Serrano tossed a glance to the stairs. "Let's head up to my office. I'd like to introduce you to the sergeant and then we can discuss next steps." He led the way to the stairs and reached the second floor. "Right this way."

Peck followed him into the hall and Serrano opened his office door, where the sarge awaited. He got to his feet and offered a hand. "Mr. Peck, I'm Sergeant Abbott. Thank you for agreeing to meet."

"Sergeant." He accepted the greeting. "I've known the lieutenant since long before he was a lieutenant, so I trust him, and now I guess I'll have to trust you too."

"Take a seat." Serrano made his way to his desk.

Peck sat down and looked at the men. "I have a contact who is willing to offer information. He has access to sensitive files and has agreed, given the dire circumstances, to grant me access to those files. But he'll *only* send them to me. And that is the main reason I've agreed to see you both this evening. If I'm to be in receipt of such information, I'll require complete anonymity. I will not testify. I will not admit to helping you in any way. Can you guarantee me that?"

Serrano nodded. "Yes, sir. That won't be a problem. Will you tell us who your source is?"

The corner of Peck's mouth ticked up. "I'm afraid I can't do that."

Serrano pulled back his shoulders. "Getting these documents, I assume, will allow us to shut down the plant, but I'd like to make one thing clear. We won't let whoever's responsible for committing the murders off the hook. And you will tell me whether Hank Ellis is a target."

"I'm afraid that is what your detectives will have to work on then, Lieutenant. The murders, I mean," Peck replied. "I can only get you so far. If I push harder, and others find out, they'll push back, and that's where I draw the line. The rest will be up to your people."

AMID THE SOUND of woodland creatures, Ellis swiped open her phone. "We need backup. I don't want to come out of these woods without it. They'll come at us again."

Bevins peered out into the darkness. "I still don't get how the hell they found us."

"That's a question for another time," McCallister replied. "Right now, someone's here. I don't know if it's *a* someone or multiple, so it's time to call it in. Once more units arrive, they'll leave. We just need to keep our eyes peeled until they do."

Ellis dialed the number. "Sir? We need back up ASAP. I'm with McCallister and Bevins. Someone's taking pot shots at us. We think it's just one, but it's impossible to know for sure."

"Where are you?" Abbott asked.

"City Forest, just outside the preserve. We came here to look for evidence that might've been left behind from the first victim. We were followed. I don't know how, but it's clear we were."

"Stay vigilant and sit tight. Help is on the way," Abbott replied.

"Thank you." She ended the call. "He's calling in units now. We need to keep up our guard for twenty, maybe thirty minutes."

McCallister trained his eye ahead. "Easier said than done. This won't be the last time they come at us. Not as long as we're on this case."

"They're the ones out over their skis on this." Ellis peered out. "I haven't heard anything for several minutes. You think they're willing to stick around?"

"Hard to say," McCallister replied. "They'd have to assume we'd call for backup. Would they risk hanging around?"

"If they're here, then maybe the reason is because they were looking for something too," Bevins added. "Something that got left behind and we were the ones who happened on them, not the other way around. That would make more sense."

Ellis nodded. "It's possible if they learned that Byrd contacted you earlier today. That suggests they've been looking for something Satchel held on to as well."

When another round fired off, the detectives ducked.

"Son of a bitch," McCallister said. "I guess they aren't finished with us yet."

Ellis readied her gun again and stood her ground behind the tree. "I don't see any flashlights."

"They're just reminding us they're still here, would be my guess," Bevins said. "We can't stay here. We need to get to higher ground."

Ellis glanced over her shoulder. "Behind us is the visitor's center. We can try to get up there. At least we'll be out of these woods and out in the open, which will expose them. We have to know who they are."

"And us, Becca. It exposes us, too," McCallister added. "But I'm not sure we have another option till our people get here." He waved them on and started up the mild incline.

Ellis aimed her weapon ahead. In the darkness, she carefully navigated the terrain. It occurred to her as they made their way to the building that Bevins might've been right. Maybe they hadn't been followed. Maybe someone else was looking for something too.

Several shots rang out and headlights flashed on.

"Shit, they've seen us." McCallister darted deeper into the woods. "This way!"

Ellis and Bevins trailed him, and she looked back. "They're coming."

"I see the building ahead. Run toward the back for cover." McCallister ran ahead and as he reached the end of the trail, the parking lot appeared. He thrust out a hand to stop Ellis, who was behind him. "Hold up. Let me go first."

Sirens sounded in the distance.

"That's our people," Bevins said.

"We can't sit here," McCallister pressed on. "We have to get to the building. We're exposed."

The headlights drew near.

"Damn it." Ellis peered out over the empty parking lot. "If

we stay close to the tree line on the left side of the lot, they won't be able to spot us." She jogged ahead.

"Becca!" McCallister called out. He looked back at Bevins. "Move!"

They hurried to catch up to Ellis, but she was already several yards ahead. She peered at the headlights that hadn't moved. No shots had been fired. She wondered if they'd heard the sirens too. It was the only way her team was getting out of here alive.

She reached the side of the building and looked out at her partners, waving them over. "Hurry!" Ellis kept an eye on the vehicle as the sirens grew louder.

Within moments, McCallister and Bevins arrived, and McCallister set his gaze on her. "Jesus, Becca, what the hell was that?"

"I saw the opportunity and I took it."

"You tried to draw their attention," Bevins said. "You took an unnecessary risk."

She aimed her finger ahead. "They're leaving. They know backup is coming. We're almost in the clear." Ellis looked at the building and headed around to the front. "I'll call and tell them where we are." She made her way to the entrance with her phone at her ear. "Sarge, send them to the visitor's center. We made it up here and whoever was here turned around. It's a half-ton truck, newer model. I don't know the make, but it appeared dark in color. Plates weren't visible."

"We're coming, Becca. I'll put out a BOLO on the truck now. Just sit tight."

She ended the call. "Abbott's coming."

Bevins peered into the distance. "If they were willing to come at us again, we have to know that they won't stop."

Ellis noticed a metal box affixed to the railing in front of the entrance. She carried on toward the doors and peered at the label. "It's a suggestion box." She turned back to McCallister with a curious gaze. "I mean, it's worth a look inside, right?"

He shrugged. "What are you hoping to find? You think Satchel made it up here and put his evidence inside it?"

"It's protected from the elements. The workers would eventually empty it, and the season's only just begun, so maybe it makes sense to hide something inside it to be discovered later."

"Then by all means," McCallister gestured to it. "Take your shot in the dark."

Ellis raised the lid. With her flashlight aimed inside, she continued. "I see note cards. A few rocks. And...Oh my God." She looked at him, her face nonplussed.

McCallister stepped toward her, mirroring her expression. "Do not tell me you found something."

Ellis thrust her hand inside and pulled out the item. "It's a phone."

"There they are." Bevins pointed ahead. "Looks like Abbott's with them."

Four patrol cars raced up the long roadway to the visitor's center, with Abbott's SUV leading the charge.

"And it appears to be undamaged," Ellis added.

"You don't actually think this is what they were looking for?" McCallister crossed his arms. "No way are we that lucky."

"I don't want to jump to conclusions and be overly optimistic. I understand the odds. But we could use a win right now. It's probably nothing. Someone found a lost phone, or whatever, but I'm taking it anyway." Ellis waved at the approaching vehicles and stepped into the beams of light. They stopped nearby and she noticed Abbott step out of his SUV.

He marched toward them and wore anger on his face.

"You three want to tell me what the hell you're doing out here?"

THE WATERFRONT BAR was practically empty as it neared 9 o'clock. Ellis waited for the barman, and when he returned he set down the bottles of beer. "You want to start a tab, Becca?"

"Sure. Thanks, Austin, I appreciate it." She carried the drinks to the table where the team had gathered. "Euan, would you mind going to get the other drinks?"

"No problem." He pushed off his stool and returned to the bar to grab the rest of the bottles. On his return, he continued, "Compliments of Becca, everyone."

"Thanks, Becca," Lewis replied. "I'm damn glad you all made it out of there safely."

"Same here. The paperwork would've been a nightmare." Fletch smiled.

"We wouldn't do that to you, Fletch," Ellis replied. "And thanks to you guys for showing up when you did."

Pelletier raised his bottle to her. "I'm just glad it worked out. What you guys did was risky."

"We didn't see it that way at the time," McCallister said. "We were looking for evidence. Had no idea people would be there, coming at us." He looked at Ellis. "Still, maybe we got lucky. We'll see."

"Hey, how's your dad doing?" Lewis shrugged. "Abbott might've mentioned it. We all know how you are, Becca, but you should know we're here for you. I think we proved that already."

Ellis looked down a moment. "Yeah, I know. But he's doing fine now. In fact, I need to put in a call to him soon. Doctors are supposed let him come home tomorrow."

"I'm sorry that happened, Becca," Pelletier said. "Your dad's a good guy. But I'm happy he'll recover."

"Thanks, Bryce. I appreciate it." She noticed the hurt in his eyes and regretted not telling him about Hank.

"What's your plan for this case?" Fletch asked. "This thing just got very real."

"It got real the moment we were shot at," Ellis replied. "The phone we found. It's a long shot, but why would it have been there in the first place? It wasn't like someone accidentally dropped their phone inside a suggestion box. My best guess is, if it belonged to Satchel, he knew he was about to be killed." Ellis grabbed her jacket from the back of the stool. "I should get going. I need to swing by the hospital and check on Hank before the end of visiting hours. Thanks again for tonight, guys. You saved our asses." She started away, when Pelletier caught up to her.

"Hey, Becca."

She stopped and turned to him. "Yeah?"

"With all that's been going on, you probably haven't had a chance to follow up on Sutton—or Lazaro, as it turns out."

"No. I had planned on calling the business and looking into him, but things have been happening pretty fast," Ellis replied. "Listen, why don't you come with me to the hospital and we can talk about it? I'll bring you back here for your car."

"Yeah, sure. I'd love to. Let me grab my things."

She waited while he returned to the table and appeared to mention that he was leaving with her.

Pelletier returned with his coat. "Let's go."

Ellis pushed through the exit and walked out into the cool night air. She was already exhausted after dodging more bullets these past couple of days than during her entire career. As they reached her Tahoe, she stepped inside and waited for him to get in. Ellis pressed the starter and buckled her seat belt. "I don't think you've seen Hank in a while, have you?"

"No, not in months."

She reversed out of the parking lot. "He'll be happy to see you. So what else did you find out about Lazaro? Does he have a record? He obviously offered Piper a fake name."

"No record, but according to the bartender he did frequent that place. As far as he knows, there were no complaints or rumors about him doing that kind of thing to anyone else."

"Doesn't mean he didn't," Ellis replied.

"No, it doesn't. I'm glad Piper wasn't hurt. She was brave to come to you."

"I think so too. Like I said, I'll check out his employer. I'm not sure how I'm going to make this guy pay for what he did, but I'll figure out something." She hesitated to mention the possibility Piper's attack and Hank's stroke were a result of this case. And after tonight, it seemed whoever was behind this was willing to do whatever it took to shut down the investigation, even if that meant involving those she loved.

Ellis arrived at the hospital and parked her Tahoe. "Listen, what I said before about being friends—"

"We are friends. First and foremost. Nothing will change that." He opened his door. "Come on. Let's go check in on your dad."

They walked on and entered the first floor of the hospital, and soon reached the elevators that carried them to the third floor.

"He's back here. Room 308." Ellis headed into the corridor and, on reaching his room, she gently knocked. "Dad?" She opened the door and slowly entered, noticing his eyes were closed. She turned back to Pelletier. "I think he's sleeping."

"I'm not sleeping," Hank called out. "Come in. I hear you went through the shit tonight." He turned to them. "Bryce, good to see you, son, but I have a beef with my daughter just now."

"Dad, listen—"

"No, you listen to me." Hank tried to raise up from the pillow but couldn't find the strength. "Serrano told me what happened. I know he filled you in on the case that we worked back in ninety-eight. Why'd you go and press the issue when he had it handled, Becca? You jeopardized yourself and your partners. You really think that was the right call?"

Pelletier raised a hand. "Sir, if I could just—"

"No, you can't." He returned his gaze to Ellis. "It was a reckless move that could've cost you your life. You understand that?"

Ellis hadn't been chastised this way since she was a teenager. She grew irritated by Hank's admonishment and especially in front of a colleague. "Dad, this is my investigation. I needed proof about who murdered these people. The lieutenant had other ideas that wouldn't get the results we needed—at least, not soon enough. I won't apologize for my decision. Things went south, yes, but no one could've foreseen that. Not you and not Lieutenant Serrano. Now, you just had a stroke, so I'll give you a pass, but this is my time now. I'm the detective, not you. And while I greatly appreciate your advice, you're the one who taught me to follow my gut. Am I wrong?"

Hank's face softened. "You're not wrong."

"Thank you." She continued inside. "Now, tell me how you're feeling."

21

The phone on Ellis's bedside table lit up with an incoming call. The vibration woke her and she turned to glance at it. She wiped her eyes and answered. "Euan, what's wrong?"

"I'm outside your door," McCallister replied.

"What? You're here?" She pulled upright and swung her legs over the side until they landed on the cool wood floor. With a deep intake of breath, she stood from the bed in her dark room and shuffled to the bench at the end. A robe lay across it and she pulled it on. "I'm coming. Hang on." She pulled the phone from her ear to double-check the time. "It's three in the morning."

"I know. I'm sorry."

"All right. Hang on." Ellis ended the call, eventually making her way to the front door. On opening it, she noticed McCallister on the other side. "Are you okay? Come in."

"Thanks. I'm sorry, Becca, but I didn't know who else to turn to."

She closed the door behind her and walked into the living

room, turning on the lamp. "It's okay. Do you need anything? Water? I can put on a pot of coffee."

"No, thank you." He stood in the middle of her living room. "I need to tell you something. I thought about it when we were at the bar, but there were too many ears. And then after what we just went through...Can we sit?"

"Of course." She ushered him to the sofa. "Okay, what's going on?"

McCallister rested his elbows on his thighs and placed his hands under his chin. "I should've told you. I should've told all of you."

She sat down next to him. "Told us what? Euan, what are you talking about?"

He turned to her with eyes that held regret. "Last night, I got a call from a journalist. She works for the *Boston Globe*." He swallowed hard. "She ask me questions about a case from a year before I left Boston PD. That case saw a fifteen-year-old kid lose his life."

"Oh my God."

McCallister drew in a deep breath. "I didn't ask, but I'm sure it's about the lawsuit the family filed with the city. I assume it's been settled, and she wanted a comment."

"Lawsuit?" Ellis asked.

"Yeah. The family sued the city for wrongful death, which they had every right to do. But, Becca, I killed that boy." He slowly nodded. "It was, of course, an accident. The boy was holding a toy gun that looked real as hell. It was late and dark, and I thought it was a gun. And I didn't think he was a kid."

She placed her hand over her mouth.

"I shot him. And that's the reason I left Boston. I was cleared of wrongdoing, but my co-workers, none of them looked at me the same. I was put behind a desk for a long time. My captain called me in after about six months or so and asked me if I wanted to transfer. He'd seen how everyone treated me. Not that I blamed them. And he knew a lawsuit was coming. So, he gave me a recommendation because, apart from that incident, I'd been a pretty good detective. But that changed me, Becca."

"Of course it did. I'm so sorry, Euan. I had no idea. Does Abbott know?"

"He does. It's on my record. Honestly, I think the only reason he agreed to hire me was because my captain asked for the favor. He'd called around other departments. Larger departments. They all said no. Abbott said yes."

"Okay, so, do you think this reporter is looking to, what, stir up sentiment again?" she asked.

"Maybe. But maybe also to try to make a name for herself." He held her gaze. "I wanted to tell you so many times, but I was afraid. I didn't want you to look at me the way my former colleagues did—like I was a monster. I have no right to feel badly. That family lost a son. But I don't want you to look at me differently. Not you, Becca."

Her heart bled for him. She knew what it felt like when a single event defined the rest of your life. It fundamentally changed a person. "We all wondered why you came here to Bangor."

"Now you know," McCallister replied. "I have to get out in front of this. I can't let the people in our department learn about it that way. It has to come from me. Whether that'll make a difference, I don't know, but I have to try."

"No one will think differently of you, Euan."

He scoffed. "Yes, they will."

"No, you're wrong about that. I don't see you differently. If anything, this makes you more human. The rest of the team won't see you differently either. You're going to have to trust me on that. None of us has gone through what you're going through now, not in the same manner. But whatever happens as a result of this article, or whatever the reporter has in mind, I'll stand behind you."

He captured her eyes, and she felt her heart climb into her throat. The way he looked at her now, with regret and fear, with self-loathing. But there was something else too. She saw his humanity; in his deep brown eyes that look of longing and desire, of pleading for absolution. All these things he held, and she couldn't look away. He drew near and then she felt his lips touch hers.

The attraction was there almost from the moment she'd met him, but her resolve to keep everyone at arm's length was strong. Until this moment. But when thoughts of Bryce entered her mind, how he'd confessed his feelings for her, confusion reigned.

She pulled away. "Euan, with everything that's happened, we're both feeling vulnerable. This isn't a good idea."

"Why not?" he asked.

"We both could've died tonight. This would be a mistake. I'm sorry."

He returned a closed-lip grin and looked down at his feet. "No, I'm sorry, Becca. I crossed a line." He stood from the sofa. "I got myself worked up over this and I knew I needed to tell you."

She joined him. "And I'm glad you did. What a terrible burden to carry. You should be able to talk to your partner. In this job, we need that."

"I should go. Maybe with this case and what happened earlier, I just let it get to me, like you said. We still have a long road ahead of us and you're right, this would be a mistake." He pressed his soft lips against her cheek and lingered a moment. When he pulled back, he wore a tender smile. "Get some rest and I'll see you in a few hours."

ON HER WAY TO WORK, Ellis was consumed with what had happened in the woods the day before. For the second time in as many days, she'd been a target. Yet she was no closer to getting to the truth than when she'd started. Then there were the two men she worked with. Both of whom had disclosed their feelings for her.

This wasn't who she was. A woman in the middle. It was almost laughable. For years, her ex-husband had insisted he was the best she would ever get. And she believed him. Her confidence lay in the work she did, not her personal life, which was why it was always on the back burner. Now, it had been thrust to the forefront. Not to mention the risks of dating someone she worked with. Those things always ended badly, and if they went bad this time, which was all but assured, the entire team's cohesiveness could be destroyed.

A call came through on her phone and she answered. "Ellis here."

"It's Brown."

"Yeah, hey, good morning."

"Are you at the station?" he asked.

"Not yet. I'll be there in about five minutes. Why?"

"Come see me as soon as you get in. Bring your buddies too. Everyone's going to want to see this." Brown ended the call.

She soon arrived at the station and hurried upstairs to CID. There was no time for awkward greetings with the men who'd burrowed themselves into her psyche. This was the time for action.

It was McCallister she spotted first, as he appeared from the hall with a cup of coffee in his hands. "I just got a call from Brown. He has something for us."

"Now?" he asked.

"Now." She carried on into the bullpen. "Connor, let's go. Brown wants to see us. Has to be about the phone."

"Shit, that was fast." He pushed up from his desk and headed toward her. "You okay?"

"Yeah, why?"

He turned down his lips and shook his head. "Uh, no reason."

Ellis headed back downstairs toward the Computer Forensics lab on the first floor. She pushed through the doors and searched for Brown, finally spotting him as he walked back to his desk. "We're here. Tell us what you found."

"Morning to you too, Ellis." He eyed the others. "All right. So the phone you guys found was in working order. I had to charge it, but otherwise it was in fine condition. No service, of course."

Ellis stood with great impatience. "Was it Satchel's phone?"

"No," Brown replied.

Her shoulders dropped. "Then whose is it?"

"The phone is registered to a man named Evan Fulton."

"Who the hell is he?" Bevins asked.

"I have no idea," Brown replied. "But I'm going to assume he worked at the visitor's center or with the Bangor Land Trust. I couldn't say."

"You said you had something for us," Ellis cut in.

"And I do." Brown retrieved the files on his computer and opened them. "I have a friend who works for Blackshift."

"What's that?" McCallister asked.

"It was founded by a former Apple engineer. It's one of the ways law enforcement can gain access to suspects' phones," he replied. "There are two companies, that I know of, who offer this service to police departments nationwide. Some departments have the money to buy the software, others send the phones to the companies and have them break in for a fee. But since I have a friend—"

"He got in for us at no cost?" Ellis asked.

"Let's just say he owed me a favor," Brown replied. "Anyway, I got the phone back. I accessed all the data." He handed her a file folder. "Look at the photos."

She grabbed the file and opened it, picking up one of the printed images. "What the hell?"

McCallister and Bevins peered at the photo. McCallister began, "It looks like the truck from last night, only we can see the make, model, and plates. Are you serious right now?" He looked at Brown. "I don't understand. When was this picture taken?"

"The data on the file indicated it was taken on December fourth of last year."

"That was the approximate date Satchel was killed," Ellis cut in. "This guy, Evan Fulton, he got a picture of the truck, and it looks to be in about the same location as where Satchel's body was found. Any other photos?"

Brown swiped through them. "Random pictures of the area. You guys got lucky this was captured."

"But how did this phone end up in the suggestion box?" Bevins asked.

"Who knows? Maybe the guy dropped it, lost it. Someone came along and found it, decided to drop it in the box. I mean, I don't know how it got there, but you should be glad it did," Brown replied.

"The owner of this phone captured the vehicle of the person who shot at us last night. It's safe to say he's also the guy who murdered Satchel. But where is Satchel's GMC?" Ellis asked. "It was found on the side of the road, near where that truck is in this picture, but it doesn't show up in any of these photographs."

McCallister regarded her. "Maybe because it was brought back later. Whoever killed him had to then stage it, like we talked about. Left it there to later be towed away. The impound officer said it was towed in on the sixth. And the chemicals found inside Satchel's truck? I'll bet the killer put them there and spilled them to make it look like Satchel carried the chemicals himself."

"Abbott put out a BOLO last night on the truck. Now we have a plate number. We got 'em." Ellis turned to Brown. "Thank you for this. I owe you and your friend." She turned on her heel and made her way through to the hall once again.

Bevins hurried beside her. "Okay, we have this, so is this enough to bring charges?"

"For coming after us, I'd say so. The rest?" Ellis began. "We need to get with Abbott and Serrano. It's the same truck from last night, and it just so happened to be at the location where Satchel was killed back in December. It sounds like enough, but we'll have to find out."

They arrived at Abbott's office and Ellis hurried inside. "Sir? Can we have a minute with you and the lieutenant? It's important."

"I'll call him in." Abbott made the call. "Yeah, they're all here. We'll wait. Thanks." He ended the call. "The lieutenant's finishing up a meeting. He'll be here in a few minutes." Abbott pulled back in the chair and laced his fingers over his stomach. "How's Hank?"

"Much better. He's getting out today," Ellis replied.

"Do you need to pick him up?"

"Uh, no. I've asked a friend of mine to drive him home. A nurse will check in on him a few times a day for the next couple of weeks."

"That's good news." Abbott nodded. "I'm glad to hear it." He looked up and spotted the lieutenant. "Come on in, sir. I believe our people have something to share with us."

Serrano walked inside and stood tall behind Abbott. "The phone?"

"Yes, sir," Ellis jumped in. "Brown pulled a rabbit out of his hat and got into the phone. It belongs to someone unrelated to the investigation, but it contained a photo of the same truck from last night and it was seen on or about the day of Satchel's murder." She pulled out the image from the folder and laid it on Abbott's desk. "That's it, there."

Abbott put on his reading glasses and studied the image. "Plates are visible." He looked over his shoulder at Serrano. "I can update the BOLO."

"Yeah, let's do that," he replied. "And in the meantime, Becca, pull the vehicle's registration details. Find out who owns it and let's bring him in ASAP."

Ellis stood from the chair. "Thank you, sir. We should also check DOT cameras in hopes of spotting the vehicle we're all but certain drove Buxton off the road and into a tree. Could be this same truck."

"We'll have to get with Portland PD on that. They might already have that information," Bevins cut in. "Now if we had the plates on that Cadi, we'd stand a shot at making a solid connection. One thing seems certain, we're dealing with at least two people. One who drives the Cadillac and the other who drives the Ford truck in that picture."

Serrano eyed Ellis. "Work on getting the registration information on the truck first. We know for a fact that it was involved. From there, let's work on a connection to whoever owns that vehicle to the folks over at Connex. The connection's there. We just have to find it."

The motor vehicle search Ellis conducted on the truck in the photograph returned a name so wholly unexpected she hardly believed her eyes. It took a moment for the result to sink in. But there it was, on the laptop screen in front of her. "Why?"

McCallister had been working to link the Connex Board of Directors and officers to the scandal from twenty-five years earlier that Lieutenant Serrano and Hank Ellis had worked. So far, most of the previous staff had retired or passed on. He turned to Ellis when she spoke. "Did you say something?"

"Wayne Byrd." She returned an incredulous gaze.

"What about him?" McCallister asked.

"The truck in the picture is registered to him. He's the one who killed Terry Satchel, or at least was there to get rid of the body."

McCallister deadpanned. "His name came back on the motor vehicles search?"

She nodded almost imperceptibly. "He came after us. And Buxton? Littleton?"

"Why? He cooperated multiple times. Even offered company files," McCallister said.

"Maybe he did that so we wouldn't dig too deep into him," she replied. "He made it look like it was the company's fault. That they were killing people."

"But we know they are," he added. "How do we explain the slow deaths of those who retired and were paid to keep quiet about the fact they were sick?"

She set her gaze far beyond the window to the outside. "I don't know. But we have to get to him. We have to find him and bring him in."

McCallister stood from his desk. "Then we go now." He cast his gaze to Bevins' desk. "It's Byrd. We need to pick him up."

Bevins jumped from his chair. "Are you sure?"

"He owns the truck. It's him. Come on." Ellis led the way through the bullpen but stopped short. "We need to relay this to Abbott and Serrano. Last thing we want is for Serrano to put his own plan into action with his guy on the inside." She turned on her heel and headed into the corridor, arriving at his office. "Lieutenant, we know who owns the truck."

Serrano glanced up at her from his desk. "Who is it?"

"It's Wayne Byrd," Ellis said. McCallister and Bevins stood behind her in the doorway. "We're leaving now to track him down."

Serrano pulled back. "Son of a bitch. Yeah, okay. Go. I'll brief Abbott."

"Thank you, sir. Before anything else happens, we have to get to the bottom of his involvement."

"Understood," Serrano replied.

A final nod and Ellis headed toward the stairs and jogged to the first floor. "We start at the plant, then his house."

McCallister kept her pace. "I'm not sure he would go back

to the plant. He has to know we'd find out, especially after coming at us in the woods."

"You're certain he acted alone?" Bevins cut in. "We had multiple shots fired. and then we have the driver of the Cadillac who shot at you two at the abandoned restaurant."

"I saw one set of headlights when the shots rang out in the woods. They came from one direction. I think he was there on his own. We won't know for sure until we find him." Ellis pushed through the exit. "Let's also consider the possibility that he's acting on behalf of someone inside Connex." She unlocked her Tahoe and stopped to turn back as an idea struck. "I initially thought that these murders and what's happening at Connex may not be related. We discussed reasons why Connex would only be digging themselves a deeper grave if they took out their own employees, given the status of those who've gotten sick. So there must be some reason why Byrd would kill Satchel, and possibly the others. We have to dig deeper."

"If we find him, he'll do the digging for us," McCallister replied.

She knitted her brow a moment before looking to Bevins. "Hang on. In your review of Buxton's phone records, did you note the date of the last call she had with Satchel, or, for that matter, Satchel's final calls?"

"The last call Satchel made to Buxton was on December third. It was also the only call he made that day," Bevins added. "I didn't dig into it any more than that because Buxton was killed soon after."

Ellis considered her theory a moment. "First of all, go back and find out who she talked to the night of the accident, besides us. And can we pinpoint where that Satchel call originated?"

"Sure. I can go back to the cell phone provider and ask

them for the information. What's the goal here? I don't follow," Bevins continued.

She grabbed the driver's side door handle. "We don't know what was said in that final call, but if we can determine where it came from, there's a chance we can put Byrd in that same location."

"And that would tell us what, exactly?" McCallister asked.

"Satchel may have suspected Byrd was on the wrong side of this, so he calls Buxton, a trusted friend and former girlfriend, and talks to her about it," Ellis continued.

"She never mentioned any alarming conversations with him before he vanished," McCallister said. "If she suspected he was in danger, or if he mentioned as much, she would've come forward with that information."

"Look, we won't know anything until Connor can get us details. But what I'm suggesting is that it's possible Satchel made the call to her and said he was meeting with Byrd. Maybe he did that just before the meeting as a precaution. It may not bear fruit, but if it does, it'll set us on the path to learning where Satchel was in the hours before his death and who might've been with him." She looked at Bevins. "Connor, I'd like you to work on that while we search for Byrd. If we split up, we stand a chance at finding him."

THE MORNING SHIFT at Connex Solutions was in full swing. Armed with proof that Wayne Byrd's vehicle had been seen at the preserve around the day of Satchel's murder, Ellis and McCallister could bring him in for questioning. This was the same man who'd offered to help the investigation, apparently to throw them off his scent. And it had worked. Byrd was smarter than they'd given him credit for; even if his motives remained unclear. But the chances he would come back to work were slim and none. Nevertheless, they had to start somewhere.

Ellis cut the engine and stepped out of her SUV. Waiting for McCallister to join her, she took in the view of the massive facility. As he neared, she began, "If he's here, HR summons him, but they can't tell him why. If he knows it's us, he'll bolt."

"I'm not holding my breath the guy's here, but don't you think we should meet with Goyer and do this through him?" McCallister asked.

"Bringing him into this right now could backfire," she began. "We don't know whether Goyer's in on it. I'm with you on our odds Byrd isn't here, so we'll make this quick and then head to his home." Ellis started on and felt his hand touch her shoulder. She stopped and turned back to him, noticing a hint of remorse in his eyes. "What is it?"

McCallister raised his shoulders. "I'm sorry about last night. I crossed a line."

Now wasn't the time to get into this, but she could see he needed to clear the air. "No, you didn't. I'm glad you came to me. We were both under stress and it happened. No big deal. I hope we can have the kind of relationship where we can show up at each other's houses at three in the morning."

He grinned. "Yeah, me too."

Ellis glanced at the entrance to the factory. "For now, we hit hard at Byrd and whoever's backing him." She opened the door to step inside. It seemed Josie, the young woman at the front desk, recognized them as they reached her.

"Good morning, Detectives. How can I help you?"

"We'd like to see the HR manager, please," Ellis said.

"Of course. Should I inform Mr. Goyer as well?" Josie asked.

Ellis plastered on a tight-lipped grin. "That's not necessary."

"All right. I'll call her up now." Josie appeared hesitant as she made the call.

They stepped away a moment, and Ellis gazed at the patent drawings framed on the wall of the lobby. "I can't wrap my head around the fact Byrd came to us and offered help. And this was after we caught up to him at that bar. The man had seemed terrified he was being watched. So he comes at us, what, twice now?"

"He and Satchel didn't get along. We know that from what Littleton said." McCallister appeared to think on it. "I have to believe someone else is pulling the strings and using Byrd as bait. If this is a trap—"

"Detectives?" A woman in black dress pants and a silver button-down blouse approached. "I'm Ginney Wegner. How can I help you all this morning?"

Ellis approached her. "May we speak in private?"

"Of course." She spun around, her high-heels clicking on the concrete floor as she entered the hallway to a nearby meeting room. She opened the door. "We can use this room. Come in and take a seat."

After she closed the door behind them, Ellis sat down and began, "As I'm sure you're aware, we've been investigating the deaths of some of your employees."

"Yes, ma'am. I'm well aware." Wegner returned a wary gaze. "Do you know who's responsible? Is that why you're here?"

"This is where your discretion would be appreciated," McCallister jumped in. "Wayne Byrd is a person of interest, and we'd like to speak to him."

"Wayne? Oh, my gosh. Okay, I didn't know you were looking for him. I can see if he's in."

"You don't know?" he asked.

"No, sir, I don't. We have more than three hundred people working here. I don't keep track of those who are or aren't in the building at any given time. But I can find out. It'll only take me a moment."

"That would be great, thanks," Ellis said. "Just do us a favor, and don't alert anyone that we're here. Find out if he's in and bring him down as soon as possible."

Wegner nodded. "I understand."

After the woman stepped out of the room, Ellis narrowed her gaze. "She seemed surprised. My concern is that she'll alert Goyer, or maybe their in-house counsel. We shouldn't have let her go without one of us."

"Too late now," McCallister replied. "But she certainly didn't look like she had any idea Byrd could be responsible. I think we're safe, regardless of the fact it's unlikely Byrd's here. On the upside, if he's not, it doesn't bode well for his innocence."

"There is that." Ellis turned her attention to the door when it opened, and Wegner stepped inside.

She stood at the entrance. "I'm sorry, Wayne didn't come in this morning. His supervisor informed me he'd called in sick today."

"And his supervisor is Harry Carver?" Ellis asked.

"It is, yes, ma'am."

Ellis got to her feet and retrieved a business card from her laptop bag. "Thank you, Ms. Wegner. We're sorry to have wasted your time. If anyone hears from him, please contact me. And again, this must be in strict confidence."

"Of course," Wegner replied.

They started into the corridor, as Wegner spoke again. "Can I ask, Detectives, should we take precautions if Wayne does show up? I mean, a lot of people work here. People with families."

Ellis picked up on the fear in Wegner's tone. They suspected Byrd was a murderer, so it was possible, if he believed he was about to be caught, that he would act. And then there was Hank and Piper to consider. She couldn't yet prove one way or the other if they'd been targeted too, but it sure as hell seemed like it. So to have Wegner possibly alert the higher-ups would jeopardize the investigation. It was a roll of the dice and Ellis was about to gamble with people's lives.

"Detective?" Wegner continued.

Ellis felt McCallister's eyes on her as she wavered. But when she donned a reassuring gaze, fighting back against the voice in her head, the decision was made. "He's a person of interest at this time. I wouldn't worry about anything else."

BEVINS WAS IRRITATED that he'd been asked to stay behind. He had done most of the leg work on this investigation and, of course, it was Ellis and McCallister who were going to take the credit. All he'd wanted was a chance to prove himself. And he'd let Wayne Byrd convince him he was on their side. Maybe that's what this was about. Ellis was punishing him for letting Byrd get the drop on them.

He went back to the task at hand and viewed the phone records of Terrance Satchel. He highlighted the days before Satchel's murder and picked up the phone. "Good morning, this is Detective Bevins, Bangor PD. I'd like to get your help in identifying a location of where calls were made to a now-deceased man whose phone was registered to you."

"Do you have a subpoena, sir?" the man asked. "I'm afraid we can't release that information to you until we do."

Bevins closed his eyes. "Check the file. I've already submitted one to obtain the records in question. Sir, I'm on the hunt for a killer. Do not throw procedure in my face when I've already complied."

"Of course, Detective. I'm sorry. I'll pull the file right now. Please hold."

It was no wonder everyone he worked with thought he was an asshole. He knew he was and so did the guy on the other end of this call. Still, he'd worked hard to be a better detective and a better person. He thought he'd proved that to Ellis already. She was the only one who defended him, and he'd still been a jerk to her. But maybe this would change things. Everyone expected a lot from him because of his military-school training. But what they hadn't known was that he'd almost been kicked out.

"Sorry for the delay, sir." The man returned to the line.

"It's fine. Do you have the information?" Bevins pressed on.

"I do. I can email you the report, if you'd like."

"Yes, please." Bevins relayed his email address. "Send it now, while I have you on the line."

"Yes, sir." He typed the message. "There you go, Detective. You should receive it any moment."

Bevins refreshed his screen. "Yes, I have it. Thank you for your help." He ended the call and opened the file. After viewing the coordinates, he plugged them into the map and the location turned up. Bevins narrowed his gaze and leaned into the screen. "Where the hell is this?" He zoomed in on the map and cocked his head. "A bar? You were at a bar the day before you went missing. Okay." He picked up his phone. "Becca, I have the location. Satchel was at a bar called the Mainer on December third. It was where he made the last call to Buxton."

"Where is it?" Ellis asked.

"I'll send you the location. It doesn't look far from the manufacturing plant. Minutes away, by the look of it." He paused a moment. "And one other thing. I went back and checked Buxton's phone records too. Guess who called her the night of the crash?"

"I'll take a shot in the dark...Wayne Byrd," she replied.

"Gee, how'd you know?"

ELLIS ENDED THE CALL, as she and McCallister sat inside her SUV at the plant. "Connor's sending us the location where Satchel made his final call to Buxton. It was at a bar not far from here. And it turns out Byrd called Buxton the night she died. What are the odds he's the one who ran her off the road?"

"Sounds like your hunch was right, and our case is even stronger if we can prove Satchel was with Byrd when he made that call to Buxton. Satchel may have wanted Buxton to know where he was and who he was with," McCallister replied. "We won't know the contents of the call, but it's worth stopping by the place and asking questions."

"Not yet. It's probably not open this early anyway. For now, let's stick to the plan and go to Byrd's home. If he's not there, then we hope someone calls in a tip from the BOLO Abbott sent out."

She drove on toward Byrd's home, which was about fifteen minutes from the plant. "Do we know if he's married?"

"We don't know a whole hell of a lot about him. We didn't have reason to, until now," McCallister replied. "Which means we'll need to be prepared."

Ellis continued down the main parkway and eventually exited into the neighborhood Byrd called home. "He should be down that road, next right." She made the turn and rolled down the quiet street. "Older neighborhood. If he's getting paid by someone higher up the food chain at the plant, he's doing a good job keeping it hidden."

"The new truck could be a giveaway," McCallister said. "It still doesn't make sense why he'd be some sort of middleman."

"Could be a setup. Everyone seemed to know Byrd and Satchel didn't get along. But until we can get hold of him, it doesn't make much sense to me either." She slowed down as the home appeared. "It's that house two doors down. The beige home with green shutters."

"I see it." McCallister peered through the windshield. "No truck in the driveway."

As she neared, Ellis squinted for a better view beneath the bright sun. "We're here. If he's not, then our last shot is checking out the bar where Satchel made the call. And if we strike out there too, Byrd's long gone, and so is proof that whoever he worked with may have tried to kill Hank."

McCallister eyed her. "We won't back off, Becca. We know too much about this company now to let it go. If they came after Piper, your dad, and us?" He peered at Byrd's home. "We'll find a way to take them all down."

BYRD DROPPED the curtain at the front window and turned back into the living room. "Just keep the curtains closed, all right, Ma?"

"What have you done, Wayne?" she asked. "You show up in the middle of the night, scaring the hell out of me, and now I can't look out my own damn window?"

He walked toward the petite, white-haired woman. "It'll be fine, Ma, okay? I've got it under control. I just need to stay here for a few days at the most. I won't get in your way, all right?"

"Why aren't you at work?" she asked. "Did you get fired? Is that it? Where's Maggie and the kids?"

Heat rose under his collar. "No, I didn't get fired. I just need time to figure things out. Figure out where I can go. I sent them to her mother's house. It's only for a little while."

"What do you mean by that?" she asked.

He sighed and dropped onto the sofa. "Nothing, Ma. I just need time to think."

She stared at him with small brown eyes. "I know you, son. I know you better than you know yourself. Now you better tell me what the hell you did, because by the look of you it was nothing good."

23

T he hole-in-the-wall bar was only five miles from the plant. At ten o'clock in the morning, it remained closed. Ellis pulled into the parking lot and stopped at the front. She peered at the brick-clad building with a worn, green-striped awning and noticed the windows covered in grime from the harsh winter that had passed.

"Place almost looks abandoned." Ellis opened her door.

McCallister thrust out his hand. "Wait. What are you doing?"

"I was going to knock to see if anyone was inside." She stepped out and closed the door, walking toward the entrance. When McCallister joined her, she continued, "Look, I don't know if Byrd came here, or if he was with Satchel at the time. But someone was in that preserve looking for something last night. Maybe they followed us, maybe not. We didn't find anything, and I doubt he did either. But if this was the place Satchel chose to contact Janice Buxton, then I'm hoping to hell there was a reason for it. And, right now, we need any leads we can get."

Ellis knocked on the door and stepped toward one of the

windows. She used her hand to shield her eyes and peered inside. "Doesn't look like anyone's here." She turned out toward the road and placed her hands on her hips. "Might as well have a look around."

McCallister gestured to her. "After you."

Ellis walked along the concrete porch lined with metal posts. She reached the corner of the building. "More parking and no sign of cameras. Figures." She continued down the side of the building until she reached the back. "Nothing back here except dumpsters, and another exit, probably for staff." Her attention was drawn to the back exit when the door opened.

A man walked out with a bag of trash in his hand and jumped at the sight of them. "Oh, jeez, you both scared me." He eyed them with caution. "Who are you and what are you doing back here?"

Ellis retrieved her badge. "I'm Detective Ellis, this is my partner, Detective McCallister. Are you the owner of this place?"

"For now, yes. Why?"

"We knocked a few minutes ago," McCallister said. "But you didn't answer."

"Sorry about that. I was in the back. Hard to hear there sometimes." His gaze shifted between them. "What can I do for you both?"

"Do you know a man named Wayne Byrd?" Ellis asked.

"Course I do. He used to come in here a lot." He placed his thumb and index finger on his narrow chin. "Not so much anymore, come to think of it. Why?"

"And what about Terry Satchel?" she continued. "Do you know him?"

He gazed up as if in thought, but only for a moment. "Well, if he's the guy Wayne got into that fight with a few months' back, then I suppose I do."

Ellis perked up, "Mr. Byrd got into a fight?"

"Not surprising, if you know him. He's a bit of a hot-head."

McCallister shoved his hands in his pockets. "You say this was a few months ago. Did something stand out in your mind about that encounter because I'm sure you must get your share of bar fights."

"Yes, sir." The man set down the bag of garbage. "Wayne was getting fed up by this man, tall man, if I remember correctly. I believe they worked together. Started going on about, I don't know, people leaving the company or retiring or something like that. Got on Wayne's nerves and they came to blows. Of course, I tossed them both out on their ears shortly thereafter."

"Did either of them return inside?" Ellis asked.

"No, ma'am. That was the last I saw of either one, now that I'm thinking about it."

Ellis turned to McCallister. "It's starting to make sense now, what Littleton said about the two of them fighting."

"Guess they didn't leave it at the office," McCallister replied. "So what are we thinking here?"

Ellis looked at the owner again. "You don't have any security cameras out here, do you?"

"No, I sure don't. We don't get much trouble and it's just too darn expensive."

"Witnesses?" McCallister asked her.

"Good question." She turned back to the man. "Do you know who else was around that night? Any regulars who still come here?"

"Oh, gosh." He raised his gaze in thought. "It was such a long time ago. I couldn't really say. I'm sorry."

"We understand. Thank you so much for your time, sir." Ellis started back with McCallister beside her.

"Oh, you know what?" he called out.

They stopped and Ellis set her sights on him. "Yes, sir?"

"I do remember a good bit of damage someone did that night to the front of the building." He started ahead. "Hang on. I'll show you."

She waited for him to catch up and then they both followed the owner back to the front of the bar.

The man reached the far right side of the building, where a chunk of brick had broken away. "Right here. I had a nice little planter here and then, of course, you see where the brick came down." He pointed to the damage.

"What caused that?" Ellis asked. "Was it that fight Mr. Byrd got into?"

"I'm almost certain it was. Like I said, I didn't see what all went down after I gave them the boot, but I came out after I closed up that night. Saw this right here. And I found a broken cell phone near the back of the planter. Figured it slipped out of someone's pocket and landed on its face. I still have that phone, you know. Thought maybe someone might come back for it. I guess I forgot about it." He looked at her. "But it's sitting in my desk drawer."

"We'd like to see it, please," Ellis said.

"Okay." The man opened the front door with a key and walked inside. "I'll show you."

They followed him inside the worn-down establishment. A few pool tables with felt that needed replacing. An old projection television tucked into a niche. As she walked through the place, Ellis tamped down her expectations. She'd been down this road already, but it was worth a look.

"All right. Here you go." The man opened his desk drawer and retrieved the phone. "Have a look at it."

Ellis gently took the phone by its edges because the glass screen was shattered. She looked at McCallister. "What do you think?"

"I think it's a broken phone. The fact it was found outside

when those two apparently went at it." He shrugged. "Maybe. Maybe it's something."

She looked back at the owner. "You mind if we take it? We're happy to return it to you when we're finished."

He swatted at the idea. "Keep it. I have no use for it. Although, it does actually work. I charged it up after I found it. Can't see anything on the screen, but it did hold a charge. Which was why I was surprised no one came back for it. But take it. See if it helps with whatever you got going on."

"Thank you." Ellis headed back to her SUV with McCallister beside her. "We can charge it up again and see what Brown can get from it."

"It can't hurt, but I think we have a better shot at finding Byrd than we do of finding anything helpful on that phone. The interesting part of this whole thing is that Byrd never mentioned this scuffle. Littleton only talked about the words exchanged at the plant, but this was after-hours."

"I agree." She examined the phone again. "The last call from Satchel's phone was from this place here. And it just so happened that Wayne Byrd was with him."

ABBOTT SAT AT HIS DESK, tapping his fingers on the top of it. Serrano stood behind him and Ellis and McCallister waited for someone to speak.

She decided to break the silence. "Sir, we have the BOLO, but we need more. We need to know who Byrd would turn to. Family. Friends. Clearly, he knows he's been made. I have to assume it was because of last night. I'm sure it didn't go down the way he'd wanted."

Abbott set his sights on her. "We have no evidence one way or another that he operated alone, but I can't for the life of me figure out why he would come at you, or more importantly how he knew where you were." He looked at Serrano. "You have any idea? Does any of this make sense to you?"

Serrano scratched his pointed chin. "I've been racking my brain, trying to see how this all fits with what I know Connex Solutions has done in the past and what it appears to still be doing. That can't be overlooked. Wayne Byrd played us. We all know that now. But is he acting alone? Is he the sole person responsible for the murders of three Connex employees?"

"Until we find him, we won't have the answers," Ellis said. "What about getting the BOLO issued state-wide?"

Abbott nodded. "We can do that."

"And it would be a good idea to set up teams at his house and at the plant," she continued. "We can ask Bevins to run a search for family members and talk to them. But I think right now this has to be an all-hands-on-deck situation. We need the entire team on this, or we risk losing him."

"Becca's right," Serrano stepped in. "We've lost enough time. We move now." He looked at her. "I'm going to push for a warrant to search the plant. They'll push back hard, but, given the history, the judge will grant one. In that regard, Abbott and I will handle that."

"And your inside man? Did he come through?" Ellis asked.

"We were given details on the actions of an employee. He was a shift leader back in ninety-eight, but runs the floor now."

She cocked her head. "Harry Carver?"

"That's the one," Serrano replied. "I don't recall him being a player the first time, but he's the only one still there after all these years."

"Byrd found the material sheets and purchase orders inside Carver's office and handed them over to us," Ellis added. "They can't be working together if he was willing to do that."

"If there's no connection, there's no connection," Serrano continued. "We get inside the place, we'll get our answers."

"Sergeant Moss's people are going to help with the search," Abbott cut in. "We'll home in on the Byrd files, the other deceased employees' files, Satchel's included. You and the others will zero in on Byrd himself. He'll roll, so let's get it done. Now."

Ellis stood. "Yes, sir." She looked at McCallister. "You ready?"

"I am."

The two returned to the bullpen, where all but Fletch were there. Ellis approached Lewis. "Gabby, have you seen Fletch?"

"No, sorry. I just got back myself. What's going on?"

"We need to brief everyone. Can you spare a few minutes?" she continued.

"Yeah, of course."

"Good. I'll gather up the team and we'll meet in the briefing room." Ellis continued on and reached Bevin's desk. "We have a new plan. Can you sit with everyone in the briefing?"

"Now?" he asked.

"Yep."

"All right."

She moved on to Pelletier's desk. "Bryce, we need help. You in?"

He looked up at her. "Do you need to ask?"

Ellis smiled. "Briefing room. Right now." She returned to her desk to gather the files and noted McCallister on his phone. He quickly ended the call, and she spotted the look on his face. "Everything okay?"

"Yeah, yeah. Everything's fine." He returned his phone to his pocket. "Is everyone on board?"

"Yep. We're meeting now." She retrieved the files. "You sure you're okay? Is this about that reporter?"

McCallister pursed his lips. "Yeah, well, the ship has sailed, so we'll see what it churns up." He followed her into the hall.

Distractions were the last thing anyone needed right now. Ellis included Hank and Piper in there too. She knew this reporter situation was a problem for McCallister but could do nothing about it. What happened, happened, and the team would find out. She was unsure whether it would sway anyone's opinion of him. And while she believed she hadn't been swayed, maybe a part of her had. He had kept this from her, and if there was one thing she hated more than anything, it was being kept in the dark.

Ellis hustled to the briefing room and set down her things at the podium. "Okay, so you guys know Euan, Connor, and I have been working on a triple homicide. It hadn't started out that way, but that's where we're at right now. We're also dealing with a company with a shady past and an old investigation. So now, with Abbott's and Serrano's blessing, we're going to divide our resources and find the man we're looking for. We're certain he's the one who came after us last night. There may be more, but the likelihood is high he is also the murderer."

She opened her laptop and cast the image onto the wall-mounted monitor. "This is Wayne Byrd. He works for Connex Solutions, same as our victims. We're assuming he's on the run."

"How long?" Pelletier asked.

"Probably since last night after the ambush. We checked his workplace, we checked his home. No signs. A BOLO's been issued on the Ford F-150 he drives. So far, no bites."

"You think he's hiding out?" Fletch walked into the room. "Sorry I'm late."

"No problem," Ellis added. "He could be. Friends, family. We'll need to search them all. At least the ones in the state."

"Tell us what you need, Becca," Lewis said. "We'll move on it now."

Ellis rested her elbows on the podium. "We have Computer Forensics Officer Leo Brown working on another phone that was found. There's no telling if it's important, but he'll work on it anyway. And so as far as to how we tackle this..." She let her eyes roam. "I'd like Gabby and Fletch to find friends and family. Gabby, that will probably mean a social media search. Backgrounds. You know the drill."

"You got it," she replied.

Ellis looked at Pelletier. "Bryce, Connor has been in on this case since the beginning. He knows the players. In fact, it was Byrd who reached out to him to begin with. So, I'd like you guys to set up one each at Byrd's home and the plant. There's a chance he'll return to one or both places. And we're going to assume he'll be armed, so be prepared."

She looked at McCallister. "Euan and I will request a trace on Byrd's credit cards, debit cards. Phone. Anything we think that will lead us to him. He'll need money if he is on the run. And when Gabby and Fletch get names of family and friends, he and I can run down the family members. You two can run down the friends."

"What about highway checkpoints?" Pelletier asked. "Are we there yet?"

"At the very least, we get MaineDOT to put someone on the cameras to see if they get a sighting on his truck."

"I agree." McCallister looked to Pelletier. "Good suggestion. So if there's no other questions, we should get going."

Ellis nodded. "Thanks, everyone." She waited while they

filed out and stopped McCallister before he had a chance to leave. "Are you with us on this?"

"Of course I am. What do you mean?"

"I mean, whatever this reporter said or did—I have to know it's not screwing with your head right now."

"No offense, Becca, but I've been doing this a long time. I got it handled." He started out again.

Ellis grabbed her things and returned to the bullpen as Pelletier called out.

"Hey, Becca?"

She headed in his direction. "Yeah?"

"I'll take the guy's home. Connor's taking the plant. We'll be heading out in the next thirty minutes. We can get a warrant to search the house. You want me to work on that? Better to see if any evidence exists than sitting outside waiting for him to show."

"Definitely. That's a good point. I wasn't sure if we had enough, but given that it appears he may have already taken flight, yes. Get hold of the judge and see what she can do quickly. Let Connor know, too."

"You got it."

Ellis headed back to her desk. "DOT cameras. You want me to move on that?"

McCallister turned to her. "I just called and put in the request. They'll be on it within the hour."

24

Abbott marched into Serrano's office with the papers in his hand. "I got the search warrant on Connex. If we want to get a jump on it before their lawyers learn about it, then we need to move now. Have you talked to Moss yet?"

"He's got four guys we can use for the search," Serrano replied. "What's the warrant cover?"

"Personnel files of the victims. Byrd's file. Compliance records," Abbott said. "We'll find out if those sons of bitches have been following the rules or if they were skirting them, who made the call, because I can guarantee you, whoever it is, is working with our killer."

Serrano pushed up from his desk and started out. "Let's get with Moss and get the team lined up." He led the way downstairs and headed into the patrol sergeant's office.

Moss peered up at them. "You come to take my people from me?"

"I'm afraid so," Serrano replied. "But we owe you for this."

"It's no problem. I can lend you Triggs, Whitaker, Ortega, and Gainey. How long do you think this will take?"

"A couple of hours, most likely," Abbott replied. "The warrant isn't overly broad."

"Then I'll let them know you're ready. Are you heading there now?" Moss asked.

"Yes, sir."

"Good luck."

Abbott and Serrano were leaving his office when Serrano got a call. "Hank? You all right?" He listened on the line. "You're out of the hospital, though, right? Good. Glad to hear it. We were just—" Serrano slowed his steps as they reached the lobby. "That was the plan, why?"

Abbott listened with growing interest. He hadn't been involved in the ninety-eight investigation, so he wondered what it was Hank knew. Did his tentacles reach as far as the courts? Did he already know about the warrant?

Serrano ended the call and looked at Abbott.

"What was that all about?" Abbott asked.

"Hank Ellis. You know all that's been going on with him, right?"

"Of course. Is he all right? Do we need to pull Becca?"

Serrano raised his hands. "No, no, it's nothing like that. No, he said something about the case. I guess Becca updated him just a short while ago. Checking in on him probably, but you know how Hank likes to keep his thumb on the pulse of what goes on in this department."

"I know that all too well, Lieutenant. So, what did he have to say?"

Serrano's face pinched. "He thinks Becca's on the right track. But that we aren't."

"What the hell does that mean? Wrong track in what way?"

"He says if we want to catch Connex red-handed, it's best to have the place shut down and request an OSHA inspection.

Claim dangerous chemical exposures as evidenced by multiple employees, the dead ones included. Says OSHA will shut them down in a heartbeat. Then it'll give us a shot at searching the place before they can torch anything that makes them look bad."

Abbott nodded. "It's extreme, but then again we have three dead bodies." He eyed Serrano. "Don't suppose Hank knows folks over at the local OSHA office?"

"He doesn't, but I do." Serrano spun on his heels. "Let's hold off on our current plan till I can put in a call."

"You want me to tell Moss it's off?" Abbott asked.

"Not off, postponed. And only for a short while. I'll see what I can do with the information we have to get OSHA in there and red tag the sons of bitches."

Gabby shot up from her desk and started toward Ellis. "Becca, I have names." She handed her the slip of paper. "Byrd has a wife and kids. I tracked down the wife through social media. She's with her mother in Portland. It's possible he's there too, but—"

"He wouldn't risk their safety is my guess," Ellis cut in.

"My thoughts exactly. I'd still have Bryce call his friends at Portland PD and do a drive by, maybe a knock on the door to confirm. But we also have Byrd's mother. That's her on the note there. She lives in Bangor. No father. No siblings. Fletch is still connecting with friends, but this is a start. You said you two wanted to run on the family? Well, here you go, my friend."

Ellis raised her brow. "A lifesaver as always. Thanks, Gabby."

"Anytime. We'll keep on it, though."

Ellis set her sights on McCallister. "We should go talk to

this woman right now. He could be there, or she might know where he is."

"Let's go." He snatched his jacket from the back of the chair. As they started on, he stopped to see Bevins. "How are you coming along?"

"We're getting ready to leave now. I'm just waiting on Bryce. He'll go to the house, I'll go to Connex. We'll keep you posted." He looked at Ellis. "Where are you two headed?"

"Byrd's mother lives in the city," she began. "We're going to talk to her and see if she knows where her son is. We'll touch base soon."

As they started into the hall, Brown jogged to meet them. "There you are. I just called your desk."

Ellis turned back to the bullpen. "Sorry about that. I didn't hear the phone ring. What's up?"

Brown held out the phone. "This is Terry Satchel's phone."

She glanced at it. "What? Are you sure about that?"

"How do you know?" McCallister asked.

"The guy who kept this thing?" Brown continued. "Said it held a charge? He was right. I got a charge on it, and the damn thing lit up. Couldn't see shit because of the screen, so I connected it to my Mac and it displayed the image."

"Wait." McCallister raised his hands. "How did you get into it? You call in another favor?"

"No, that would've taken at least a day. We got lucky. Terry Satchel didn't have his phone password protected."

Ellis pulled back and glanced at McCallister. "Who the hell doesn't use a password on their phone?"

"Maybe a guy who knows he's about to lose and wanted someone to find the phone."

Ellis furrowed her brow. "You're saying, he suspected he would be killed, probably by someone at Connex, and so he made sure whoever found the phone would get into it?"

"Hey, he called Buxton, didn't he? Is this so far-fetched?" McCallister replied.

"Look, I don't know how or why this guy didn't use a password," Brown interrupted. "But he didn't. So, do you want to know what I found or what?"

AS THE AFTERNOON SET IN, Byrd grew anxious. His knee bounced as he sat on the sofa inside his elderly mother's home. He knew he couldn't stay here and questioned whether he'd jumped the gun; made a move before it was necessary. Last night had been a fluke. Byrd had spent more time searching for Satchel's phone since they found him than he had figuring a way out of this mess. So he went back to the scene to look one more time.

There had been so many cops and BLT, and all the rest, that he hadn't had time to see if the phone was there. When he did get the chance to go back, goddam cops were there. He didn't have some sort of death wish and decided to take on a bunch of cops in a shoot-out. He'd heard movement and fired off a round in panic. It was a miracle he wasn't killed or hadn't killed one of them. If he had, the entire police force, hell, the entire state's police force, would've come after him. The worst part of it was that he had no idea if they'd seen his truck. No idea what was going on, or whether they were coming for him, but he had to assume the worst-case scenario.

Satchel had gotten under his skin for the last time; coming to him at the bar that night after mouthing off at the plant. If he would've just left him alone, Wayne wouldn't be in this situation. But Satchel had pushed him.

So when the fight erupted and the bar owner tossed them out, Satchel kept at it. It was a goddam accident. Satchel hit his head on some brick planter at the front of the bar. Byrd panicked, loaded up Satchel into his truck before anyone noticed.

He'd had only minutes to come up with a plan. And then it hit him. He'd grabbed Satchel's keys to move the truck. That was when he saw the chemicals in the back. Dumb son of a bitch must've stolen them from the plant. Probably thought he could use them as some kind of proof of his claims.

Byrd snatched the chemicals and drove Satchel to the preserve and tried to make it look like the company did it. But then he couldn't find the damn phone. He knew Satchel had recorded the beginning of the confrontation.

Byrd had killed three people, not that they could prove he ran Janice off the road. But if they found Satchel's phone... Never mind, he wasn't going down alone. He'd tried to shift the blame, sending the cops the photos of the purchase orders. Now, he was going to have to beg.

He walked to the phone mounted on the kitchen wall and dialed the number. The call rang through and he waited for the line to pick up.

"Yeah, this is Harry."

"You gotta help get me out of here, man," Byrd said. "I think they saw me last night."

"And that's my problem? You've been blackmailing me for months. Now you want my help with the other two people you killed?"

"I had no choice. Look, are you going to help me, or do I let them take me in and tell them everything, including your part in this? You think you're getting off scot-free?" He waited while the line went quiet.

"Meet me at the old plant. Half an hour."

BROWN WAS at his desk and typed in the commands while the detectives waited with seemingly growing impatience. He opened the video files. "Okay, you'll want to see this."

Ellis and McCallister huddled close and peered over Brown's shoulder.

The first video began to play.

"It's Satchel," Ellis said. "Strange to see him alive."

Satchel was behind the wheel of his GMC truck and held his phone while it recorded. "I'm going to see Wayne Byrd," Satchel said as he drove on. "I'm going to talk to him about the chemicals. He knows what gets ordered and where they come from. I know he does. Problem is, I'm not sure I can trust him after what happened on the shop floor today. But I'm sending this video to you, Janice, so you will have proof. Everyone thinks I'm crazy, but I know I got sick from what the company did, just like all the others. So, I'm going to get proof from Byrd, then I can take it to the feds."

Brown stopped the video. "That's the bulk of it, but there is another." He opened another file and pressed play. "Take a look at this."

Ellis eyed the monitor and waited. "Looks like Satchel's inside the bar."

McCallister pointed at the screen. "That's Byrd, right there."

"I think he's about to confront him," she added.

They continued to watch as the video played.

"*I warned you, Terry, you're barking up the wrong tree, now fuck off,*" Byrd said.

"*How can you go along with this, man?*" Satchel asked. "*You know what they're doing is killing people, right? Why are you helping him? What are you getting in return?*"

"Who are they talking about?" Ellis asked.

"*Helping who? You don't know what you're talking about, okay?*" Byrd shot back. "*Just go home, Terry.*"

Satchel grabbed Byrd's T-shirt. "*Hey, look, if you think I'm going to walk away from this—*"

Byrd whipped around in the bar stool and slugged Satchel in the jaw.

Ellis flinched. "This was what the owner talked about."

They watched as a fight ensued and, a moment later, the owner walked out.

"*Go on, both of you. Get the hell out of here before I call the cops.*"

"They're going outside, but look at Byrd's face," McCallister began.

The video went black. "What happened?" Ellis asked.

"That's the end of this video, but hold on. He wasn't finished." Brown opened another file. "This is the last one."

Satchel was outside and held his phone to his face. "*Wayne Byrd struck me in the face. Janice, you have to take this to management. I'm going to send—*"

The phone dropped onto the ground and aimed at the underside of the bar's awning.

"Holy shit. What's going on?" McCallister asked.

"Listen," Brown replied.

"*All you had to do was your damn job and keep your conspiracy theories to yourself. But you wouldn't listen, would you?*" Byrd said off-camera.

The sound of an altercation continued, but they saw nothing.

"*You think Harry is going to get away with this?*" Satchel said, while he was out of view.

A loud crash sounded, as the phone slid away and the screen went dark.

Brown ended the file. "That's it. That's when the phone broke." He turned to them. "You have a name. I told you this was something you'd want to see."

Ellis raised her brow. "Harry Carver's the floor supervisor. Why would he be behind this?"

"More importantly," McCallister began, "is there someone behind him?"

"But what this means is that Byrd killed Satchel by accident, a result of a bar fight," Ellis continued. "Then he must've taken him to the preserve, poured the chemicals down his throat. And that was the end of it." She glanced at McCallister. "What would be the point in doing that?"

"To make it look like someone at the company killed him," McCallister replied. "But it still doesn't explain why he would take out Janice Buxton and Scott Littleton. Satchel said he was sending her those videos, but she never mentioned it."

Ellis tilted her head. "It's safe to assume she never received them, but maybe Wayne Byrd hadn't known that. And then when she came to us, he thought she might have proof of what he'd done. Same thing for Littleton." She creased her brow. "All these people died because Byrd was covering up for the accidental murder of Satchel?"

McCallister rocked back on his heels. "Byrd wanted to lay the blame at Carver's feet, but why? He never once mentioned him to point us in that direction."

Ellis eyed him. "No, but he did get photos of the purchase orders that came from Carver. Maybe that was his way of shining the light. What if Carver's behind the illnesses? He orders the chemicals. Where does he get them from?"

"You're thinking it's a kickback situation?" he asked.

"Possibly." She considered how Hank and Piper had been pulled into this. "Serrano said Carver was the only person left who'd been there during the original investigation. He knows Hank."

Byrd arrived in his pickup truck to the site of an old plant that had been shut down years earlier after the jobs had been shipped overseas. The steel mill stood tall on the edge of the city but withered and crumbled with each passing day.

He stepped out of his Ford F-150 amid the weeds that pushed through the cracked asphalt parking lot. Broken windows, rusted metal, and rotting wood were just about all that was left of the plant. Ahead, he spotted Harry Carver standing next to his car. And as Byrd approached his supervisor, he tossed a glance behind him. "If you don't help get me out of this, Connex is going to look like this place when I'm through."

Carver removed his glasses and tilted his head. "You're in no position to issue threats, Wayne. If I recall correctly, you've killed three people."

"And you've killed at least three, too, for now. More coming down the line," he replied. "So, what are you planning to do to get me out of the cops' line of fire? If you want me to keep quiet, you gotta help me."

Carver scoffed. "You're the one who blackmailed me into telling everyone that Satchel took off after you killed him, and now you're threatening me again? What the hell were you thinking, going after Janice and Scooter?"

"First of all, I'm not the only one. You think I don't know how you and your friend operate? Don't tell me you're innocent in all this."

Carver crossed his arms. "I had them watched, but I didn't have them killed. That's all you, Wayne."

"Look, I didn't know what those two said to the cops, okay? But I do know Scooter told them about the argument I had with Terry at the plant. I know he started acting squirrelly the other day, so I followed him to the grocery store. I saw the lady detective go inside shortly after." He kicked the dirt with his shoe. "Then Janice...I knew she'd met the cops."

Byrd shook his head. "Goddam it, Harry, I never wanted any of this. You shouldn't have been taking money from Beecham. You helped kill our own people with those chemicals they used, all so you could make a few extra bucks."

"Enough of this shit." Carver raised his hand. "You're going to keep your head low, you understand? I'm working on a way to get you out of the state, up to Canada, but it's going to take time."

"I don't have time. They know who I am. They'll know what I drive," Byrd said. "The last thing I have is time."

"So long as you keep your mouth shut, then I can help," Carver added. "But you even think about going to the cops, you won't survive the day, you understand?"

"I wasn't going to do that to you, all right?" Byrd replied. "I just need a way out of here. No one knows about you."

Carver peered at the approaching car. "Your ride's here."

Byrd turned at the sight of a black Mercedes. "Who is that?"

"A friend who's willing to help without asking questions. He'll get you someplace safe until I figure out how to get you clear of the city."

The car continued its approach and Byrd eyed the driver. "You sure I can trust him?"

"I trust him and that's all you need to know."

The car stopped and the driver stepped out. "Mr. Byrd, let's go." The dark-haired man, with a thick brow, walked around to the passenger side and opened the door. "We don't have much time, so I suggest you hurry along."

Byrd was reluctant. He glanced at Harry. "When will I hear from you again?"

"Tonight, maybe the morning at the latest. You let me worry about this now. Keep your mouth shut, and I'll make sure no one finds you."

Byrd started toward the vehicle and slid onto the

passenger seat of the Mercedes. The tall man in the dark suit walked closer to Carver and appeared to whisper. Byrd couldn't hear the conversation, as dread fell over him, but he kept watch. Carver eyed Byrd as he spoke to the driver. That dread turned to fear. "You're not going to let me go, are you, Harry?"

It was then he spotted the gun under the driver's jacket secured at his waist. His heart raced. *Get out, run.*

Byrd stepped out of the car and darted toward the plant. There was no other place to go, but if he could get inside, he could hide. He could find a way out.

He heard the gunshots ring out. "Shit." Byrd pumped his legs, as the plant loomed in the distance. Fear gripped him, his eyes watered from the cold air, and the feeling that death sprinted after him kept him going.

Another shot rang out. The bullet pierced his back right between the shoulder blades. Byrd collapsed to the ground. The irony that this was exactly how he'd murdered Littleton didn't escape him. He fell on his stomach. His heart slowed. His breaths turned shallow. With his gaze out to the side, he saw black dress shoes approach. No words would come.

"You know, we all had a pretty good arrangement. You shouldn't have tried to pin this on Harry, Wayne."

CARVER STOOD next to the body of Wayne Byrd, a man who'd dug himself into a hole no one could've helped him out of. And now he had to clean up his mess. To look at Harry Carver was to see a humble man. A man who didn't rock the boat. But that all changed when he was given the responsibility of awarding contracts for materials needed for production.

Companies from all over the world courted him, but one

in particular, Beecham International, offered Carver a little something extra on the side. It was more than a little, if he was honest. It was enough to set him up well into retirement.

The past two years saw that relationship blossom right along with Carver's bank account. It wasn't until last year that the complaints rolled in. Employees were getting sick, but surely it had nothing to do with the materials used on the line? He knew the struggles Connex had faced to regain the trust of the community and of the government. And when he confronted the people at Beecham, they said they'd talk to their supplier, but it wasn't his concern. Carver hadn't known who their supplier was, and they made sure he didn't find out.

Only now had the real problems begun. Byrd's temper. Satchel's foil-hat theories. Goyer had agreed to the settlement payouts for those who'd gotten sick, with the promise Carver would fix things and no one would talk. But when Satchel died and Byrd shone a bright light on Connex, it became Carver's mess to clean up.

The tall man in the dark suit buttoned his jacket, as he stood next to Carver and the now-deceased Wayne Byrd.

Carver offered his hand. "I can take care of it from here, Tom. Appreciate the help."

Tom Lazaro eyed the body. "And Detective Ellis? She'll figure out what we've done. And when that happens, how long do you think it'll be before she realizes we tried to kill her father and went after her best friend?"

"I did warn you it was a mistake to go after her people. She's her father's daughter," Carver replied. "I suggest you pull back and let me handle things from here. Rest assured, Byrd will take the fall for all of it."

25

Armed with new information about an accomplice in the murders of three Connex employees, Ellis and McCallister returned to CID and to Abbott. Ellis walked in. "Sir, we know Byrd killed our three victims, but we also know that he was protecting someone at Connex."

"Who?" Abbott asked, as he sat at his desk.

"The supervisor, Harry Carver. Video from Satchel's phone surfaced, and his name was thrown out. It appeared to have been an accident, initially, after a bar-room fight, but it spiraled," Ellis continued.

"Serrano and I are in the process of getting OSHA to shut down the plant. I believe he's working on that now," Abbott replied.

"Sir, if that happens, I think this man, Carver, will do everything in his power to destroy evidence. We don't have proof he's done anything. All we know is that Satchel mentioned his name and we know that Carver approved the purchase orders for the chemicals," Ellis said. "Can you hold off on that? It'll give us a chance to look into him. To find him and bring him in for questioning."

Abbott eyed her a moment. "What about Byrd? He's your killer."

"We have the rest of the team helping to locate him now, sir," McCallister replied. "Becca's right. Can you give us time to track down Carver and bring him in? So far, we have no idea how far up the food chain this goes. If we bring him in, he might be willing to talk if it means he'll get a deal."

"Where do you plan on looking?" Abbott asked.

"We'll find out where he lives. Whether he's married. We'll go to the plant," Ellis said. "Sir, we will find him. We have the advantage because he has no idea we know about him. He won't be on the run like we believe Byrd is now. This is our shot at getting ahead of the game."

Abbott nodded. "I'll do my best to pull Serrano off, but I guarantee you, if you don't get results, he'll move forward, and I'll agree that he should."

<hr>

ELLIS SAT behind the wheel of her Tahoe and headed north toward the Connex plant. "Connor is already there looking for Byrd's truck and we've got Bryce at the guy's house. It's possible, since the two are working together, that Byrd will seek out Carver and ask for help."

"The question of others' involvement is what concerns me at the moment," McCallister replied. "Carver may be the only one, but I can't believe that's true, given the non-disclosure agreements signed by the former employees who later died. That means others are in on this, just as Serrano suspected."

"Maybe, but I think Carver will be the fall guy," Ellis said.

"And like we told Abbott, he could turn on whoever is behind this."

She arrived at the plant and made the call. When the line answered, she began, "Connor, where are you? We just pulled into the parking lot at the front."

"I'm around the side. They have cameras here, but they don't know my vehicle. I haven't spotted Byrd's truck. What are you two doing here? What's the plan?" he asked.

"We're here for someone who we think Byrd is working with. We're about to go in, but if you don't see Byrd soon, just get with Bryce and you two hit the mother's house. He hasn't been spotted on DOT cameras. He could be holed up there." Ellis ended the call and stepped out of her SUV. McCallister joined her and the two of them started toward the plant once again. She thrust out her hand and stopped him a moment. "We say we're bringing him in to help us find Byrd. Any other suggestion could trigger a cover-up from above."

"Copy that."

They walked inside and Ellis approached the desk. She was immediately greeted with a familiar smile.

"Afternoon, Detectives," Josie said. "I'm surprised to see you here again so soon. What can I do for you?"

"We need to speak with Harry Carver. We have some questions for him," Ellis replied.

"You know what, I saw him arrive just a short while ago, actually." Josie picked up the phone. "I'll call back to him and let him know." She held up a finger when the line answered. "Harry, yeah, those detectives are back and want to talk to you. Do you have a few minutes?" She nodded. "I'll let them know, thanks."

Ellis felt relief, knowing the man was here. This cat-and-mouse game had grown tiresome.

"He says you can go back, if you'd like. Do you remember where his office is?"

"Sure do," Ellis said. "Thanks for your help." She waved on McCallister and they headed back through the doors marked "Employees Only."

The machines hummed and the conveyors looped around the shop floor. People wore earplugs and stood at their stations, putting together parts for the assembly line.

Ellis started on toward the foreman's office, which had a large window that looked out onto the floor. She opened it and the two walked in. "Afternoon, Mr. Carver."

"Detectives Ellis and McCallister," he said. "What brings you two by this afternoon?"

"We'd like to ask you a few questions about Wayne Byrd," Ellis began.

"Of course. I'm here to help." He eyed them. "What can I answer for you?"

"Is Mr. Byrd here at the moment?" McCallister asked.

"No, sir. He didn't show up today, as a matter of fact. Not too surprising, all things considered. We've had a lot of that around here lately."

Ellis noticed his eyes. Calling bullshit was sort of her specialty and she wanted to call bullshit right now, but they needed him to willingly accompany them back to the station. It was best to keep things civil.

"I see." McCallister glanced away as if in thought. "I don't suppose you'd mind coming down to the station to speak with us? I think you might've known Mr. Byrd well enough to offer insight."

Carver raised his chin. "What's this about, exactly?"

"I'll be honest with you, sir," Ellis interrupted. "We think Mr. Byrd knows more about the murders of your employees than he's let on. Would you mind coming with us? We think it would be best to do this away from here. We don't want to upset your staff." She watched as he appeared to consider the proposal. The slight uncertainty in his gaze. The shifting of his feet.

"I suppose that would be okay. Sure." He grinned. "I can go there for a little while. They can manage without me."

BEVINS NOTED the exit of Ellis and McCallister from the building, with the man he knew to be Harry Carver in tow. He wondered if he was the guy Ellis had said was working with Byrd.

He caught her gaze, but she offered no indication of whether the plan had changed. He picked up the phone. "Bryce, you have any luck there at Byrd's house?"

"He's not here, but I got the warrant and went inside. He'll have to fix his window later."

"And?" Bevins asked.

"Found a laptop and I don't think it belonged to him," Pelletier replied. "I think it could be Terry Satchel's."

"Oh wow, okay. That's something. I'm still sitting at the plant and looking at Becca and Euan usher out Byrd's supervisor."

"The supervisor?"

"Yep. They think he might know where Byrd is," Bevins continued.

"What does she want us to do? Clearly, something popped, or they wouldn't be hauling that guy in."

Bevins peered through the windshield. "Yeah, I don't know what the hell's going on right now, but I don't want to be sitting here on my thumbs before she lets us know."

"You got a plan to find Byrd?" Pelletier asked.

"Becca wants us to hit Byrd's mother's house." He paused a moment. "I'm going to call Gabby now. She and Fletch were working on hunting down family and friends. Let me see if they have an address for us. I'll call you back." He ended the call and reached out to Detective Lewis. "Hey, Gabby, it's Connor. You and Fletch have an address for Byrd's mom?"

"We do," she replied. "I was just about to call Becca and let her know. She and Euan were going to talk to any family members while Fletch and I talk to friends. Why? What's going on?"

"I'm sitting here on my ass waiting for Byrd to show up at his job. Meanwhile, Becca and Euan are dragging out the guy's supervisor, but she wants us to run down there and check it out."

"Okay. I'll text you the address now."

"Thanks, Gabby." He ended the call and waited for the text to arrive. "Now, I'll send this to Bryce." He typed a message.

> Just meet me there and we'll talk to his mom.

A moment later, a reply came.

> On my way.

Bevins pressed the starter on his Mustang and headed out of the parking lot. "All right, dude. Let's see if you ran home to Mommy."

ELLIS HELPED Carver from the back seat of her SUV and when McCallister joined her, she led him inside the station. "If you'll follow me down the hall, we can sit in one of the private rooms."

"Sure. Fine," Carver replied.

She opened the door. "Go on inside. Can I get you a bottle of water?"

"No, thank you. I'll answer your questions, but then I really ought to head back to the plant," Carver said.

"Of course. I'm going to grab a bottle for myself. We'll be back in just a moment." Ellis closed the door, while McCallister waited in the hall. She turned to him. "Did you see the look on his face?"

"He's wondering what we know," he replied. "What's our play?"

"We'll ask him about his relationship with Byrd and that we're certain Byrd came at us last night. Then we'll go into Byrd's last meeting with Satchel."

"And that's when we drop the shoe," McCallister said. "You know he'll ask for a lawyer after that."

"Oh, I have no doubt he will, but as long as he doesn't have a chance to contact anyone at the plant. In fact, I'll run up to see Abbott now. It's time they move in while we work on this guy." She walked away and started upstairs to CID, but before she headed into the hall to find Abbott, Lewis called out to her. Ellis turned to see her and Fletch together. "Hey, we just got back and we've got Harry Carver here. What's happening on your end?"

"I gave Connor the address of Byrd's mother," Lewis began. "We got it handled, Becca. You do what you need to do. Connor and Bryce are going to question the mom. We'll see where that goes."

"Anything else you need from us?" Fletch asked. "Byrd didn't appear to be active on social media, just his wife. We know she's in Portland."

"Right. If Byrd's not at his mother's place, we'll get Bryce in touch with his friends in Portland and see if he's gone to his in-laws. Thanks for your help, guys. I'm just about to brief Abbott. Catch up with you later?"

"You got it," Lewis replied.

She arrived at Abbott's office and noticed Serrano inside as well. "Good, you're both here. We have Carver downstairs. He doesn't know why he's here other than to help us find Byrd."

"So it's time to move on shutting down the plant," Abbott said.

"I think it has to happen before Carver has a shot at contacting anyone there," Ellis replied.

Serrano nodded. "Yes, sir. It's time we put an end to this right now because I'm certain Carver isn't working alone. I remember him from back in the day. He's not that smart."

"We'll have to see if he's willing to talk. I'll keep you posted." Ellis turned around and headed back downstairs. As she arrived in the hall, McCallister stood outside the interview room holding two bottles of water.

"Here." He handed one to her. "How'd it go?"

"Abbott and Serrano are ready to move forward on the plant closure. Connor and Bryce are headed to Byrd's mother's house."

"I guess it's you and me up to bat. Let's aim for a triple hitter." He opened the door and stepped inside. "I'm so sorry to have kept you waiting, sir."

"That's okay, but I really do need to think about getting back to the plant. Maybe I can call my manager and just let him know?"

"Sure, yeah." Ellis sat down. "But honestly, we won't take up much of your time." She retrieved the laptop that contained Satchel's files from the broken phone.

"What's that?" he asked.

"Just something we thought you should hear." Ellis opened the file and pressed play. She eyed McCallister as it began and then shifted her focus onto Carver as he listened.

"What is this?" he asked.

"It's Terry Satchel and Wayne Byrd," Ellis replied. "Just listen."

It took several moments before he seemed to understand what was happening. And then he heard his name and shot a glance back at Ellis.

She leaned back in her chair. "So, is there anything you'd like to add to this, Mr. Carver?"

BEVINS KNOCKED on the front door where Byrd's mom lived. Pelletier stood beside him. Several moments passed before it opened and an older woman with sharp features and a petite build appeared on the other side.

"Afternoon, ma'am. I'm Detective Bevins, this is Detective Pelletier. We'd like to talk to you about your son, Wayne."

She returned the kind of glare that could only come from a disappointed mother. "I knew it. Come on in. Figured he'd done something stupid." She stepped aside and they walked in. "Can I get you anything?"

"No, thank you," Bevins said. "Is Wayne here?"

"No, sir, he is not," she replied.

"Can you tell us when you last saw your son?" Pelletier cut in.

She turned around and started toward the kitchen. "A few hours ago. He went to meet with someone, and I haven't seen him since. I knew he was in trouble. I could see it on his face. What'd he do?" The old woman turned on the faucet and filled a coffee carafe with water.

Bevins stepped toward the doorway between the kitchen and living room. "Uh, ma'am, do you have any way of contacting your son?"

"I suppose I can call him on his cell phone." She tilted her head. "What, you can't tell me what he's done?"

"We'd just like to talk to him about some people he worked with," Pelletier said.

"Oh, dear Lord. I told him that job was going to get to him eventually. People always getting sick and whatnot." She picked up her phone. "I'll call him now, but you know what? I can't recall his cell number off the top of my head. I have it written down in my bedroom. I'll be right back."

Pelletier noticed the phone on the wall. "Do you think he would've used the landline to contact whoever he was trying to meet?"

Bevins looked at the old avocado green phone with plastic buttons for a keypad. "It's possible, especially if he hadn't wanted to leave a record of the call on his cell. Why?"

Pelletier walked over to the phone. "I can check the last number dialed."

"Oh, shit." The corner of Bevin's mouth tilted up. "Yeah, you can. I forgot about that."

"Good thing I'm a little older than you." Pelletier pressed the star button and then the numbers 6 and 9. "Some things are good to remember." He listened when the automated operator came onto the line and scrambled to find a piece of paper. "I need something to write with."

Bevins grabbed his phone and opened the screen. "Repeat it back to me."

As the automated voice called it out, Pelletier relayed the number and hung up the phone.

The old woman emerged from the hallway. "I have that number here, Officers."

"That's good news. Would you mind making the call?" Bevins asked.

She dialed the number and waited for the line to answer. "Well, shoot. I got the voicemail. You want me to leave a message?"

"No, thank you, ma'am," Bevins replied. "We appreciate

you trying, though." He retrieved a business card and handed it to her. "If you do see or hear from him, could you call me, or better yet, have him call?"

"Yes, sir, Officer." She glanced at the number. "Is Wayne in real trouble?"

Bevins raised his shoulder. "I don't know for sure, ma'am. I'm sorry."

The detectives returned outside and Bevins grabbed his car keys. "I hate lying to old ladies."

"It's not a lie. Truth is, we don't know the kind of trouble he's in." As they reached the car Pelletier continued. "You want to call this number we got from the landline and see who answers?"

"Yes, I do." Bevins dialed the number and placed the call on speaker, as he leaned against the passenger door. The line answered. "Connex Solutions. You have reached the office of Harry Carver, who is not available to take your call…" Bevins raised his brow. "What do you know? Byrd finds himself in trouble and he calls his boss."

Pelletier scoffed. "The same man who's now sitting inside the station."

26

The raid on Connex Solutions included not only OSHA, but Bangor PD and the state police as well. Abbott and Serrano orchestrated the operation within hours of the detainment of the supervisor, Harry Carver, who had, so far, refused to speak without an attorney present.

The team had returned, and all gathered in the bullpen.

Bevins' phone rang and he answered the line. "Yeah, this is Detective Bevins." He listened to the caller. "The BOLO on the Ford truck. Dark gray, that's right." He eyed Ellis. "And you're sure he matches the description? Thanks, man. I appreciate the heads-up." Bevins ended the call and peered at his colleagues. "State police got a call about an abandoned truck matching our BOLO."

"Byrd's?" Ellis asked.

"Yep. Unfortunately, his body was found nearby. He'd been shot in the back and left for dead."

"Son of a bitch." McCallister punched the air with his fist. "The call he made at his mother's house was to Carver. Now the guy's dead."

"He must've met up with him. Carver figured out we were close and turned on him." Ellis heard her phone ring on her desk and spun around. "We'll want to get moving on ballistics, and then search Carver's car for the weapon." She snatched her phone. "Ellis here. Uh-huh. Got it. Okay, thanks. We'll come down now." Ellis ended the call and eyed McCallister. "The lawyer's here. Now that we know about Byrd, I don't think any lawyer is going to be able to get Carver out of here tonight."

They returned downstairs, and Ellis offered her hand to the woman in the blue suit. "Ms. Lunt, nice to see you again."

"Sadly, it's under these circumstances, Detective. I'm here to represent Connex Solutions, and I'd like to offer you everything we have on Mr. Carver."

The unexpected news forced Ellis back on her heels. "You're willingly handing over employee files on this man?"

"Yes, ma'am," the lawyer replied. "First and foremost, Connex Solutions would like it to be known that they are in full cooperation with your investigation. As such, we will give you whatever it is you need to see to it Mr. Carver pays for any wrongdoing."

Ellis looked at McCallister a moment. "A word?" She glanced back at the lawyer. "Excuse us for a moment." She stepped several feet away and, in a low voice, continued, "Before we say anything, we need to get with the sarge and find out the results on the raid. This could be a way for them to get in our good graces, if what turned up was damning enough."

McCallister glanced back at the lawyer. "I'll find him now. Keep her occupied for a few minutes. We'll see how Abbott and Serrano want to handle this."

Lieutenant Serrano was in the hall when McCallister spotted him on his way to see Abbott. "Sir?"

Serrano stopped a moment. "Yes?"

McCallister thumbed back. "A Connex lawyer is here, and she says they're prepared to give us anything we want on Harry Carver. But before we even talk to her, Becca and I thought to check with you first. Is this a ploy to get reduced charges for Connex?"

Serrano waved him over. "Let's sit with Abbott and go over the situation." He started ahead and they soon arrived at the sergeant's office. "Jim, we need to chat." Serrano walked in. "Connex sent a lawyer. I don't know who sent her, but my guess is it's Goyer." He turned to McCallister. "After the raid, he admitted to giving our guy, Paul Peck, the files on the NDA agreements and other details." He turned back to Abbott. "This lawyer claims Connex is willing to give us anything we need as it relates to Carver."

Abbott pulled off his reading glasses. "Now, that is interesting. Sounds an awful lot like Goyer's covering his ass and the company's."

"How so, sir?" McCallister asked.

"We hauled in boxes upon boxes of documentation this morning. OSHA's shut down the plant altogether, giving us time to go through all of it," Abbott continued. "Two of Connex's officers said they'd be willing to speak to us in exchange for immunity. One of them was Alex Goyer."

"Figures," McCallister said.

"Yes, and no." He eyed Serrano. "You want to tell him?"

"At first glance, it appears Harry Carver awarded contracts to companies that provided Connex with the chemicals needed for production. The contracts, of course, were approved by Goyer and those on down the line. Nothing appeared out of the ordinary, according to them." Serrano crossed his long arms. "However, on closer inspection, the chemicals did not meet US standards. Elevated levels of deadly benzene, for one. And we suspect Carver was getting kickbacks for these contracts."

"What was the name of the company?" McCallister asked.

"Beecham International," Serrano replied.

"And Byrd knew about this?" McCallister pressed.

"That'll have to come from Carver, himself, unfortunately, since Byrd's dead," Serrano replied. "But it's entirely possible."

"So does this mean Connex didn't intend to harm its workers?" he asked. "But then how would that explain the non-disclosure agreements and the large payouts?"

"Those are things we are still working on," Abbott said. "Along with state police, and now the FBI."

McCallister drew in his brow. "And if this lawyer wants to turn over what they have on Carver, is it a way to help exonerate the company?"

"I would say so," Serrano replied. "But at this point, unless Carver asks for a deal, let the lawyer hand over whatever she wants. Our goal is to make sure Carver pays for what he's done. Byrd's already paid with his life. That said, Ballistics will almost certainly tie him to Littleton, I have no doubt."

"And Hank Ellis?" McCallister raised his chin. "Did someone at Connex come after him because of the old investigation?"

Abbott turned up his palms. "I don't know, but we damn well better find out."

"Okay, thank you both. I'll let Becca know and I guess we'll see what the lawyer has to say." He headed back down to the first floor interview room and noticed Ellis waiting for him in the hall.

"So?"

"We let the lawyer give us everything. According to Serrano, it looks like Carver went out on his own. He contracted with a company called Beecham International that used substandard materials. It caught up to him."

Ellis looked away for a moment.

"What?" he asked.

"Beecham?" she continued. "I know that name. I can't remember how, but I do."

"We'll get the names of all the suppliers," McCallister continued. "Connex may want to let Harry Carver take the fall, but I want to make sure they all go down for what they did to the workers there. And we still need to understand whether what happened to your dad was those guys too."

"Yeah." Ellis pushed inside the interview room. "Your lawyer is still on his way, Mr. Carver. Apologies. We thought the Connex lawyer who just showed up was for you."

He was silent for a moment while the detectives sat down. "You think I'm the only one involved in this? You have any idea how many people were in this with me?"

Ellis regarded him. "We're all ears. Why don't you shed some light, because I will say this, the people at Connex Solutions are prepared to hang you out to dry. If others are responsible, now would be the time to speak up."

"We're happy to wait for your lawyer," McCallister began.

"What's in it for me, if I give you names?" Carver asked.

Ellis returned a crooked smile. "At this point, Mr. Carver, the only thing that's going to be in it for you is the knowledge that you won't be the only one to go down."

He appeared to consider his options. "Do you have something I can write with?"

McCallister patted his shirt and pants pockets until he found a pen. He set it on the table.

Ellis pulled out his file from her laptop bag. "Write anything you want on here."

Carver eyed them a moment before he began to write. "This is the man I've been working with at Beecham

International. They supplied the chemicals. I can tell you more, but I'll need assurances." He slid the file folder back to Ellis.

She glanced down at the name. Her pulse quickened and her gaze darted to McCallister.

He creased his brow. "What is it?"

Ellis reached into her laptop bag and retrieved the business card Pelletier had been given by the bartender that night. She handed it to McCallister. "Tom Lazaro, Beecham International."

"Piper?" he asked.

She returned a stony gaze and nodded. It took a few moments for the information to sink in. It seemed impossible this was the same man who came after Piper. And if he knew who she was, then how hard would it have been for him to find out about Hank? She returned her attention to Carver. "Did you know my father, Detective Hank Ellis, Mr. Carver?"

He glanced up, appearing to think about the question. "You know what, I believe I remember him from a situation at Connex a long time ago." Carver returned his gaze to Ellis. "Is there a problem, Detective? You look upset."

THE CASE WAS OVER. They'd found their killer, but they'd found a hell of a lot more than that.

Pelletier caught up to Ellis at her desk as she prepared to head home. "What happens now?"

"Now, I find Lazaro and arrest him. Carver didn't say as much, but he mentioned Beecham and Tom Lazaro is behind them. Serrano's talking to the DA, but given what Connex's lawyer said, my guess is they'll work with Goyer to get what they need."

Pelletier glanced at McCallister, who was on a call at his

desk. He turned back to Ellis. "I can tell you where he is right now."

She returned a deadpan stare. "You know where Lazaro is?"

"I do, but listen, this guy, he's rich. I mean, like really rich, which means he probably has some powerful friends. He didn't get the deal with Connex on his own. Who knows how many other companies he does business with? And when word of this gets out, it might be hard to take him down. He'll be lawyered up ten deep, I promise you."

Ellis considered his words. "I can't let him get away with what he did, to Piper or Hank. I don't know how he got to Hank, but he did. And we already know he tried to hurt Piper." She eyed him. "Where is he?"

"At the same bar."

"How do you know this?" she pressed.

Pelletier shrugged. "I might've figured out where he lives and happened to catch up to him after I left the station earlier. I imagine he's still there."

"He really thinks he's off scot-free, doesn't he? Of course, without a gun, I can't prove he killed Byrd. I can't prove he messed with Hank's meds either." She turned to McCallister, as he ended the call. "We could use some backup. Care to join us?"

He tilted his head. "What's going on?"

"You want in or not?" Ellis grabbed her jacket from back of the chair and snatched her keys.

"Yeah, I'm in."

She headed into the hall with Pelletier at her side. "You, me, and Euan, we'll go there now and place him under arrest."

"His lawyers will get him out inside the hour," McCallister cut in.

"Doesn't matter. He might get bail, but he won't get away

with what he's done. Aside from Carver calling him out, I'll find out how he got to my dad. How he got to Piper. I'll make sure that man doesn't see daylight for a decade or more." Ellis walked into the parking lot and headed to her Tahoe. She looked back at them, as they appeared hesitant. "I'd rather not do this alone, but I will if I have to."

THEY ARRIVED at the spot where it happened. Where Piper barely made it free from a man who would've done God knows what to her if given the chance. Ellis needed proof regarding Hank, needed proof regarding Byrd, but given Carver's admission, she would get it from him one way or another.

Ellis parked her Tahoe and looked at her team; her friends. "I'll go in first. Stay several steps behind me, then go inside after a minute or two. Sit down somewhere near the back. He won't want to make a scene, so let me get what I can from him and then we get him outside, slap cuffs on him."

She walked into the bar that was loud, dark, and over-crowded even at seven p.m. on a weeknight. It was hard to know whether he'd been made aware they had Carver in custody. Carver was allowed his one phone call, but it wasn't to Lazaro. But if Pelletier had managed to track him down to here, chances were good he hadn't known.

Ellis made her way through the crowd and figured the guy would be at the bar somewhere. People crowded the twenty-foot-long bar, but she pushed in, eventually spotting a well-dressed man leaning with an elbow on the bar top. She peered at her phone and the picture Pelletier had sent to her of this man. "That's you."

Ellis continued her approach and stood next to him, attempting to garner the attention of the bartender.

"Evening," Lazaro said to her.

"Hey," she shot back. When the bartender approached, Ellis started to speak, but the man cut in.

"Whatever she wants. Put it on my tab," he said.

"You got it," the bartender replied.

"I'll have a whiskey and Coke, thanks." She turned to the man. "I appreciate it. It was unnecessary but appreciated."

"Never unnecessary to buy a beautiful woman a drink, Rebecca." He offered his hand. "Nice to finally meet you in-person."

She let her gaze roam over him. "I'm surprised you're here, Mr. Lazaro."

"And why is that?" he asked.

She wore a closed lip grin. "Harry Carver had an awful lot to say about you when we brought him in a couple of hours ago." Ellis noticed the look on his face. "Oh, you hadn't heard?"

"Sorry, I'm not sure who that is," he replied.

"Now, that can't be true. And I'm pretty sure you know my friend, too."

He returned a sideways glance. "And what's this friend's name?"

Lazaro wore that slick smile, like he'd just rubbed Vaseline on his teeth. It took Ellis a moment to talk herself out of slugging the guy in the jaw. "Just a friend." The bartender set down the drink and Ellis picked it up to toss back a swig. "Oh, and I'm certain you're familiar with my father. Retired Detective Hank Ellis." She watched his expression shift. "So you do know who I'm talking about? Good. Then we cut the shit and you can tell me how you got to him."

He appeared irritated, on the verge of anger, but exhibited restraint. "Well, Rebecca, it was a pleasure meeting you. Enjoy the drink."

Just as he started to walk away, she called out to him. "Tom, can I ask you something?"

He reluctantly stopped and turned back to her. "What's that?"

"Do you enjoy attacking women?"

He chuckled and looked around nervously. "Sorry?"

"That friend of mine I was telling you about. You bought her drinks. Got her a little bit tipsy, maybe more. Took her outside, then threatened her."

"I have no idea what you're talking about." He turned around again.

This time, Ellis stepped toward him and reached out for his shoulder, spinning him around to face her. "I know who you are, Mr. Lazaro. And I know what you've done." She reached for her handcuffs and eyed McCallister and Pelletier. They pushed through the crowd toward her. "You're under arrest for the attempted murder of Hank Ellis, attempted sexual assault on Piper Dixon, oh, and the murder of Wayne Byrd. And I know there will be plenty of other charges stemming from the contract you had with Connex Solutions that ended up killing at least three of their employees."

"Get off me." He flicked away his shoulder and started on again.

"I wouldn't do that," McCallister squared up to him.

Ellis put Lazaro in cuffs and led him out of the bar, with McCallister and Pelletier behind her. "Thanks."

IT WAS ALMOST midnight by the time Ellis returned home. After booking Lazaro and filing her reports, she could hardly keep her eyes open. The case was finished, but she wasn't finished with Tom Lazaro, not by a long shot.

The other Connex stuff, well, that was mainly on Abbott

and Serrano. She and her team did what they set out to do, which was to find out who murdered Terry Satchel. And in doing so, uncovered an even larger -scale operation of deceit from someone inside an organization that had a history of such acts. It made for good cover, for a while.

She dropped her laptop bag next to the sofa. Hank was back home, and she'd stopped in to see him, holding back on the Lazaro situation until she had proof. Hank wouldn't want to know unless she could prove it. But he was safe and that was all that mattered to her.

Hank could rest, knowing that Connex hadn't gone back to their old ways, but had nevertheless been complacent in the actions of its staff. Turned out, Terry Satchel was the lone voice of reason, not the crazy conspiracy theorist everyone thought he was. Well, everyone except Janice Buxton.

Just as Ellis slipped off her shoes, a knock came on her front door. She turned to unlatch the dead bolt and open it. "Oh, hey."

McCallister stood on the other side. "Can I come in?"

"Yeah, of course." She stepped aside.

"I'm sorry to drop in."

"It's okay. You want a beer or something?" she asked, heading into the kitchen.

"I'd love one, thanks."

Ellis grabbed the bottles from the fridge and returned to hand him one. "Have a seat." She gestured to the sofa.

"I just wanted to know, Becca, if what I told you changes your view of me."

She sat down beside him and noticed his downturned gaze. "About what happened in Boston? I already told you it doesn't. Look, I don't know all that happened, but I think I'm starting to get to know you and there is no doubt in my mind that what happened eats away at you."

"It does, but that doesn't make what happened right."

"No, of course it doesn't. I didn't say it excused anything or made it right. It was a decision made in the field. I've never faced anything like that so I can't compare it, but it happened. Have you talked to your old captain?" she asked.

"Not yet. We've been a little busy, but I will. In fact, I'm sure he'll reach out to me sooner rather than later."

"Like you said before, Euan, nothing can change what happened. You can't bring that child back to his parents. They wanted justice and I can understand their point of view. It's a lose-lose proposition, unfortunately. Point is, you have to face whatever happens. I will say this—Abbott won't fire you. You've become a crucial part of this team and he sees that."

"Well, the heat might get to him if he doesn't let me go," McCallister said.

"Then he'll get hot, but he won't burn—himself or you."

He nodded. "Listen, I should go and let you get some rest. I suppose I don't feel much like going home, so maybe I'll go for a walk along the river." He stood to leave and when Ellis joined him, he stopped and turned back. "You were right, what you said about the kiss. The stress of the job and all. So, can we just forget it ever happened?"

"Yeah, sure. I'm here for you, Euan, just know that." She opened her door. "Try to get some sleep."

ELLIS CHANGED her clothes and climbed into bed, staring at the ceiling. She checked the time on her phone. "It's one in the morning?" She sighed and set down her phone again. The gratitude she felt toward the two men who had come to be pretty important to her left her confused. Pelletier's confession replayed in her mind. Then she thought about McCallister and the brief kiss they'd shared. In light of what was about to come for him, he was going to need a friend to lean on for a while. And she hadn't been certain all would turn out okay for him, no matter how hard she tried to convince him of that.

Ellis reached for her phone on the nightstand once again and swiped open the screen to make a call. "Hey."

"Did I forget something?" McCallister asked.

Ellis kept her eyes at the ceiling. "No, uh, I just got to thinking."

"About the case?" he asked.

"Not the case. The kiss." He was quiet for a moment and she raised her brow. "Euan? Are you there?"

"I'm here. What about it?"

"I was thinking, maybe I wouldn't mind trying that again sometime in the future. I don't know when in the future—"

"Are you sure you want to go down that road? It could complicate things—for a whole lot of people."

"You mean Bryce?" she asked.

"It's pretty clear he has feelings for you," McCallister said. "I don't want to get in the middle of that."

"And what about you?" Ellis continued.

"I think you know I do."

Ellis inhaled a deep breath. "Well, I don't know what's going to happen either. I'm not a fortune teller. But I'm willing to find out, if you are."

WE HOPE YOU ENJOYED THIS BOOK

If you could spend a moment to write an honest review on Amazon, no matter how short, we would be extremely grateful. They really do help readers discover new authors.

ABOUT THE AUTHOR

Robin Mahle has published more than 30 crime fiction novels, many, of which, topped the Amazon charts in the US, Canada, and the UK. Also a screenwriter, she has adapted some of her works into teleplays, which have gone on to place in film festivals nationwide. From detectives to federal agents, and from killers to corruption, her page-turning tales grab hold and refuse to let go. Throw in tense action and thrilling twists, and it becomes clear why her readers come back for more. Robin lives in Coastal Virginia with her husband and two children.

www.robinmahle.com

ALSO BY ROBIN MAHLE

Detective Rebecca Ellis Series

No Safe Place

A Frozen Grave

The Dead Lake

Leave No Trace

No Way Back

Made in United States
Orlando, FL
26 August 2024